Snow Blind

P. J. TRACY

PENGUIN BOOKS

PENGUIN BOOKS

Published by the Penguin Group
Penguin Books Ltd, 80 Strand, London WC2R 0RL, England
Penguin Group (USA), Inc., 375 Hudson Street, New York, New York 10014, USA
Penguin Group (Canada), 90 Eglinton Avenue East, Suite 700, Toronto, Ontario, Canada M4P 2Y3
(a division of Pearson Penguin Canada Inc.)
Penguin Ireland, 25 St Stephen's Green, Dublin 2, Ireland (a division of Penguin Books Ltd)
Penguin Group (Australia), 250 Camberwell Road, Camberwell, Victoria 3124, Australia
(a division of Pearson Australia Group Pty Ltd)
Penguin Books India Pvt Ltd, 11 Community Centre,
Panchsheel Park, New Delhi – 110 017, India
Penguin Group (NZ), 67 Apollo Drive, Rosedale, North Shore 0632, New Zealand
(a division of Pearson New Zealand Ltd)
Penguin Books (South Africa) (Pty) Ltd, 24 Sturdee Avenue,
Rosebank, Johannesburg 2196, South Africa

Penguin Books Ltd, Registered Offices: 80 Strand, London WC2R 0RL, England

www.penguin.com

First published in the United States of America by G. P. Putnam's Sons,
a member of Penguin Group (USA) Inc. 2006
First published in Great Britain by Michael Joseph 2006
Published in Penguin Books 2007
1

Set in 12/15 pt Monotype Garamond
Typeset by Rowland Phototypesetting Ltd, Bury St Edmunds, Suffolk
Printed in England by Clays Ltd, St Ives plc

978-0-141-03460-7

Prologue

They had to sit for a time after dragging the body so far in this heat – two young women in sleeveless summer dresses, hugging their knees on the hillside while the hot wind danced in their hair and crept up their skirts and a dead man lay behind them. They both looked straight ahead across the rolling fields of prairie grass, and nowhere else.

'We should have tied him to a board or something,' Ruth said after a few minutes, 'so he wouldn't get tangled up in the grass like he did.'

Laura opened her mouth, then closed it abruptly. She'd almost said they'd know better next time. She closed her eyes and saw big, raw hands dragging through the grass, fingers curled, almost as if he'd been trying to hang on. It was high summer and the grass was long, whipping in the wind and wrapping around the rough fabric of his sleeves.

'Shall we start?'

Laura felt her heart skip a beat. 'In a minute.'

But it was impossible to keep Ruth still for very long. She was like one of those little birds whose wings beat so fast you couldn't see them, darting here and there like they were always on the edge of panic. She was trying to be still to please Laura, but her hands were busy, almost frantic, shredding one piece of grass and then another. 'I have a headache.'

'It's those combs. They always give you a headache.'

Ruth took the combs from her hair and shook it free,

lovely blond curls falling down her back like liquid sunshine. Silly Ruth, as old-fashioned in appearance as the name she'd been saddled with: hair too long and skirts too short; maybe that was what had brought this whole thing to a head. She managed to sit for almost a full minute, and then started to fidget again.

'Stop fussing, Ruth.'

'Don't yell at me.'

Laura heard the hurt in her voice, and knew without looking that Ruth's lower lip was starting to tremble. Soon the tears would spill over. She hadn't yelled, exactly, but perhaps her tone had been too sharp. That was wrong. Ruth had always been the fragile one, even before her belly had started to swell, and you had to be careful. 'I'm sorry if it sounded that way. Have you thought of a name for the baby?'

'Stop trying to distract me. We have to dig this hole.'

'I just want you to be still for a bit. Rest.'

'Rest?' Ruth looked at her as if she'd just uttered a profanity. 'But we have so much to do.'

'Just this one thing.'

And then Laura smiled and felt herself relax for the first time in years. It was true. Kill a man, bury him – that was all that was on their list today.

After a few seconds Ruth said, 'Emily.'

'What?'

'Emily. I'm going to name her Emily.'

'What if it's a boy?'

Ruth smiled. 'It isn't.'

This was the story Emily was remembering on her last day, and it amazed her that she could remember it at all. She'd heard it only twice in her life – once from her aunt Laura, who'd told her on the sly when Emily had turned thirteen, as if it were a strange and secret birthday present; and again from her mother on the day Emily had left the home farm to marry Lars and make her own life. Her mother had giggled during the telling, which her aunt had never done, and that had frightened her a little. And then she told her to remember the tale, that it wasn't really so funny, in case a day should come when she would need it.

Today she needed it, Emily thought, wondering if she could finally do it, after all these years. And if she did, what would all those wasted years have been for?

It was the last day; the last day of secrets. She lay on her back in bed, right hand pressed against her flat stomach; pushing, pushing the pain back inside; holding the evil, growing mass that writhed inside with hungry tentacles reaching for open nerves. God, it hurt.

A perfect, thin line of light pushed up the black curtain on the horizon outside her bedroom window, and the quality of dark inside the room began to change. This room, where love and hell had happened, all in the same lifetime.

Emily's feet were on the floor before the first chirp of the earliest-rising bird had sounded, and the rush of agonizing pain pushed her head to her knees. She squeezed her eyes tightly closed and saw rolling, sparking pinwheels of light.

Old, ravaged huddle; tiny woman; folded into a small package of gray hair and sharpened knees, alone in a chamber of agony where, inexplicably, birds welcomed the morning in gay, sporadic disharmony.

She did things that seemed odd, considering her chore list for the morning. Prepared and ate her oatmeal; drank her precious single cup of coffee; carefully washed the bowl and cup and saucer with their faded rose patterns, knowing those patterns had always been there, amazed at her years of indifference. Everything seemed sharper, clearer, as if she had seen the world for years through a lens just barely out of focus.

And then she walked to the old gun cabinet in the dining room.

The pistol lay in her right palm, and she folded arthritic fingers around it. It felt good. It felt right. She hadn't used it for years. Five? Six? Since she had shot the squirrel that the oil truck had left, panting and mangled, eyes glazing in the driveway.

Emily was an excellent shot. Lars had seen to that, back when fox and bear still wandered freely in and out of the chicken coops and the isolated barnyards of rural Minnesota. 'You will learn to shoot, Emily; and you will shoot if you have to,' he had answered her shudder when he first lay the new pistol in her palm; and she had. How impossibly far from her mind then was the final use to which she would put this gun. How inconceivable it would have been. To kill, with careful thought and planning; with only cold, dismal dread, as for any other unpleasant task.

Appalling, evil woman, she thought as she stepped out onto the back porch. To feel no remorse, no guilt. How hideous. How deeply sinful.

The sun had not yet topped the cottonwoods when she walked out from the house toward the looming barn, and the path through the tall grass was still dim with early morning.

She saw in her mind an image of how she must have looked at that moment, and laughed aloud at the sight: a crazy old woman, hustling in a faded dress and orthopedic shoes, gun in hand, out to kill quickly, out to finish the job before it was too late.

She stopped when she rounded the turn at the bushy hydrangea, just as the enormous, ancient barn sprang into view, tractor door gaping like a bottomless black mouth.

Suddenly the pain in her belly moved. Now it was a bright piercing in her head, and then without warning, a deadness spread down her arms.

It didn't get the gun, she thought senselessly. It didn't get the gun. I can still feel it. It's heavy, hanging so heavy from my hand.

But the pistol was on the ground, winking sunlight off the long, polished barrel, mocking her as Emily fell beside it. Her lips wouldn't move, and the scream stayed inside her head.

No, God, please no. Not yet. I have to kill him first.

I

Minneapolis hadn't had much of a winter. Every promised storm had veered far to the south, dumping Minnesota's fair share of snow on states that neither wanted nor deserved it, like Iowa.

Meanwhile bitter Minnesotans watched their lawns green up in the occasional rain, and their snowmobiles gather dust in the garage. A few die-hard riders made the short trek to Iowa to try out new machines, but they never talked about it at the water cooler on Monday morning. It was simply too humiliating.

Today was going to change all that, and the whole state was giddy with anticipation.

The snow started at ten o'clock in the morning, falling with a gentle vengeance, as if to apologize for its late arrival. Within an hour there wasn't a blade of grass visible in the whole city, the surface streets were slick with new snow hiding the black ice beneath it, and the average freeway speed had dropped to seven miles per hour. Reporters' mini-cams picked up shots of lunchtime drivers behind the wheels of cars barely inching along in the kind of stop-and-go traffic that normally fosters road rage, but all the drivers were smiling.

In City Hall, Detectives Leo Magozzi and Gino Rolseth were totally oblivious to the little surprise nature was cooking up outside. They sat at their facing desks in the back corner, grinning at each other. It wasn't the kind of picture you saw often in Minneapolis Homicide, but this was a banner day.

Gino propped his feet on the desktop and laced his hands behind his head. 'We are never going to have another day this good. Not on the job, anyway.'

Magozzi pondered that. 'Maybe we should retire right now. Go out in a blaze of glory, get jobs as golf pros on some course in Hawaii.'

'Golf pros never get a high like this.'

'Probably not.'

'And neither one of us knows how to golf.'

'How hard can it be? You hit a little ball into a little hole. Pinball on grass, is what it is.'

Gino's grin widened. 'We are probably the only homicide detectives in history where the homicide victim lived.'

'Nah. Must have happened a hundred times before.'

Gino made a face. 'Yeah. I suppose. But not in this department. And she could just as well have died, if it weren't for the two greatest detectives on the planet.' He shook his head in happy disbelief. 'Man, this is almost better than sex.'

Magozzi thought that was a load of crap, but he was feeling too good to take issue with it.

They'd been called out on a probable homicide four days ago. Bloody bedroom, drunken ex-husband with a history of abuse and assault, and a missing woman who'd had a restraining order against the dirtbag ever since the divorce. Magozzi and Gino had found her early this morning, locked in the trunk of a car in the long-term lot at the airport, barely breathing. The docs at Hennepin General said she was going to make it, and they'd been floating ever since.

Gino rolled his chair around to face the window, and his

silly grin turned upside down. 'Oh, crap. That stuff's still coming down.'

'Good. People hardly ever kill each other when it's snowing.'

'Oh, yeah? Homicides were up six percent last quarter.'

'Because there was no snow. It'll get better now. Man, look at it come down.' Magozzi walked over to the window and looked down at the mess the storm was making of the street.

Gino joined him, shaking his head. 'Those homicide stats never made sense to me. Should be the other way around. Winter in this state is enough to make anyone homicidal. Boy, this better stop soon.'

Magozzi shoved his hands in his pockets and smiled. 'We're supposed to get at least a foot.'

'Aw, jeez, come on, don't tell me that.'

'Sorry, buddy. Looks like there's going to be a Winter Fest after all. Baby's got snow.'

'Goddamnit.' Gino's happy-camper mood was officially deceased. 'So I'm going to end up spending one of my two days off building a stupid snowman for a stupid kids' festival in the freezing cold. Those so-called computer wizards at Monkeewrench ever get a lead on who the hell is doing this to me?'

Gino was the very reluctant fall guy for every charity gig the MPD sponsored, thanks to some anonymous donor who kept doubling the proceeds on the condition that Gino had to participate.

'I don't think so.'

Gino narrowed his eyes. 'Well, that's pretty interesting, if you ask me. We've got four geniuses who developed the most sophisticated crime-solving software in the world, can hack into the NSA database with their brains tied behind their backs, and yet they can't put a name to a bank routing number. That smells, and you know it. Monkeewrench is behind this. Specifically, Miss Grace MacBride herself.'

Magozzi smiled a little at the mention of Grace. 'Now, why would she want to do that? She likes you.'

'Well, gee, let me think. Maybe because in the past I've been a little negative about you two trying to have a relationship. She's still mad about that.'

'Grace doesn't get mad.'

'Tell me about it. She gets even.'

By noon there were five inches on the ground, most of the city schools had started bussing the kids home, and people were cross-country skiing on side streets the plows hadn't hit yet. By mid-afternoon four more inches had fallen, along with the mercury, and the freeways were at a dead standstill, clogged with remorseful commuters who'd made the bad decision not to leave work early.

By nightfall the storm was still dumping its load of white at the rate of an inch an hour. The streets were a mess, and most of the city had locked itself down for the night. Tommy thought of all the fools sitting in front of their fireplaces sipping hot toddies or whatever it was such people drank, missing the first real snow of the season and the sights and silence of a big metropolis that had ground to a halt.

It was spooky, in a way, to be in the park when it was this empty. As far as he could tell, the only people around were over on the lighted sledding hill, all the way across the big field. They looked like colorful ants from this distance, and he could barely hear them. Even though it was the first time in this long, snow-free winter that the city had opened the cross-country ski trails, all but the die-hards would wait for daylight and perfectly groomed trails before snapping on the skids. Tomorrow the trails would be jammed, but tonight they were his.

Even in perfect conditions, not many skiers used the higher, wooded trails in the park, especially after dark, which was why Tommy liked them. No shuffling kids, no pokey old-timers to block the narrow passageways through the big trees, break his rhythm, and slow him down.

The groomers had hit the trails once today after the first six inches, but since then another several inches had fallen, and he liked the challenge of muscling the long skis through it, making his marks the first in the new snow.

The big hill up to the woods had been a bitch, though, and Tommy could already feel the strain in his thighs and shoulders, and they'd only been skiing for an hour. His daily workouts at the gym kept him tight and strong, but there was no way those stationary ski machines could prepare you for the real thing, no matter how high you set the resistance. They couldn't duplicate the jittering bumps of a rough trail, or a skid on a slick spot that tugged your legs sideways instead of forward, using a whole different group of muscles. Maybe he'd invent one, make a million dollars.

He stopped for a breath, shook out his legs and hands, then went still for a moment, listening for the shushing sound of Toby's skis behind him. He was back there somewhere, probably struggling on the incline up into the woods, which was pretty much the story of Toby's whole life. He'd always been a little slower, a little weaker, and some kind of bull's-eye for just about every bad shake that can hit a guy. Best thing that ever happened to him was hooking up with Tommy way back in the fourth grade, when every other kid wanted to beat the crap out of him just because they could. Tommy fought off the bullies, Toby idolized him, and it was still that way, all these years later. The bullies were bigger and meaner, but Tommy was still fighting Toby's battles for him, whether they were with guys on the street or their superiors at work, and that was just fine with him. He liked being the hero, and most of all, he liked the hero worship that went along with it. He supposed it didn't matter if your battles were on a playground, in a war, or on the street, they made a bond between men that couldn't be broken. Women just didn't get that.

He'd been still for too long, and the cold was starting to seep in through his Gore-Tex suit. He was just opening his mouth to holler back at Toby when he finally heard the shush of skis heading toward him. He listened for a second, frowning, because the sound wasn't coming from the trail behind; it was moving toward him sideways, through the woods. And then he saw the little beams from skier head-lamps, jittering through the big tree trunks.

He snorted out a plume of frost, irritated that he'd have company on the trail in a few seconds, and unreasonably angry that he was no longer the best, strongest, and fastest skier in the park. Skiing off the trail through unmarked woods with nearly a foot of new snow took a lot of strength and endurance – more than he had – and nothing pissed off Tommy more than being second best.

He thought about shooting off down the trail while he still had a little head start, then thought about the humiliation of skiers that strong passing him. No way he was going to let that happen. *I'm just waiting for a friend to catch up*, he'd tell them, standing there casually while they skied away, as if he could have taken them if he really wanted to.

He side-stepped off the trail to give them space, then watched them come, his own headlamp showing a glimpse of black suits and ski masks moving steadily toward him. They might be strong, but they sure were stupid, he thought, wearing ski masks when they were working up a sweat like that.

Twenty feet back on the trail, Toby was shoving himself along by the poles, trying to keep his skis in Tommy's tracks to make the going easier. He didn't have his ski legs yet this winter, and the trip up the long hill into the woods had left his thighs weak and quivering.

It surprised him a little when he spotted more than one headlamp through the snow just ahead, especially since he'd been following only one set of tracks. A few feet closer and he could make out Tommy, standing loose and casual off the trail, watching other skiers approach from the woods. He shook his head at the foolhardy souls who'd ventured off the trail at night, dug in with his poles, and gave a last, strong push that sent him gliding toward them. In the middle of his glide, he saw the first skier out of the woods slide in close, raise a gun to Tommy's head and pull the trigger.

Toby Myerson kept drifting in and out of a delicious sleep, and each time his eyes fluttered open, the landscape changed, as if someone had pushed fast-forward on a movie.

Earlier, the big sledding hill across the field had been a rush-hour kiddie freeway, jumbled with the primary colors of a hundred miniature snowsuits, and the air had been sweet with the delighted squeals of children. Happy music that warmed him from the inside out.

Toby loved watching the little bodies sailing down the snowy hill, tumbling off saucers and sleds and the occasional toboggan at the bottom. They rolled like balls and then skittered up the slope like colorful insects; so animated and tireless, so very alive. Occasionally he would focus on one child who seemed a little taller and more coordinated than the others, and he would wish with all his heart that the child would cross the stretch of open parkland and walk up to greet him. He was feeling a bit strange at that point, and worried that he might seem intimidating. Youngsters frightened so easily, and if they were frightened, they would run from him, and Toby thought he would just die if that happened, because he had to tell someone about ... something ... something bad. He just couldn't remember what it was.

Things seemed darker when he opened his eyes again. At first he thought the park lights had been turned off, but that couldn't be it, because when he moved his eyes up to look at them he could still see pinpoints of brightness, as if none of the light could get out of the bulbs. Odd.

Only a few shadowy stragglers remained on the sledding hill now, and the only sounds he heard were the shouts of the last parents calling their kids up the hill, home to bed, because the park was closing.

Don't go. Please don't go.

And then Toby realized he was very, very cold. He'd been still for so long, watching the children. Probably hours. My God, what had he been thinking? He had to move, get the blood flowing, get home and warm.

Funny how the scenery remained exactly the same, no matter how far he went. And the really funny part was that his mind recorded every movement of his legs and arms, and yet he couldn't feel the snow sliding beneath his feet or the good stretch of his triceps.

That's because you're not moving, Toby.

Oh, my God.

There was a brief flutter of heat as his body tried to find some adrenaline to send to his heart, and he concentrated on not blinking, on screaming as loud as he could to the last kid climbing up the hill, omigod he was almost to the top, screaming, screaming, splitting the silence with terror and outrage because now he knew he was dying and he couldn't move and *Why didn't the kid turn around?*

At the top of the hill, the last child grinned up at his father, and the two of them turned to look out over the empty, absolutely silent park.

2

Traffic on Theodore Wirth Parkway was an unmitigated disaster – the twelve inches of yesterday's fresh snow had been churned into treacherous slop before the overworked battalion of snowplows had been able to catch up, and when the temperature had plummeted overnight, the slop froze into icy furrows. Instant bobsled track. Magozzi had stopped counting fender-benders long ago.

Still two blocks from the park's main entrance, he'd been sitting in his car at a dead standstill for almost five minutes, watching enviously as throngs of pedestrians waddled cheerfully and unimpeded past the gridlock in their warmest winter garb, heading for the Winter Fest Snowman Sculpting Competition. There were too many to count, all of them braving the wind and cold and traffic just to watch people play in the snow, and amazingly, they all looked happy about it.

This town was absolutely nuts for winter. Or maybe they were just nuts; Magozzi hadn't decided. Once there was enough snow on the ground, streets were always blocked off for one thing or another – sled-dog races, cross-country ski marathons, hockey demonstrations, or bikini-clad residents making a big fuss over the idiocy of diving into a frozen lake or river. Every winter sport the world ever thought of had a home base here, and when they ran out of sports, they took art outside.

Give Minnesotans a block of ice and they'll harvest

twenty thousand more from whatever lake is handy and build a palace. Give them a little snow and you're likely to find a scale replica of Mount Rushmore or the White House on someone's front yard. Ice and snow sculpture had been elevated to artistry here, and competitors came from all over the world to participate in any number of winter festivals. Who would have thought that a snowman contest that the department sponsored just for kids would attract this much attention?

He moved another half-block by inches, past a wooded section of the park, and got his first glimpse of the open field that fronted the boulevard. Like all the drivers before him, he slammed on his brakes and stared out his window in amazement.

The park opened up here onto a good thirty acres of empty, rolling land that looked a lot like a golf course in summer. Today it looked like a blindingly white battlefield for an invading army of snowmen. Magozzi gaped at what looked like hundreds of them sprouting up every few yards, up and down the hills, staring out at the boulevard with their black lifeless eyes and silly carrot noses.

When he finally got into the park, he pulled into the first illegal spot he could find, between a Channel Ten satellite van and a NO PARKING AT ANY TIME sign. He grabbed his gloves and a thermos from the passenger seat, and stepped out in time to catch a frigid gust of wind square in the face.

Hundreds of spectators were milling around the park, watching piles of snow take shape under frozen hands, and Magozzi wondered how he was ever going to find his partner in such a vast sea of anonymous bipeds swaddled head-to-toe in fur, down, and Thinsulate.

He finally spotted Gino on the far side of the field, his modest five-foot-nine-inch frame cutting a towering figure amid all the crazed, screaming little munchkins who swirled around him in a rainbow of brightly colored coats, scarves, and hats.

Gino, on the other hand, was dressed all in black, as if in mourning, bundled up in a huge down parka so puffy he could barely bend his arms. He had some kind of animal on his head, and his hands were encased in leather snow-mobile mittens big enough to be pizza paddles. It was obvious that his mood was even blacker than his outer-wear, because he was planting nasty kicks to the base of his nascent snowman.

'Nice parka, Gino. How many ducks died for that thing?'

'It's about time you showed up. And to answer your question, not enough. I can't feel my extremities. I think I have frostbite. And hypothermia. Goddamnit, I hate winter, I hate snow, I hate cold. Remind me why I live here again?'

'Because you love mosquitoes?'

'Wrong answer.'

'Must be the change of seasons, then.'

'No, it's because every goddamned winter, the brain cells that know how miserable it is here freeze and die. It takes 'em all summer to grow back, and then it's winter again and the whole ugly process starts all over.'

'But you look great – most places you just can't get away with earflaps anymore.'

Gino adjusted the black pelt on his head a little self-consciously. 'Laugh now, freeze your ass off later, Leo. The wind chill is about fifty degrees below zero, and dressed like that, you're going to be running for the car in five minutes.

What, are you shopping with the Chief now? You look like a mobster.'

Magozzi smoothed the front of his new cashmere overcoat – a Christmas gift from Grace MacBride. 'I heard it was supposed to warm up. Look, the sun's coming out already.'

'When the sun comes out in Hawaii, it warms up. When the sun comes out in Puerto Vallarta, it warms up. When the sun comes out in Minnesota in January, you just go snow-blind.'

'And therein lies the real truth as to why you live here.'

'So I can go snow-blind?'

'No, so you can complain about the weather.'

Gino mulled that over for a good, long time and finally nodded. 'That's actually a good point, Leo. The only thing worse than bad weather is boring weather.' He bent down and swept up a mitt full of dry, powdery snow. 'You want to tell me how the hell I'm supposed to build a snowman out of this?'

Magozzi gestured toward a group of kids who were working with spritzer bottles full of water. 'Watch and learn. You use the water like glue.'

'Okay, Michelangelo, go pull your gun on them and requisition a water bottle for the MPD.' He looked hopefully at the thermos Magozzi was carrying. 'Tell me you got schnapps in that thing.'

'Hot chocolate. You're not supposed to drink in the cold. It dilates your blood vessels and you get hypothermia faster.'

'I already have hypothermia, so what's the difference?' Gino turned back to his misshapen, pathetic half-snowman that was shedding vast portions of its body with each gust of wind. 'Christ, look at this. This is the worst snowman in the whole contest.'

Magozzi took a few steps back and eyeballed it. 'Maybe there's a conceptual-art category. You could enter it as *Snowman with Psoriasis.*'

'You're just full of wisecracks today, aren't you?'

'I'm trying to cheer you up. Aren't Angela and the kids coming?'

'Later, for the judging. And I want to get at least an honorable mention, so help me out here.'

'Okay, I'm ready. Where do we start?'

'I think we need a theme.'

Magozzi nodded. 'Good plan. Like what?'

'Hell, I don't know. Maybe we should do something cop-related, since we're cops.'

'I'm with you. I think a cop snowman would be appropriate.'

'But nothing too flashy. See that one over by the woods?' Gino pointed to a nearby snowman that had cross-country skis sticking out of its base, ski poles propped against its torso, and a pair of Elvis-style reflective sunglasses perched atop a carrot nose. 'It's too skinny if you ask me, but nice execution overall. I'm thinking we could use it as a template.'

'Whatever you say. You're the visionary, I'm just the free labor. Tell me what to do.'

'Make me a head that won't fall apart.'

Gino and Magozzi started working fast, rolling and molding and shaping. The sun was on their side, because it was bright and high in the sky now, softening up the snow and making it easier to work with. A half hour later, they had a respectable-looking basic snowman.

'That's a damn fine start,' Gino said, stepping back to admire their handiwork. 'A few details, maybe a couple trimmings, and we'll have ourselves a contender. What do you think?'

'I think its butt looks fat.'

Gino rolled his eyes. 'Snowmen are supposed to have fat butts.'

'Maybe some arms would balance him out a little.'

'Great idea. Go get some twigs from those bushes over there.'

'It's illegal to pick foliage in parks.'

'I don't give a shit. I'm not signing off on this thing until it has some limbs. And don't make any smart-ass remarks about the Disability Act.'

Magozzi wandered over to the straggly thicket that bordered a margin of woods, stopping to look at the skiing snowman on the way. The sun was hitting it full-on now, and its left side was starting to look glazed and a little mushy. With any luck, it would melt before judging and they'd have one less competitor.

'This yours?'

Magozzi looked down at a little red-haired kid who'd suddenly appeared at his side.

'No.'

The kid couldn't have been more than eight or nine, but he was circling the snowman with the critical eye of a seasoned judge. 'It's pretty good. Better than that one the fat guy's working on.' He pointed to Gino.

'That's my partner you're talking about.'

The kid looked up at him, nonplussed. 'You don't look gay.'

The ever-evolving English language, Magozzi thought.

Seemed like every word had multiple meanings nowadays. Somebody was going to have to make up some new ones eventually. 'Not that kind of partner. We're cops.'

Now the kid was impressed. 'Did you ever shoot anybody?'

'No,' Magozzi lied.

'Oh.' Disappointed, the kid turned back to the skiing snowman, dismissing Magozzi as quickly as he'd engaged him. Clearly, inanimate objects were more interesting than cops who didn't shoot people.

Magozzi looked around to make sure Park Service wasn't hovering in the bushes, waiting to ambush him, then started harvesting illegal arms for their snowman.

A few seconds later the screaming started. Magozzi spun toward the source, his hand on his holster even before the pivot, and saw the red-haired kid standing in front of the skiing snowman, staring up at it with wide blue eyes and an impossibly wide mouth.

He was at the kid's side in seconds, looking at the carrot nose tilting downward in the melting face, the sunglasses sliding down the carrot, and the big, terrorized milky eyes the sunglasses had been hiding. The real nose behind the carrot was a waxy white, right off the color palette of the dead.

Oh. Shit.

The kid was still screaming. Magozzi put his hands on his shoulders and turned him gently away from the snowman that wasn't a snowman, toward the red-haired man and woman running frantically toward their terrified son.

3

Immediate damage control out on the snowman field had been a challenge. The kid's scream had started a stampede, and by the time Magozzi and Gino realized what they were dealing with, at least fifty people were bearing down on them as fast as they could, knees pumping high over the deep snow, shouting, 'What do you think you're doing?' 'Get away from that kid!' and other more colorful phrases that made it perfectly clear what they were thinking.

There were a lot of things you could predict with a hundred-percent accuracy in this city – one of them was that if a child screamed, any adult within earshot came on the double. No waiting for the second scream, no thought of personal safety, no hesitation at all. Four attempted child abductions had been foiled in just such a way within the past year – during the last attempt, the cops had to pull what seemed like an entire neighborhood off a sleazebag who would never again recognize his own face in the mirror. Last Magozzi heard, the creep had filed suit from his prison cell against every one of the people who stopped him from driving away with a five-year-old girl.

It was one of the things that made Minneapolis a nice place to live, but in this particular case, it was going to make the job a lot harder. He wasn't sure what worried him more: the impending destruction of a crime scene, or getting beaten to a pulp by well-meaning citizens.

He stepped away from the boy and held his badge high,

showing it to the crowd. It slowed them down a little, but neither his nor Gino's furious shouts stopped them until they were close enough to see the boy unharmed and in his father's arms. Unfortunately, that also put them close enough to see the exposed, cookie-dough face and cloudy eyes that had been concealed by the skiing snowman's Elvis sunglasses. That was the sight that finally stopped them in their tracks and dropped every mouth into a horrified gape. But more were coming in from all directions, including a few park police, who rushed past them, probably expecting a fistfight or a heart attack and getting a lot more than they bargained for. They were as stunned as the rest of the gawkers, and any crowd-control training they might have had went out the window.

Magozzi called it in on his cell while Gino stomped around like an asylum escapee, flailing his arms, waving people back, screaming *'MPD! Keep clear!'* until he was red-faced and hoarse. The crowd ebbed a little, but not far enough, and Gino felt like he was sticking his finger in a bursting dam. Frankenstein and the angry mob came to mind.

Fortunately half a dozen MPD patrols had been trolling the Winter Fest area and got to the scene fast. The uniforms took charge immediately, clearing the area around Gino and Magozzi within a minute.

'Damnit anyway,' Gino grumbled, watching the suddenly obedient citizens nodding respectfully to the patrols and backing off as they were told. 'This is the kind of thing that makes you want to put on the blues again. I'm waving my badge all over the place and it didn't mean crap. Those guys show up in brass buttons and, bingo, everybody listens.'

Magozzi was looking over the cops holding the line,

hoping for someone he knew well enough to work. 'You should have lost the hat. Earflaps diminish authority.'

'Yeah, well, you weren't doing so hot either, Mr Topcoat.'

The two of them were silent for a moment as they stared at the snowman, thinking and feeling things they would never talk about, not even to each other.

'That couldn't have been easy,' Gino finally said, shaking his head.

'What do you mean?'

'You ever think about how hard it would be to get a body inside a snowman?'

'Not until this minute.'

'I mean, how do you get a floppy dead guy to stand up while you pack snow around him?'

Magozzi thought about that. 'I don't know. Maybe he wasn't floppy.'

'You mean, like rigor or something?'

'Yeah. Or something. The killer could have had help.'

Gino thought about it for a minute, then shook his head. 'I don't know. This is so damn weird, and the really weird stuff is usually a solo job. I'll bet you a million bucks we plug this into NCIC and won't get a match.'

'No bet.'

'Damn. And I had you pegged for easy money.' Gino backed up a few feet and continued his scrutiny. 'He could be propped up with something, I suppose.'

'We don't even know if there's a body under there. It could just be a head.'

'Jesus, Leo.'

'Hey, you're the one who's obsessed with the logistics, I'm just sharing some possibilities. But I think a better question is why you'd want to put a dead guy in a snowman in the first place. That's not exactly a body dump of convenience. This guy took some serious risks, doing something like this in a public park the night before an event like this.'

Gino went through three stages at every homicide scene. The first stage was that single moment when he saw the victim as a person. He usually moved out of that one pretty fast, before it weighed him down too much. The second stage was the disconnect, when what you had to do at a crime scene overcame humanity. The third stage was out-and-out rage, and once it hit, it stayed with him until the day they closed the file. It was coming too fast this time, Magozzi thought, watching his partner's face turn red.

'Goddamnit, this really pisses me off, you know? This is a contest for kids, for Chrissake. What kind of a sick bastard would plant a body where kids could find it?' He tugged out his cell phone and punched speed-dial. 'I gotta stop Angela before she heads over here with our kids.'

While Gino was talking to Angela, Magozzi waved over a couple of uniforms who were slogging through the snowy field of snowmen, looking for a crime scene to mark, rolls of neon yellow tape looped over their wrists. 'Give me a fifty-footer around the snowman.'

'No problem. Which one?'

Magozzi jerked his thumb over his shoulder and the cops took a closer look.

The younger of the two caught his breath and took a quick step backward. The older one looked at the dead eyes inside the snowman, then moved even closer as his face went slack. 'Jesus, Mary, and Joseph,' he whispered. 'That's Tommy Deaton.'

Magozzi dug in his coat pocket for his notebook. 'You know this guy? You're sure?'

'Hell, yes, I know him. Rode with him for a couple weeks before he shifted over to the Second.'

'Wait a minute. He's one of ours?'

The old cop nodded, keeping his stone face on. 'Damnit, he was a nice kid. Loved the job.'

Magozzi felt like someone had just punched him in the stomach. He turned his head to look hard at the face inside the snowman, trying to see something familiar. In a city with this many cops, a lot of them changing precincts, changing shifts, changing jobs, no way you could know them all. Magozzi felt guilty for not knowing this one.

He glanced at Gino, who was tucking his cell back in his pocket. 'You heard?'

'Yeah, I heard. Man, this just keeps getting worse.'

There was a sudden commotion by the parking area as the Bureau of Criminal Apprehension crime-scene van inched its way through a massing crowd of media, gawkers, and the frazzled patrols who were scrambling to clear a path. Reporters shouted questions from behind the barrier of blue the minute Jimmy Grimm and his techs got out and started unloading equipment.

'Look at that,' Gino said in disgust. 'They're worse than buzzards. What the hell do they think the BCA is going to tell them now? They haven't even been on scene yet.'

'Jimmy never talks to the press. I think there's a bounty on his head. First reporter to get a grunt out of him goes national.'

Magozzi was still staring off into the distance, watching Jimmy Grimm and his team as they tromped across the field toward them in their white jumpsuits, looking too much like animated versions of the snowmen they were dodging.

'Happy new year, Detectives,' Jimmy said morosely as he approached.

'It was, up until an hour ago,' Gino muttered.

'I hear you. I caught the story about you saving that woman in the car trunk yesterday and figured that was a good omen.'

'More like a harbinger of doom.'

'Apparently.' Jimmy sighed and his eyes coursed the field, taking a mental inventory for later reference. 'So, show me what you've got.'

Magozzi and Gino stepped aside and watched Jimmy take a long, hard look at the snowman. If he was surprised, he didn't show it. 'We're going to have to bag the whole damn snowman. There could be trace anywhere in there.'

Magozzi moved a little closer to him and kept his voice low. 'There's a possible ID, Jimmy. Tommy Deaton. Works out of the Second.'

Grimm kept his eyes on Magozzi's for a long moment, took a shallow breath, then turned to his team and started barking out orders like a drill sergeant. 'Shoot the pictures, then get some polyurethane around Frosty here and peel him like an egg. Make damn sure you don't lose a flake, and for God's sake, be careful. I'm guessing we're going to find some kind of a support somewhere under all this snow, and I want some more photographs of him in situ before we take him down . . .'

The old cop stringing tape eased over to Magozzi and Gino while Jimmy was still talking. His radio was silent, but his hand was still on his shoulder unit. He looked at them for a minute without saying anything, then took a deep breath. 'We've got another one,' he said quietly. He tipped his head toward a circle of blue surrounding a snowman on the other side of the field. 'And it's another one of ours, name of Toby Myerson. He worked the Second, too.'

Jimmy was still talking in the background; uniforms on the line were still herding onlookers back from the scene; the media reps were still shouting questions – everything in the park looked and sounded exactly as it had five seconds ago. The three men who knew it wasn't – Magozzi, Gino, and the old cop – just looked at each other silently for a few seconds, afraid to look anywhere else.

Finally Magozzi let his gaze travel around the field, focusing on one snowman, then another, then another. 'How many you figure there are?'

'At least a hundred,' Gino said.

The old cop shook his head. 'More like twice that. What do you want us to do?'

Magozzi and Gino exchanged a glance, then both looked back at the parking lot where all the long lenses were recording everything.

'Knock 'em all down,' Magozzi said.

4

There were well over a hundred officers of one sort or another in the park, but it still took a good half hour to destroy the work of children. Gino and Magozzi had moved to the center of the open field so they could see as much of it as possible, busy eyes and knotted stomachs waiting for a blue-coated arm to rise or a cry to go out announcing another terrible find.

They were just snowmen, but for some reason, Magozzi felt as if he were watching a massacre as crime-scene techs and cops systematically and carefully dismantled them one by one. With each one that went down, he cringed and held his breath, expecting the worst – pessimism was an occupational hazard that moved in fast and stuck around for the long haul – but so far, the rest of the field was clean.

Most parents had whisked their children away long ago, but there were a few left who watched the proceedings with feral glee, oblivious to the terrorized expressions on the faces of their offspring.

'Jesus Christ,' Gino fumed. 'Can we arrest those assholes for child abuse?'

'I don't think it would hold up.'

'You know what's going to happen, don't you? All their kids are gonna wake up screaming every night for a month, and then they'll sue the department for not providing grief counselors. And why? Because they just had to stick around for the peep show, hoping like hell they'd see some poor dead bastard and feel happy that it wasn't them on a slab at the end of the day.'

The sad thing was, Gino was only half-joking, and probably more than half-right.

One of the younger uniforms broke away from an anonymous sea of blue at the far side of the field and crunched over, his ears and nose bright red from the cold, his expression a mix of relief and misery. 'That's all of them, Detectives. Nothing else.'

'Thank God,' Gino said, releasing a sigh.

The cop nodded, his eyes preoccupied with the decimated field that had turned to slush under heavy foot traffic and the afternoon sun. 'Did you know them?' he finally asked.

Magozzi and Gino shook their heads somberly.

'Me either. But I feel like I did.' He drifted off without another word, no doubt contemplating his own mortality for the first time.

Magozzi and Gino followed, and ran into Jimmy Grimm halfway.

'I was looking for you guys. We've got the first one uncovered. Come over and take a look.'

The first thing they noticed was that Tommy Deaton's body was lashed to a wooden ski trail marker with common yellow synthetic rope – the kind you could find just about anywhere, from gas stations to grocery stores. His chin had dropped to his chest without the packed snow to brace it up, and Gino thought it was the saddest thing he ever saw.

'Oh, man, can't you cut him down?'

'Not until Dr Rambachan sees it in place. He got caught behind a twenty-car fender-bender on 494, but he should be here soon.'

'There's the answer to your question, Gino,' Magozzi said.

'What question?' Jimmy wanted to know.

'How you get a dead body to stand up straight so you can build a snowman around it.'

Jimmy nodded. 'And the skis weren't just a prop. This guy was hard-core. That suit he's wearing goes for six hundred bucks minimum, add another thousand or so for the skis and poles.'

'You been watching the Home Shopping Network again?'

'I wish. Three kids, two of them on the ski team, and I'm broke every Christmas. Been trying to talk them into something cheaper, like the debate team, but no joy.' He walked over to Deaton's body and pointed at the side of his head. 'One shot, small caliber, probably dropped him on the spot. No exit wound, so we should get a slug out of the autopsy. And there's stippling on the scalp, so it was real close.'

He stooped down in front of a tray of neatly arranged evidence bags and plucked one out that held a tooled leather wallet. 'I just pulled this off him. ID, credit cards, two hundred seventy-eight bucks cash.'

Magozzi's eyes drifted down to Tommy Deaton's belt holster, where his service piece should have been but wasn't. 'But no weapon.'

'Right.'

'How about Myerson? Is he uncovered yet?'

'I've got a team over there now. Let's take a walk while my guys get the shots of Deaton without the snowman.'

They were careful to give wide berth to the crime-scene tape that cordoned off the ski trail that wound through a sparse patch of woods – the only trail that drew a line directly from Tommy Deaton to Toby Myerson. Of course the hundreds of people tromping through here before the tape went up hadn't been so careful, and Magozzi knew the chance of getting any tracks was beyond hope; but there were a couple BCA guys in the woods proper, and they were crouched by a skinny maple, carefully collecting shredded bark with pairs of tweezers – a good sign.

'Did you find something?' Jimmy asked hopefully.

'Maybe. We've got lots of fresh bark confetti, and as far as I know, beavers hibernate, so we're hoping for a slug.'

'Pull some guys from the field and widen the grid around the trail a few hundred yards. Take a look at every tree.'

'They're on their way. We'll keep you posted.'

Toby Myerson looked very much like his Second Precinct partner, right down to the skis and the yellow rope that held him upright against another trail marker, but this man's right arm hung at an awkward angle, and the sleeve of his ski suit was shredded and stained almost black.

Magozzi stood quietly, moving only his eyes, taking it all in. 'That arm wound had to have bled like crazy. So where's the blood?'

Jimmy actually smiled at him. 'Good question, Grasshopper. We uncovered a little that filtered down through the snow, but not enough. My guess is he didn't take the arm shot here. We're looking for a blood trail between the two snowmen.'

Gino nodded. 'No glove on the right hand. You find it around here?'

'Nope.'

'Did you test the hand for GSR?'

'Nothing.'

'Huh. So he never got a shot off, but he sure as hell tried.'

Jimmy frowned at him. 'How do you figure that?'

Gino poked at his forehead with his big mitten. 'I see it

right here, that's how. Two guys skiing together right after the first snow, bad guy jumps out from behind a tree and pops Deaton, Myerson sees his partner buy it, rips his glove off to get at his weapon, but before he can get a shot off, the killer nails him in the shooting arm and he loses his piece.'

Magozzi rolled his eyes, but Jimmy looked fascinated. 'Then what happened?'

'Poor Myerson tries to get away, that's what, pumping away with his good arm, but he only makes it this far before he bleeds out.'

Jimmy Grimm looked at Magozzi. 'Where does he get this stuff?'

'He makes it up. Does it all the time. Only this time, I think he's got something. It makes sense.'

Grimm nodded solemnly. 'Except for one thing. He didn't bleed out. The arm shot shattered the bone, but it wasn't lethal.' He walked around the pole Toby Myerson was lashed to and pointed to a small hole in the back of the dead man's neck. 'The son of a bitch chased this man down and put a bullet right through his spine. Doesn't look like a killing shot, but it probably paralyzed him instantly.'

Gino frowned. 'Then what killed him?'

Grimm looked away and shrugged. 'Who knows? You'll have to wait until the doc gets inside to find that out. Could have been a heart attack, could have been hypothermia, massive organ failure . . .'

'Jesus,' Magozzi whispered. 'Are you saying he could have been alive while they were building a snowman around him?'

'Maybe. Maybe even for a long time after that.'

Magozzi closed his eyes.

5

Harley Davidson's mansion looked as if it had been styled for a Currier and Ives Christmas card reproduction. Normally it looked foreboding from the street, but dressed with fresh snow and the holiday decorations he had yet to take down, the place looked more like a fairy-tale gingerbread castle than the red-stone lair of Summit Avenue's biker-ogre. Even the wicked spikes that topped the wrought-iron fence looked whimsical with their white mushroom caps of snow. A tasteful display of twinkle lights sparkled along the eaves of the carriage house, and a lovingly restored, antique sleigh sat in front of the big wooden barn doors, as if waiting for a handsome team of harness horses to be hitched up.

Except at Harley's, horsepower had a whole different meaning, and the carriage house was really a tricked-out garage; anybody who looked inside would get the Currier and Ives fantasy blown right out of their mind. But all the priceless cars and motorcycles and the big luxury motorcoach Monkeewrench used as a sort of traveling Crime Stoppers unit were all tucked away under blankets and tarps, waiting for warmer weather and dry roads. And it was driving Harley nuts.

At the big house, in the third-floor Monkeewrench office, lights were blazing. The leather-clad lord of the manor was stationed at his mammoth desk, polishing off the last of his Carnivore Special from a local pizza parlor, while Roadrunner paced the floor with a clipboard, reading aloud from a punch list. His gangly, six-foot-seven frame was clad in a white Lycra bike suit today, and Harley thought he looked like an origami crane.

'Clean up graphics on level two,' Roadrunner recited.

Harley gave him a distracted nod while he mopped tomato sauce out of his black beard. 'I'm working on it now.'

Roadrunner made a meticulous checkmark on his list and continued. 'Okay. Fonts are inconsistent on –'

'Yeah, yeah, I know. I'm working on that, too.'

'Improve load speed between levels three and four.'

'That's your problem, buddy – my level transitions work just fine.'

Roadrunner gave him a grumpy look. 'You haven't even started writing code for your levels yet.'

'I know that, but when I do, they'll be perfect. What else?'

Roadrunner was still annoyed, but he turned back to his list without comment. 'There are some minor glitches that carried over from the beta version, but it looks like Annie and Grace have those covered . . . oh. Here's one. In all caps: HARLEY. DRESS THE DAMN ICE PRINCESS.'

Harley glowered at him. 'Who wrote that? Annie?'

'The Ice Princess needs clothes, Harley.'

'She's dressed already.'

'She's wearing a bikini.'

'Like I said, she's dressed. That's PG material.'

'This is supposed to be a children's spelling game. Ages five to ten. It's totally inappropriate.'

Harley spun his chair around and stared out the window. 'Look at that. They haven't plowed yet. You know, nothing says we can't go out and buy a couple sleds right now and shred Summit Avenue.'

‘Are you going to take care of the Ice Princess or not? Because if you don’t want to do it, I will.’

‘Great, then she’ll end up looking like Lance Armstrong.’

Roadrunner’s cheeks flared red and for a moment, Harley was certain he was going to chuck his freshly sharpened pencil at his head.

‘Christ, Roadrunner, relax. Okay, I’ll dress her in a turtle-neck, a nun’s habit, whatever you say.’

‘And you can’t impale the Snow Pixies on icicles when the kids spell a word wrong.’

‘That was a joke. Would you just take it easy? This is supposed to be fun, remember? At least that’s what you keep telling me, but you’re taking things way too seriously.’

‘This is serious. It’s for a good cause, Harley. The proceeds from this game are going to help out a lot of kids who need a safe place to go after school, and you know from personal experience how important that is. We all do – that’s why we picked this charity in the first place, remember?’

‘Kiss my ass, of course I remember. And I’m damn happy to do it, and all the other pro bono stuff. But this is the kind of programming I can do in my sleep. Plain and simple? I’m bored.’

Roadrunner sighed, moped over to his own desk, and slumped into his chair. ‘I know what you mean. But we all agreed we needed to take a few months off after the Four Corners thing. Plus, we can’t take the rig on the road in this weather.’

‘I know, but I’m ready for some action. Hey, what do you say we send out our virus and shut down a couple spammers?’

Roadrunner gave him a disapproving look. ‘Spam isn’t illegal. If we get caught, we go to jail.’

'You know what I got in my in-box this morning? A spam that said "Dikkie 2 small? Not UR falt!" That should be illegal.'

'Maybe somebody's trying to tell you something.'

'That doesn't even dignify a response.' He turned to his computer and started typing.

'What are you doing? You're not doing anything stupid, are you?'

'Relax. I'm just checking my mail.'

'You're finished working for the day, aren't you?'

'It's Saturday. I might have a hot date.'

'Then I'm going home.'

'You're not biking home in this weather.'

'Why not? It'll be good exercise. Besides, it stopped snowing.'

'It's not going to stop snowing for another day. Look it up.'

Roadrunner pouted at his computer screen. 'I'll take a cab, then.'

'Don't be a jackass. I'll give you a ride . . . Just hang on a minute.'

Roadrunner knew that 'a minute' in Harley's lexicon could end up being an hour, so he started surfing the websites of the local news channels, looking for weather reports. What he found instead were streaming video footage and photos from Theodore Wirth Park, and damned if he didn't catch a glimpse of Magozzi and Gino standing in the background of one of the stills.

'Harley. We've gotta turn on the TV.'

Across the Mississippi in a different world, Magozzi pulled the unmarked into a broad driveway carved between two fresh snowbanks and shut it down. He and Gino looked at Tommy Deaton's house through the windshield, one of the prewar brick two-stories that peppered the back streets of Minneapolis, especially near the lakes. Neither one of them made a move to get out of the car.

'Ten years ago this neighborhood was right in the toilet,' Gino said.

'I remember. Wonder what these houses go for now?'

'This close to the lake? Quarter of a mil, at least, and all thanks to the MPD. Bump up the patrols, pull the dirt-balls off the street, pretty soon you have cops living in the neighborhood and property values skyrocket. You ask me, the department oughta get a percentage. Isn't that Polish butcher shop around here somewhere?'

'Kramarczuk's? Not even close.'

'Kramarczuk's could be a thousand miles away, and it's still close enough. Man, you don't get sausage like that anywhere else in the country. I bring home a package from that place, and as far as Angela's concerned, I can do no wrong for about a week. We gotta make a run over there one of these days.'

Magozzi released his seat belt, but didn't make any move to get out of the car. 'I can't believe we're sitting out here freezing our tails off talking about some goddamn stupid sausage.'

Gino sighed. 'We do this every time we have to make a notification. Last time we spent five minutes in the driveway talking about lawn fertilizer runoff.'

'We did?'

'Anything to keep from going in there. You notice the driveway? Somebody did a real nice job with the blower on this one.'

Magozzi nodded and finally lifted the door handle. 'Maybe a service. Or maybe Mrs Deaton. We should ask about that.'

'Yeah, and isn't that a nice touch? "Gee, Mrs Deaton, I'm sorry to tell you your husband is dead, but on a lighter note, who cleared your driveway?" Christ. It's a damn miracle these people don't pull out a gun and shoot us.'

It took a long time for Tommy Deaton's wife to answer the front door, and the moment he saw her, Magozzi understood why. She was a tiny thing with bruised and blackened eyes, a swollen face, and a big white bandage over her nose. She examined their badges very carefully before letting them inside, and then their expressions as they tried not to stare at her ruined face. She was a cop's wife, and knew what they were thinking. 'New nose,' she explained with a quick, embarrassed smile. 'Thirtieth-birthday present from my husband.'

Magozzi's thoughts went off on a side track, wondering what the world was coming to when husbands gave their young wives plastic surgery for their birthday. What the hell kind of statement was that? Happy birthday, honey, and, for Chrissake, go get your face fixed.

Tommy Deaton's wife was looking at him with polite uncertainty, probably wondering why they were there. She collapsed on the foyer rug when they told her.

After she came around, Gino and Magozzi helped her make some phone calls, then had about fifteen minutes to ask all the terrible questions they had to ask, while Mary Deaton sat ramrod straight on the sofa, tears running down her face, but answering everything. She knew the drill.

The normally smart-mouthed, hard-nosed Gino was tender with her, as he always was when he did this kind of thing, his heart sticking out all over the place. 'So you had no reason to worry when Tommy didn't come home last night?'

'No. Like I said, he was crazy for cross-country skiing. Him and Toby both, and they'd been waiting months for a decent snow. Tommy said he'd probably spend the night at Toby's. He lives a lot closer to the park, and those two like a few beers after they ski. Tommy's a real stickler about driving after he's had a drink, so he stays over at Toby's a lot in the winter.'

'A real responsible fellow.' Gino smiled at her.

'Yes, he is.'

She kept talking about him in the present tense, which always made Magozzi uncomfortable when he was talking to surviving family members. It wasn't really denial. Sometimes it just took a long time for death to trickle down into speech patterns.

Gino chuckled softly. 'You know, I stay out all night, even when I'm on the job, and my wife's all over me on the cell the next morning. Where am I, what am I doing, when am I getting home . . . that sort of thing.'

Mary Deaton looked at him as if she'd never heard of such behavior. 'Really?'

'Oh, yeah.'

She almost smiled. 'Tommy wouldn't like it one bit if I tried to check up on him like that. He's pretty much his own man, you know what I mean?'

'I do.'

Mary Deaton's parents arrived then and made a beeline for their daughter, eliciting a fresh gush of tears and the pathetic, quiet wailing of a full-grown woman slipping immediately back to childhood when the arms of a parent could protect you against almost anything. Magozzi and Gino moved well back, looking anywhere but at the clustered threesome, trying not to listen to that first flush of shared grief that could drown the hardest cop after a while if he let himself hear it.

Eventually the father broke away and walked over, introduced himself as Bill Warner, and shook both their hands. He was taller than Gino, shorter than Magozzi, with a gray brush cut, a well-lined face, and a trim body he carried in a very familiar way.

Gino took one look at him and said, 'You're on the job.'

Bill Warner gave him a sad smile. 'Was. Twenty years with MPD. Retired two years now, but glad to hear it still shows. Mary says you've been real nice to her. I thank you for that. Did you have a chance to ask her what you needed to?'

'All we need for now,' Magozzi replied. 'There may be more later.'

Mr Warner nodded. 'There always is. Anything we can do. Any of us.' He took a card out of his wallet and handed it to him. 'Alice and I are going to take Mary home with us today. Home number's there, and my cell. Any chance you can give me something about what really went down? All Mary can say is he's gone, and so far the news is just a bunch of talking heads trying to reword the same old bullshit. I've got purple prose coming out of my ears and I only had fifteen minutes to listen to it on the way over here. Goddamn vultures just keep harping about all the traumatized kids, like that was the only tragedy here . . .' He stopped himself and took a breath, and cooled down the red in his face a couple of shades. 'Sorry. I'm reacting all wrong. It's just that we didn't even hear two cops had been murdered until Mary called. The news just keeps yammering about the goddamned snowmen getting knocked down ...' He almost lost it again, and apologized again.

'Don't sweat it. But for the record, the word that they were cops hasn't leaked yet.' Magozzi put his hand on the man's arm, something he rarely did when dealing with survivors, and then he broke a cardinal rule and gave the man a sketchy summary of what they knew so far, because Bill Warner was one of them, and he'd know enough to keep his mouth shut. He still had a bone-chilling image of Toby Myerson, paralyzed and helpless, still alive and maybe conscious while someone packed snow around him, dying by inches and probably knowing it. He glossed over that in a big way, guessing that the man would know his son-in-law's partner, but Warner still went pale. At least Deaton's death had been quick, and he could give him that much. Bill Warner listened without interrupting, like a cop would, but in the end he sagged into a chair and put his head in his hands.

By that time the house was starting to fill up and any pretense of private conversation became impossible. Family and friends had started to gather, and there was a steady stream of blue uniforms through the living room and foyer as the department closed ranks around one of their own.

Magozzi took a last look at Mary Deaton as he and Gino made their way to the door. She looked tiny and helpless in the swelling crowd, like a shell-shocked child surrounded by protective soldiers.

Once outside, they waited by the side of their unmarked, taking deep breaths of the frigid air while the uniform who'd parked them in moved his car. The place looked like a police convention. Patrol cars filled the driveway and double-parked on the street, which made them feel a little better about leaving Tommy Deaton's widow, and a lot worse about what had happened.

'Thank God we don't have to do this twice,' Gino grumbled. 'McLaren called when I was in the can. We'll hook up at the hall when he and Tinker get back from making the other notification.'

'Was Myerson married?'

'It's almost worse. Happy bachelor, barely twenty-eight, just moved back in with his mom when she got real sick, spends most of his off-time taking care of her. McLaren knew the guy, and he is beyond bummed. Goddamnit, Leo, he's killing cops. Good ones. And he's doing it big-time in our face, at an MPD-sponsored festival, no less. This one's so personal it scares the crap out of me. Damn, it's freezing out here. Tell me the temp didn't drop twenty degrees when we were in that house.'

Magozzi opened the car, then lifted his face toward the westerly wind. It was starting a slow pickup, and he could smell more snow coming.

6

It was Saturday afternoon and Steve Doyle should have been at home blowing snow so his wife and kids could get into the driveway that night when they came home from Northfield. He should have been cleaning up the sinkful of dirty dishes that had piled up during a week of bachelor dinners. And above all, he should have been on the couch, sipping a cold beer and watching the Gophers' hockey game. *Should* have been.

Instead, he was sitting at his desk on a precious day off, reading the nauseating bio of yet another scumbag he was supposed to babysit – all because the damn blizzard had shut down every bus and most of the roads yesterday, so the newly released Kurt Weinbeck hadn't been able to make it to his Friday-afternoon parole meeting. And for some reason known only to God and the criminal justice system, his supervisor had decided it was a good idea to reschedule and make Doyle come in on a weekend so that he could give his lecture on piss tests, gainful employment, and the halfway house that would be the scumbag's home for the next several months. As if it would make a difference.

He drained his coffee and poured himself another cup, even though he was already flying on caffeine, and turned his attention back to the file in front of him. The more he read, the more depressed he got. Kurt Weinbeck was a multiple felon with no hope of rehabilitation that he could see – one of those frequent flyers who kept getting regurgitated back onto the streets by a system that wasn't just blind, it was brain-dead. Doyle had always thought that guys like this should be turned into fertilizer, because they were nothing but bags of manure to start with.

Even though he was barely forty and by all accounts a few years away from total burnout, Doyle was pretty sure he'd already crossed that threshold. His wife had been begging him for two years to change jobs, and he was actually thinking about listening to her for a change. In fact, Kurt Weinbeck might be the very last case he'd ever take, and the thought actually buoyed his spirits a little.

He'd started this job as a young, devout Christian hopeful, believing absolutely that every criminal was merely a misguided victim in his own right, and that single-handedly he and God could reform any sinner. Five years in, he was a cynical agnostic thinking maybe the death penalty wasn't such a bad idea. Ten years later he was a die-hard atheist with a .357 in his desk drawer, because half of these guys scared him to death. You could only read so many files about creeps who sexually abused their kids and raped strangers and slashed the throats of anybody who got in the way of their next hit of crack before you started thinking that if there really were a god keeping an eye on this world, you didn't want any part of him. Year after year he'd watched the system that signed his paycheck suck them in, then spit them out so they could do it all over again. Lately he'd been fantasizing about pulling out the big gun and shooting any new parolee who walked through the door, and save the state a lot of money and the world a lot of grief.

Get out of this business, he told himself. *Right now, before it's too late.*

He got up and turned on the little TV that was perched

on a bracket in the wall, hoping to catch some college hockey while he waited, but instead saw a breaking news bulletin and a live feed showing a lot of Minneapolis cops knocking down snowmen at Theodore Wirth Park. He turned up the volume and felt his stomach flip-flop, wondering if there'd been a terrorist attack – hell, why not take out a park full of children? Of course, it wasn't a terrorist attack, not by today's standards – but leaving dead corpses for children to find qualified as terrorism in his book.

When Weinbeck showed up a few minutes later, Doyle turned down the TV, took his place at his desk, and did a quick visual inventory of his newest client. Parolees generally came in three basic models: fat and mean, muscular and mean, or skinny and mean. This one fell into the latter category, with big, bobbling eyes that raced around the room, and a sinuous, slinky body that moved and twitched like a meerkat on crack.

'You're thirteen minutes late, Mr Weinbeck. You realize I could have called in a warrant on you.'

'I'm sorry, sir. It won't happen again.'

'Make sure it doesn't. For future reference, show up early, and if you can't show up early, show up on time at the latest. That's one of the rules, and if you follow the rules, we'll get along just fine.'

'Yes, sir, I know.'

Doyle made a show of paging through his file. 'I see that this is your third time on parole. Do you think we can make this your last?'

Weinbeck nodded enthusiastically and launched into his predictable spiel of bullshit about how he was genuinely remorseful, how he'd finally learned his lesson, how grateful he was for another chance, and how he would make it work this time around, blah, blah, blah. Doyle nodded at the appropriate moments, but his eyes kept drifting back to the TV.

'Something going on?' Weinbeck asked, following Doyle's gaze.

'Nothing that concerns you.' He slid some paperwork across the desk. 'This is your bible. It lays out the rules and regs, procedures, where you'll be staying, where you'll be working . . .'

'. . . when I can eat, sleep, take a piss . . . I know the drill.'

'I'm sure you do, but look it over anyhow. If you have any questions, now's the time to ask.'

'When can I talk to my wife?'

Doyle stared at him. 'You've got to be kidding.'

'She's my wife.'

'She divorced you two years ago. You got the papers. You get within a hundred yards of her, you'll be back inside before you can take a breath.'

Weinbeck tried for a friendly smile. 'How the hell am I supposed to do that? Nobody'll tell me where she is. Besides, I just want to talk to her. A phone call is all I'm asking. They told me you'd have the number.'

'It's not going to happen, Weinbeck, and you know it's not going to happen. You've been through this before. You want to just throw in the towel now and head straight back to Stillwater, save us all some trouble?'

Kurt Weinbeck's manner changed instantly, and so did his countenance, softening into a practiced expression of deference and obedience. 'No, sir. I certainly don't. I'm sorry I mentioned it. I just worry about her. I'd like to know that she's doing okay, that's all.'

Doyle studied the man's face for a long moment. Man, he

hated these guys, hated the way they thought they could play you with a smile and a pretense of acquiescence, as if you were some kind of idiot. They were all self-serving, deceptive bastards. He really believed that. And yet somewhere beneath his hard-won shell of cynicism, a stupid, irritating flicker of idealism still lingered. He couldn't get rid of it, which was probably why he was still in this job after all the years of disappointment. His head knew better, but his heart still wanted to believe that the worst scumbag was still a human being, that if the right person offered a little charity at just the right time, he could find his way back. And what would it cost him? Just a single sentence, a few words of reassurance.

'I talked to your wife myself. She's doing just fine.'

This time Weinbeck's smile was genuine, and it made Doyle feel better about himself than he had in months.

'Thank you, sir. It means a lot to hear that. Are we finished here?'

'Ten more minutes.'

'Can I get something to drink? A Coke or something? I saw a vending machine down the hall.'

Doyle pushed a few forms across the desk. 'I'll get it. Start signing wherever you see a flag. The sooner you finish, the sooner you're out of here.' He picked up Weinbeck's file to take it with him, pausing as he walked around the desk to make sure Weinbeck was signing in the right place. Some of these guys were so dumb that, red flag or not, they couldn't figure out where to put their name.

He saw the blade as it slashed up toward him, but not soon enough.

7

Midafternoon on a Saturday, and City Hall was buzzing like a blown-out amplifier. The entrance was jammed with what looked like every reporter and camera operator in the state, and as usual, where the cameras went, the politicians followed.

As he and Gino carved a 'no comment' path through the din of shouted questions that followed their entrance, Magozzi recognized no less than three city council members, several legislators, p.r. people from the mayor's office, and bizarrely, the media spokesman for the Department of Transportation, though God knew what he was doing here. Probably looking for an increase in the snow-removal budget so they could get rid of all the white stuff someone was hiding bodies in.

Oddly enough, Homicide was the only relatively quiet place in the whole building. They heard Gloria's excessively polite phone voice coming from the other side of the door that divided the reception area from the office proper, and Magozzi didn't know which was more disturbing: that Gloria had come in on a Saturday, or that she was actually being civil to someone. 'The detectives are still at the scene, sir. Yes, I certainly will pass that on.'

She was big and black and sharp-tongued, fastidious about her appearance, and slavish to a wild style that was uniquely her own. They were used to seeing her in anything from tiny braids to colorful turbans; one day in a sari, the next in a miniskirt and platform heels, but this was something entirely new.

She was standing at the front desk, hands on ample hips, glaring down at all the blinking lights on her phone, looking like a very big, very black Priscilla Presley. Her black hair was glued into some kind of a flip; the rosy dress was full and shiny and made crinkly little noises when she moved. Gino hadn't seen one like it since his dad showed him his high school prom picture from sometime during the dark ages. He opened his mouth to say something, but Gloria glared and pointed a finger at him.

'You like your balls, Rolseth?'

'I do.'

'Because this day is too black for wisecracking.'

Gino nodded. 'I was just going to say that so far you're the best thing in it. You look good in red.'

'Hmph.' Her big shoulders relaxed a little. 'This is not red, you fool, it's cherry blossom, and you think this dress is bad, you should have seen the bride. Looked like she was wearing a big fat doily.' She plopped back into her chair with a rustle and a grunt. 'The Chief just called. He was halfway to his lake place when the news hit; won't make it back before the five o'clock news, which might be a good thing. Local media has already been all over the tube with bulletins, and CNN picked it up. They're runnin' crawl lines and calling it the Minneapolis Snowman Killing Fields. Bastards think they're cute.'

Magozzi felt his jaw muscles tighten. 'Goddamnit, we've got two dead officers here.'

'Yeah, well cop-killer is a favorite headline, but it takes

second place on the hit parade when you've got film of a bunch of uniforms knocking down hundreds of snowmen in front of a crowd of crying kids.'

'Jesus. They're showing that?'

'You bet they are. Local, national, probably international by now. They've got the damn thing on a loop. Chief's doing a live thing with the press at nine tonight; he wants everything you've got on his desk by eight so he can cull through it.'

Johnny McLaren and Tinker Lewis were halfway across the room at their desks, working the phones, already buried in paperwork; otherwise the place was empty. Magozzi and Gino rolled a couple of chairs over to Tinker's desk, primarily because McLaren's looked like the inside of a Dumpster during a garbage strike.

Tinker thanked someone on the phone and gently set it back in its cradle. The man did everything gently – always had, as long as Magozzi had known him, which was a pretty rare demeanor to find in Homicide. He had brown eyes that always looked sad; today they were downright mournful. 'Second Precinct is red-lighting over everything they've got on Tommy Deaton and Toby Myerson. Recent performance reviews, arrest reports, the private stuff they kept in their lockers, anything that might not be in the master files. Nothing flashy stood out in the Sarge's mind – not that he'd be able to think of it today, anyway. They've all got their brains wrapped in black over there.'

Magozzi nodded. 'We need to tear it all apart, see if this is a cop thing or maybe even a Second Precinct thing.'

'Yeah, they're a little worried about that.' He glanced over at McLaren, who had one ear glued to the phone while he scribbled on a scrap of paper. 'Johnny's talking to one of the guys over there that hung with Myerson off-time. You get anything from Deaton's family?'

Magozzi shook his head. 'We got what we could, but nothing that really jumps out. Wife went down like a redwood when we told her. She was pretty messed up. How about Toby Myerson's family?'

Tinker leaned back in his chair, closed his eyes, and saw Toby Myerson's mother again, braced crookedly in her wheelchair, one side of her wrinkled face sagging from the stroke that took half her body and most of her speech, but left awareness and emotion and a pair of eyes that said more than Tinker wanted to hear. 'No family except the mother. Toby took care of her. Don't know what's going to happen to her now.'

He started sliding neatly labeled file folders across the desk, some fatter than others. 'Reports are starting to trickle in, but it's going to be an avalanche soon. Must have been hundreds of people out there today; plus we've got to go through all the film and stills the media took; then there's the door-to-door on all the houses around the park, and you know how that goes. As soon as people find out there was a murder, we're going to hear about a million parked cars that, now that they think of it, looked kind of suspicious . . .' He blew a frustrated sigh out of puffed cheeks that drooped a little lower every year he was on the job. 'The book on this one is going to weigh a ton.'

Magozzi nodded. 'You have Espinoza on it?'

'Yeah. We're copying him on everything, he's plugging it into the Monkeewrench software, but there's still a lot of stuff that needs eyes on.'

'Always is.'

Johnny McLaren finally hung up the phone and rolled

bloodshot eyes in their direction. Rumor had it the flame-haired detective started every weekend with a Friday-night toot that lasted forty-eight hours, and looking at him on a Saturday made Magozzi believe it. 'I got a little. Could be good, could be bad. Toby Myerson and Tommy Deaton were together last night. Both of them were cross-country ski fanatics; couldn't wait to get off last night so they could hit the trails.'

Gino nodded. 'Yeah, that's what Deaton's wife told us. You know, I took one look at that first snowman and thought whacko serial killer posing his trophy. Then we found the second one, and I'm thinking, holy shit it's like serial-killer winter Olympics. Then we find out they were both ours, and it started to look like some asshole with a hard-on for cops. Now that we know those guys were together, we might have to look for a personal angle. Like maybe only one of them was the target, and the other just happened to get in the way.'

Tinker liked that. 'So maybe it didn't have anything to do with them being cops.'

'That would be the dream scenario.'

'I like that angle a lot better than some serial killer just plugging people at random, or cops in particular,' Magozzi said.

'Don't we all. Doesn't mean it's the way it went down.'

They all looked up at the heavy click of Gloria's heels on the floor and saw her fill the aisle between the desks with pink. 'I'm going to catch a bite before the Chief gets back. You're getting those reports pulled together for him, right?'

Skinny, red-haired McLaren looked at her and grinned, forgetting for a second that there were dead cops and a bad case and a late night ahead. 'You gotta tell me how you get that skirt to stick out so far.'

Gloria ignored him. 'Switchboard's screening till I get back, but Evelyn's on tonight, so cut her some slack. Last time she hung up on the city council chair and put through some idiot who said the CIA was planning the overthrow of the government in his living room. Chief damn near had her canned.'

'Can't really blame the woman,' Gino said. 'Chair of the city council or a paranoid idiot. Kind of a toss-up, if you ask me.'

She scowled, turned on her heel, then spun at the last moment and looked straight at McLaren. 'Crinolines,' she said, then disappeared out the door.

'What're crinolines?' McLaren whispered.

Gino gave him a look. 'You are such a fashion fetus. They're really stiff slips. They got plastic hoops in them so they stick way out. Fifties stuff. Must have been a retro wedding. Can't believe she even went to one of those things, let alone dressed up in a getup like that.'

McLaren was still staring at the place he had seen Gloria last.

It had been full dark for an hour, and Grace could still hear the irritating scrape of shovels against concrete from inside her house. In a working-class neighborhood like this, there weren't a lot of snowblowers, and the shovels had been busy all day, clearing yesterday's storm from walks and driveways. A few of them were manned by intrepid youngsters who trolled from house to house, picking up a little extra cash for a lot of hard labor. There weren't many such baby entrepreneurs these days; most kids were parked in front of the TV or a PlayStation, hands out for allowances earned by their mere existence. The few who worked the small, older houses on Ashland Avenue in St Paul never bothered to knock on Grace MacBride's door.

She'd had high-tech heating grates built into her sidewalks and driveway before she bought the place six years earlier, and you could Rollerblade on those sidewalks in a blizzard. Not that Grace minded physical labor, but she'd been hiding from a lot of people in those days, and there was no way she would expose herself long enough to shovel a path through a Minnesota winter. Supposedly no one was trying to kill her anymore, but it was just plain silly to take chances.

This evening, inside the snug little house she'd converted into a fortress, she was practicing the MacBride version of slovenliness.

No one ever saw Grace dressed like this, except Charlie, of course, and since human speech was the only trick the dog hadn't mastered yet, he wasn't talking. The flannel pajamas had been a gift from Roadrunner; soft and warm and, bless the stick man, black. Clearly a lot of thought had gone into the purchase, because the pants were wide enough to provide easy access to the derringer she kept strapped to her ankle when she was working at home. But the very softness of the lightweight flannel felt dangerous. Grace liked weighty fabrics between her and the rest of the world.

If it had been anyone but Magozzi, she wouldn't have opened the front door. He got a silly little grin on his face when he saw her outfit. 'You're in pj's. I find that enormously encouraging.'

'You're early, Magozzi.'

'I thought I could help you cook.'

'Supper's already on the stove. I was just about to get dressed.'

'Or I could help with that.'

Grace rolled her eyes and stepped aside while Magozzi hung up his coat and greeted Charlie. These days he was here so often that the dog no longer went completely ballistic when he walked in. The joy was still there, but it was a little more subdued, almost respectful, as if in Charlie's wee brain Magozzi had made the transition from playmate to master. Grace wasn't sure how she felt about that. 'You're in a pretty good mood for a cop with two new homicides on his plate.'

Magozzi didn't even look up from patting the dog. 'You heard?'

'Harley and Roadrunner called, made me turn on the television.'

He straightened and looked at her, and there was nothing good-humored in his expression. 'They were cops, Grace. Both of them.'

In the year and a half he'd known her, Magozzi had rarely seen Grace visibly express any emotion. She was closing in on the mid-thirties, and yet there wasn't a line on that face; not a smile crinkle at the corners of her mouth, not the slightest memory of a frown between her brows. It was like looking at the blank canvas of a baby's face, before the joy and the heartache of life left their lovely marks, and it always made Magozzi a little sad. But sometimes, if he looked very closely, he could see things in her eyes that never went any further.

'I'm sorry, Magozzi,' she said, and he felt a door close on the outside world and all the terrible things that happened there.

She took his hand and led him back to the kitchen, checked whatever was simmering on the stove, then poured two glasses of wine and sat opposite him at the kitchen table. 'Tell me about it,' she said, and it occurred to Magozzi that a woman had never said those words to him before. It sounded like a magic incantation.

This is what Gino has with Angela, he thought. *You come home dragged out and frustrated and there stands this amazing woman who really wants to know what kind of a day you had.* This was not a little thing. This wasn't just sharing the time you had together; this was wanting to share the time you spent apart, too, and as far as Magozzi was concerned, that boiled down to wanting to share a life. He wondered if Grace knew that was what she was doing.

'What are you smiling at, Magozzi?'

Magozzi was starting to hate his own house. It was dark, empty, and, worse yet, there was no woman and no dog. It had been unbelievably hard to leave Grace's tonight, but he had an early call and a hefty stack of accumulated reports to go through before morning, and reading would have been out of the question with Grace sitting next to him in her flannel pj's.

He grabbed a Summit Pale Ale from the refrigerator, turned on the television, and steeled himself for the ten o'clock news.

The news teams had had all day to polish up this story for maximum impact and it showed. Dramatic, inflammatory scripts laced with adjectives like *horrific, shocking,* and *ghastly* played well against the backdrop of skillfully edited montages that made what ultimately had been a well-managed, controlled crime scene look like a soccer stadium stampede.

Especially effective were the images of screaming, crying children as they watched the boys in blue knocking down one snowman after another. Without exception, every single broadcast made the MPD come off like a bunch of heartless jackasses.

They all ran snippets of Chief Malcherson's press conference, and none of it had been good. The man was a master of the calm, forthright presentation, but it wasn't working this time. He made a good case for an ex-con with a grudge going after the cops who had put him away, but the press kept hammering him with the one question that even the cops were asking themselves: What kind of killer poses bodies in snowmen? That was B-movie stuff.

Kristin Keller of Channel 3 was putting an even more salacious spin on it. As they showed the tape of him and Gino no-commenting their way through the reporters at City Hall, she did a somber voice-over in her best end-of-the-world tone. 'One has to wonder if the Minneapolis Police Department is concealing the truth, trying to avoid panicking the population of this city. A retired criminal psychologist who wishes to remain anonymous has told this reporter that the elaborate posing of these bodies in snowmen is the unmistakable mark of a psychopathic serial killer . . .' She paused dramatically, looking straight into the camera. 'A killer who will most probably strike again.'

Before he had time to put his fist through the TV screen, the phone rang, and he didn't need to look at the caller ID to know who it was.

'Gino.'

'Leo, I want you to feel free to mentally insert as much profanity as possible into my side of the conversation, because I'm sitting here with my kids and I can't do it myself.'

'I take it you're watching Channel Three.'

Gino sputtered, but apparently couldn't manage to eke out a G-rated word.

'They haven't really said anything we haven't been thinking ourselves, Gino.'

'It isn't what they said; it's the way they said it. Bunch of bullshit scaremongering. Kids are going to be afraid of snowmen. They'll stop building them. Then they'll grow up and won't let *their* kids build snowmen. The networks will never show the *Frosty the Snowman* cartoon again, and all the radio stations'll pull the song off their playlists. Gene Autry's family will never see another residual check again. This could change the winter landscape of the whole country just because Kristin Keller's got a hard-on for a network slot.' He finally wound down his rant and signed off, leaving Magozzi with a warm beer and a mountain of paperwork.

8

Kurt Weinbeck blinked himself awake, then jerked upright in the seat and looked around in a panic, wondering how the hell he'd managed to fall asleep in the first place, and what had awakened him. The cold, probably. Or maybe it was a gust of wind, rocking the little car. No, that couldn't be it. This piece-of-crap tin was locked so tight in the holes that four bald tires had dug, it would have taken a hurricane to move it a fraction of an inch.

The ditch was ridiculously deep, and any Minnesota boy knew what that meant. They'd built the damn road right through the middle of a swamp, hauling in enough fill to raise it above the water line, and not a crumb more. So all through the state you had these roads towering above the surrounding land with ditches so deep, you could drown in them during the spring. Driving on them in winter was like an Olympic automobile balance-beam competition. One tire one inch too far one way or the other, and you were toast.

He'd known it the minute he'd felt the car skid and go airborne. If there hadn't been two feet of fresh snow waiting at the bottom, he would have busted an axle when it finally smacked down. No way he was going to get it out, but still he tried, rocking back and forth as long as the tires grabbed snow, digging himself in another few inches when they spun, until the friction of the tires finally froze the snow around them into ice and they locked up tight. Worse yet, he'd dug himself in so far that the snow had packed around the doors and there was no way he could push them open.

Goddamned snow coffin, is what it was. Ol' Cameron Weinbeck just dug himself in so deep, the snow packed the doors shut and there wasn't a damn thing he could do to get out. 'Course he was pretty well pickled like always, so maybe it wasn't so bad, sitting there waitin' for his eyelids to freeze open and his fingers break and fall off. Probably had himself a high old time until he emptied the last bottle, then I suspect things went downhill from there.

It wasn't your standard run-of-the-mill eulogy, but it was the story he'd heard most, standing around his dad's coffin as an eight-year-old. And here he was, twenty-four years later, about to relive a family legacy.

He'd almost wet his pants right then, until he remembered to roll down the window and squeeze out that way.

It had been snowing hard by the time he crawled out of the car and got to the top of the ditch, and the temperature was dropping way too fast for his thin coat and tennis shoes. He looked around at the snowy woods, empty land, and deserted road and thought, *Middle of nowhere,* which was an overused phrase in this state until you realized it was the place you got to whenever you turned a corner this far north of the Cities.

The newscasters started hammering viewers over the head with the winter driving rules sometime in mid-November. You had to have a kit in the trunk: candles, matches, canned soup, blankets, and a bunch of other stuff that was supposed to save your life if you were ever stupid enough to do what he and his father and scores of other Minnesotans did every winter. Trouble was, people who were stupid enough to get stuck in a ditch in the middle of a snowstorm were apparently too stupid to carry a kit, because there sure as hell wasn't one in this car. Damn hatchback didn't even have a trunk.

So on to the second rule, and this was the big one: Stay with the car. Someone will find you. He looked around and thought that was pretty unlikely. Besides, being found wasn't exactly first on his list. He knew then that he'd have to walk out, he'd have to find himself another car, and then he'd have to get out of this damn state, and, by God, he was never coming back.

But first he had one last piece of business to take care of, and he hadn't for one second considered leaving it undone. He'd spent the last three years stewing in a cell, thinking about it, waiting for the day, and now the day was here.

So he'd cleared the snow away from the exhaust pipe, then crawled back into the car to warm up a little before his trek; see if he couldn't dry out his shoes a little. He'd turned the heater on high, leaving the window open a crack so he wouldn't gas himself to death.

A good move, he thought, because the heat had put him right to sleep for a solid two hours – it was three a.m. already – and chances were, the new snow had blocked the exhaust a while back.

He shut off the car and climbed out the window for the second and last time, and started walking. He didn't know where the hell he was, but he knew where he had to be. Back to the lake, then just follow the shore, because if there was one place in Minnesota you'd find some kind of civilization, it was anywhere near water. Damn lakeshore property sold for a small fortune, even at the tippy-top of the tall state. The lake wasn't that far back, and maybe slogging it wouldn't be so bad.

You live long enough in prison where the lights are on all

the time, you forget what real dark is like. Even in a landscape buried in white, you had to have a little illumination to reflect off it, or you were walking blind. The moon was ideal – lit up the world like a big strobe in the winter – but even starlight was enough when you had this much snow. But there was no moon, no stars, and he had to work at staying on the road to find his way back.

He found the lake after half an hour, but already, he couldn't feel his feet. The snow around the lakeshore was even deeper than it had been on the road, crawling up over his knees, soaking his jeans and then freezing them solid, until they scratched his calves every time he took a step.

Another half hour, and most of his face was stiff and the nerves had shut down, and still he hadn't seen a single house, a single structure of any kind, except the ghostly shadows of fish shacks on the ice he'd passed earlier. A lot of them had heaters, and, Lord, he'd been tempted, but he couldn't go back there.

Fifteen minutes more and he decided that this was the biggest lake in the state, the only one without houses on it, and that he was going to die. The funny thing was that it wasn't even that cold out; not by Minnesota standards. Ten, maybe even fifteen degrees, and freezing to death in that kind of balmy winter temperature would be just plain embarrassing.

So he pushed on for another agonizing ten minutes, veering away from the lakeshore, up a shallow hill to a flat, empty field that seemed to go on forever. The hill, shallow as it was, had damn near killed him. By the time he got to the top he'd fallen twice, his lungs were burning, and the sweat was freezing his hair to his forehead. That's when he started counting steps instead of minutes, and he knew that was a bad sign. Bend a knee, he told himself, then let the thigh muscles scream while he lifted a foot he could no longer feel above the snow, then stop to breathe and cough and then do it all over again with the other leg. He stopped counting at five, because he couldn't remember the number that came next. And that's when he saw it.

Such a dim, tiny light, barely visible in the distance through the falling snow, maybe a mirage, but maybe not. He started counting steps again.

It wasn't exactly the kind of shelter he'd been hoping for, but it was out of the wind, a few degrees warmer than the outside, and by God it was going to save his sorry life, and the truth was that for the first time in a long time, he had a lot to live for.

Payback, he thought, stumbling around on half-frozen feet, feeling his way in the darkness with half-frozen fingers until he found what he needed to survive the night.

9

Iris Rikker hadn't been up before the sun in ten years, and she didn't like it. By the time she stumbled her way through the dark bedroom to the wall switch, she'd cracked her elbow on the dresser and stepped in a fresh pile of cat vomit.

'Shit. *Shit.*'

The offending cat materialized when the light came on. She was sitting near her little surprise, blinking her startled pupils down to pinheads.

'Puck, you puke,' Iris muttered, then hopped on one bare foot into the bathroom and stuck the other one in the sink.

The water was freezing. Iris sucked air through her teeth when it hit her foot. It would take long minutes for hot water to rise two floors from the ancient heater in the basement, and she didn't have extra minutes this morning. New water heater. It was first on the list of home improvements she might be able to afford now. That was something, at least.

Even the sound of running water couldn't drown out the breathy wail of the wind around this north corner of the old farmhouse. Icy pellets of sleet dived out of the dark to tap at the bathroom window, where a layer of frost had built up on the inside wooden sash again. New windows. Maybe that should be first.

She scowled at the sleet hitting the window as she dried

her foot, thinking about moving to California, or Siberia – anywhere she could count on the weather to be reasonably consistent. Two days ago she'd ridden her bicycle the quarter-mile to her mailbox; yesterday the mailbox had disappeared under a foot of snow; this morning a new storm front was adding a coating of ice to the mix, just for openers.

The cat waited until Iris was sitting on the toilet, then came into the bathroom and simply stood there, staring at her.

'Voyeur. Puking voyeur.'

Puck blinked at her, then came over to rub against her legs. Iris chose to interpret this as a kitty apology, and stroked the thinning black fur. The cat was fifteen this spring, and probably shouldn't be blamed for the occasional uproar of an aging digestive system. 'Poor Puck. Don't you feel good?'

The cat began to purr, then promptly threw up on Iris's other foot.

It was six a.m. and still dark when Iris finally went downstairs to the kitchen. She wore the clothes she'd laid out the night before after an agonizing hour of indecision. Black slacks, white pullover, and a black blazer waiting, draped over the back of her chair. She had purplish smudges under her eyes this morning, and makeup wasn't helping.

She was in the middle of her first cup of coffee and a bowl of cereal when the phone rang.

'Is this Iris Rikker?' a male voice asked.

'Yes, who is this?'

'Lieutenant Sampson. We're down at Lake Kittering, public landing, you know where that is?'

'Uh . . .'

'North shore, just past the courthouse, right next to Shorty's Garage. We've got a body.'

Iris stood absolutely still, connected to a brand-new world by the length of a phone cord. She took a breath. 'I can be there in half an hour.'

'No, you can't. The roads are shit. But don't worry. This one isn't going anywhere.'

The click of a sudden disconnect made her blink. She eased the receiver back into its cradle, then took a step back from the phone and hugged her arms. She looked around at her cozy kitchen – white cupboards, dark green wall-paper, a jug of dried flowers on an oak table. It smelled like fresh coffee and the cinnamon candle she'd lit last night. It was a nice kitchen – a homey farm kitchen – and phone calls about bodies didn't belong here.

There was a full-length mirror on the inside of the closet door, and Iris looked into it as she pulled on a pair of moon boots she'd had for ten years and a black parka she'd bought last week. Something old, something new, she thought, wondering why she looked so small this morning; a little blond-haired woman with blue eyes too big for her face and very pale skin.

Damnit, there weren't supposed to be bodies. Bodies had never been mentioned, not once.

She stared holes into the eyes of her reflection, mentally reinforcing who and what she was – onetime city girl, sub-stitute English teacher at whatever school in the district would take her, and the brand-new deputy who'd been working a scant two months on night-shift dispatch because part-time teaching couldn't pay the bills – and then she closed her eyes and took a deep, shaky breath. Yesterday she had been those things. Today she was the newly elected sheriff of one of the largest rural counties in Minnesota, and some jackass named Sampson thought she was the person to call when you found a body lying around.

'Oh, yeah,' she breathed at the mirror, and then headed for the upstairs bathroom at a dead run.

Puck found her kneeling in front of the toilet.

Iris looked at her balefully. 'Watch and learn, Puck.'

Aside from the monster under the bed and other such delicious childhood scares, Iris had never really been afraid of anything. In a life that, by most people's standards, seemed charmed, there hadn't been any reason for fear. Until Mark left, the bastard. For some reason, that changed everything. Suddenly the nighttime noises of the old house became sinister, imagined faces lurked just beyond every black window, and now she stood with her hand on the back-door knob, paralyzed by the thought of stepping outside onto her own porch, simply because it was dark out there. Oh, how she hated him for that; for shattering a self-assurance she had always taken for granted.

Damnit, you have never been afraid of the dark, and you are not afraid of the dark now.

'Yeah, right,' she said aloud, then opened the door and stepped out onto the porch.

The wind picked up as soon as Iris was away from the shelter of the house. It blew off the hood of her parka and whipped her hair in crazy circles around her head. Four steps away from the porch and the circle of light from the house bled into darkness. She slogged blindly in the general direction of her SUV through knee-deep drifts, cursing Mark again, because shoveling snow was supposed to be his job. Too bad he hadn't stuck around long enough for the first snowfall – lots of people died of heart attacks while shoveling snow.

She couldn't see the truck until she almost stumbled into it, and small wonder – the damn thing looked like a giant ice cube. She swiped at the snow on the windshield and felt a solid layer of ice beneath it that was probably going to take fifteen minutes to chip off. Jesus, why had they bought a house without a garage? It was another thing she badly wanted to blame Mark for, but that particular idiocy fell squarely on her shoulders. He'd actually pointed out that little flaw about the property, but it had been eighty degrees and sunny at the time, and the charming old farmhouse, beautiful yard, and low price tag had lulled her into temporary stupidity.

She yanked on the driver's-side door and nearly ripped the handle off, but it didn't budge. Of course, the goddamned doors would be frozen shut, because it was clearly her destiny to be waylaid this morning by every possible inconvenience winter in Minnesota could dish out. In fact, she might as well start calculating odds on whether or not the truck would actually start, since she'd been a bad and slothful person and hadn't taken the time to stop off at the mechanic's and get a new battery, even though that very chore had been on her to-do list for the past three months. *It's a mild winter, I don't need it this minute, I don't have time to wait for them to install it now, it can wait until tomorrow, next week, next month, next year* . . . The litany of a born procrastinator.

She made a seamless mental transition from really annoyed to really pissed off, and started hammering her fist along the seam of the door, trying to dislodge the small glacier that had formed there overnight, and when that didn't work, she tried a modified version of a flying drop kick.

The drop kick seemed to work, and the door finally groaned open with a shower of ice shards. She said a little prayer, jammed the key into the ignition, and was greeted by the sickeningly slow, whining sound of a near-dead battery, just as she predicted. This was not good. Not good at all. Did sheriffs get demerits for showing up late to murder scenes? Would her name plaque have a little frowny face after her name? *Sheriff Iris Rikker* ☹

She kept cranking the engine because she didn't know what else to do, and started to panic as the whining got slower, but miraculously the old SUV eventually sputtered to life.

She cleared a patch on the windshield just big enough to see through, let the engine and defroster warm up for a few minutes, then gave it some gas. The truck lurched a little as it broke through a snowdrift, but at least the four-wheel drive was working and she rolled down her circular driveway until her headlights hit the drafty, spooky old barn where the ghost lived.

Shit. She put on the brakes and sat there for a moment, staring at the little door that had been closed last night, now standing ajar.

It was one of those little things the locals used to embellish the ghost stories they loved to tell about the old farmstead. Doors opening on their own, strange lights flickering in the summer dark, and a faint, howling sound some folks said they used to hear after the old lady who'd owned the place dropped dead in the driveway with a gun in her hand. Delicious nonsense, of course, concocted around the genuine mystery of the gun in the old lady's hand. Iris knew perfectly well that the flickering lights were summer fireflies, that the howling came from the coyotes that lived in the woods beyond the back field, and the mystery of the opening doors had been nicely explained the first time a weather system moved in.

It had happened a few times in the summer, when the big winds hit the back of the barn and blew through the cracks. The latch on the hundred-year-old door had long since bent out of shape, and wishes and dreams were just about all that kept it closed, and even those didn't work when the wind got busy. And the wind had been very busy last night, so of course the door had blown open. Perfectly logical. So why were her palms sweating?

Leave it. Pretend you never saw it.

And, oh, she liked that idea just fine, but the icy snow-sleet mix was piling up around the base of the door. Another few hours of that and it would freeze it right to the ground, it would stay frozen open all winter, and snow would pile up inside the barn. They never should have stored the bed in there.

It was the one and only material possession that Iris really valued – a Civil War–era four-poster that had been in her family for a hundred fifty years, and now it was sitting in a drafty old barn younger than it was because it was too big to get through the doors of the house. It was still carefully wrapped in the moving blankets, with heavy padded tarps over that, but as far as she knew, you didn't preserve old walnut by letting snow blow all over it, and it wouldn't do the mattress much good, either.

Thirty seconds, that's all it will take. Maybe a minute.

And still she sat there behind the wheel, watching the sleet mix swirl in the beam of the headlights while her silly heart sputtered a little, finally making her feel ridiculous.

She got out of the truck fast, plowed through snow up to her knees, and started kicking away the newly formed ice around the bottom of the door. When she had it cleared enough to close, she stepped through the doorway and into a cavernous dark, reaching for the flashlight she'd left on the seat of the truck.

She cursed under her breath, decided she could find something as big as a bed in the dark, and started shuffling forward. She heard the rustle of her boots moving through straw, old boards creaking in answer to a gust of wind she could not feel, and the contented murmuring of pigeons high in the rafters. She could hear the creak and the groan of the barn's old timbers complaining to the wind, and tried to find the music in it, but it just sounded like a creepy soundtrack for a haunted-house movie.

Finally the bed was under her hands and she felt the padded moving blankets, still tied in place around the legs, still layered on top of the bed and snugged under the sideboards. And then she found the corner where the wind had dislodged the padded canvas, exposing a slice of mattress.

She took off her glove, breathed a sigh of relief to feel that the mattress was still dry, then snugged the cover back in place before going back out to the truck.

Behind her in the barn, beneath the layers of padded canvas on the bed, two eyes opened wide.

10

Even with four-wheel drive, it took Iris well over half an hour to travel the fifteen miles of county highway to the Kittering Road turnoff. Lieutenant Sampson – whoever the hell he was – had been right about the roads. They were slick with the new glaze of ice, and now fat white pinwheels were spinning out of the dark to splat on her windshield. Four more inches before it was all over, the radio DJ announced with that perverted glee of a born Minnesotan.

The old-timers who lived in Dundas County liked to think of it as Minnesota's frontier. Sixty miles to the south, the twin cities of Minneapolis–St Paul beckoned to the high school seniors like a two-dollar whore; but one step over the northern county line and you were as likely to run into coyote and bear as you were a commuter.

They were coming, of course. The empty land on either side of the freeway was starting to fill up, and eventually those Armani-suited hobby farmers would venture this far north, but for now the houses on the road Iris drove were pitifully few and far between.

Her fingers tightened on the wheel as she imagined the long, cold walk for help if any of the locals on the roads this morning lost traction and ended up nose-deep in a snowy ditch. Up here there were still a lot of people – especially the old-timers – who regarded cell phones with deep suspicion.

As she made the left turn onto a twisting, narrow road she felt the tires of the Explorer spin, then catch, then spin again, and wondered if she'd die en route to her first day on the new job. Lake Kittering waited on her left, fifty feet straight down from the road that clung to the side of the hill. In a couple months there would be patches of black water scattered across the white ice like dozens of open mouths, hungry for the next car that would challenge the much-dented guardrail and lose.

Local lore had it that the road up Kittering Hill to the County Courthouse had dispatched more defendants than any judge in the district, and on this particular morning, Iris Rikker believed it.

By the time she topped the treacherous slope, Iris had eaten all the lipstick off her lower lip, and she couldn't feel her hands anymore. She loosened her grip on the wheel and flexed her fingers to bring back the circulation.

She skidded past the two-story brick building that housed the Sheriff's Office and jail, its windows throwing yellow light out into the snowy dark. Her eyes briefly darted left and she shivered, thinking of walking into that building later, facing the people who had awakened this morning subordinate to the first female sheriff in county history. She should have brought doughnuts or cookies or something. It was probably the only way they'd let her in the front door.

A block beyond the courthouse, the road started a sharp downslope toward the lake. She figured she was at the public boat landing when the road ended and the ice shacks began. Shorty's Garage was a gray metal pole building a block beyond the courthouse, right on the lakeshore. The lot was cluttered with unlicensed vehicles in various states of demise, including an ice-encrusted green junker that was tethered to a tow truck like a homely dog on a leash. An equally ice-encrusted Dundas County deputy was standing at the rear of the car.

Iris left the Explorer blocking the entrance and slogged through the snow toward him.

'You Rikker?' he asked from behind a hood that nearly obscured his face.

Iris stifled the impulse to answer 'Me Rikker,' wondering why no one in this county ever spoke in complete sentences. 'Yes. Are you Lieutenant Sampson?'

'Yeah.'

'I don't think we've met,' Iris said, sticking out a mittened hand, which Lieutenant Sampson either didn't see, or chose to ignore. The people of the county gave her seven more votes than the incumbent sheriff, but it was pretty obvious that the deputies weren't happy about it.

Sampson smacked the trunk of the junker, making her jump. 'Lottery car.'

Iris squinted through the snow at the old wreck. 'You're kidding. That car is a lottery prize?'

He snorted or sighed or made some kind of a sound Iris couldn't interpret. Or maybe it had just been the wind. 'Forgot. You're not from around here.'

She considered telling him she'd lived in the county for a whole year, that her latest pair of Keds hadn't even seen a city sidewalk, then decided against it. You were always an outsider in a place like this, unless you'd been born in a farmhouse your great-grandfather built with his two hands and a pair of mules, or some such nonsense.

'We put a junker out on Lake Kittering every winter,' he explained. 'The whole county bets on the day and hour the car will finally fall through the ice. Been doing it since I was a kid. Winner gets bragging rights, proceeds go to charity.

This time some asshole put the car over a spring, and that warm spell for the past couple weeks cracked the ice yesterday and she went down, just before the first storm hit.'

Iris suppressed a shudder and tried to look sheriff-like. 'So the body is in the car?'

'Nope. Just making conversation. Body's out there.' He jerked his head toward the lake. 'Just beyond that cluster of shacks. Come on.'

He was ten feet away and almost lost in the increasingly heavy snowfall by the time Iris got her legs to move and hurried after him down to the shoreline and out onto ice that was surely waiting for the city girl's single misstep before cracking and sucking her down into the frigid depths. She decided that that was why he'd told her about the car, the bastard. So she'd know the ice could crack at any moment beneath her weight.

Bastard, bastard, bastard, she repeated mentally as she slogged after him through the frozen drifts that looked like choppy waves, sweating inside her layers of clothing, telling herself she could do this. If she survived the walk, examining a dead body was going to be a piece of cake. After all, she'd seen bodies before. She'd been to funerals. And of course she'd imagined seeing her ex-husband dead a million times, preferably next to the nineteen-year-old slut he'd run away with less than a month after he'd moved her into a broken-down old farmhouse so far from the city that the people seemed to speak a different language – one without complete sentences.

She almost ran into Sampson's back when he stopped suddenly. Iris squinted through the driving snow and saw two deputies in winter gear just standing there. One of them glared at her, saying nothing. The other, all baby fat and blue eyes, gave her a nod. 'Morning, Sheriff. Deputy Neville.'

'Good morning to you, Deputy Neville,' Iris said, then caught her breath when the deputies moved aside, showing her what was behind them.

In one way, it wasn't as bad as she had feared – no blood, no gore, no immediate sense that what she was looking at was a dead human being – but in another way it was worse, because Iris may not have had a decent hot-water heater or an adequate furnace, but she did have a television, and she'd watched it long into the night.

'Oh, Lord,' she murmured, looking at the fat, ice-encrusted snowman leaning against one of the ice fishing shacks. Snowman head, snowman body – not as storybook perfect as the ones she'd seen on the news last night, but close enough – totally encased in hard-packed snow, except for the hands. Those were exposed, whitish blue, and unmistakably human, wrapped around a fishing pole.

'I take it you saw the news last night,' Sampson said.

Iris could only nod.

'From the look of it, I'd say we've got snowman number three out here.'

Iris found enough to breath to ask, 'Have you called the coroner?'

'Right after you.'

'Then where is he?'

'Mexico.'

'Mexico?'

Sampson shrugged. 'It's January in Minnesota. Everybody's in Mexico. MPD and the BCA are going to want to cover this one anyway. My guess is they'll beat feet to get up here five minutes after our call.'

'From Minneapolis?' Iris blew frosty air out into the coming dawn. 'It's going to take them hours to make the trip on these roads.'

'Yep.'

'When did you place the call?'

'Didn't.'

'Why not?'

'Don't have the authority.'

Iris blew an exasperated sigh into the frosty air of the coming dawn, wishing she'd spent a few of those quiet nights on dispatch reading the department handbook, if they even had such a thing. 'Well, then, who does?'

'Just the sheriff.'

Iris closed her eyes, then fumbled in her parka pocket for her cell phone. 'So whom do I call, and what's their number?'

Sampson kicked at the snow with heavy lace-up boots that looked a lot warmer than hers. 'Well, if it was me, I'd call Minneapolis PD and ask for Detective Magozzi or Detective Rolseth. They caught the snowman scene down at the park yesterday. But you're going to need a landline for that, especially in this weather. I had to go inside just to call you.'

'Fine. In the meantime, are you the department's homicide investigator?'

'Nope.'

'Well, whoever he is, get him out here to take charge of the scene.'

'Homicide investigator's here already.'

Iris's eyes fixed on the other two deputies stretching crime scene tape in a rectangle around the snowman. 'Which one is he?'

This time Sampson rolled his head all the way left to look at her, and she could see his face for the first time. He was smiling, just a little. 'That would be you, Sheriff Rikker.'

11

Magozzi awakened at five a.m. to the sound of sleet hitting his bedroom window. He rolled over, jammed pillows to his ears to block out the sound, then remembered that someone was killing cops and stuffing them in snowmen.

Half an hour later he was showered and dressed, scrambling eggs and deli ham in the same skillet, ignoring the evangelist who had popped onto the television screen when he'd turned it on. Shit. Sunday morning. Even in a state of news and weather junkies, religion topped the bill on the airwaves one day a week, and if you wanted to hear if the world had ended overnight, you had to wait until the men in black robes finished telling you that God's love was everywhere. Magozzi figured none of those guys ever watched the news.

He channel-surfed while he ate and found a local news brief that was little more than all the stuff they'd run last night, but a couple of the cable news channels were running with the Minneapolis story, mostly because the video was so good. There were a couple of shaky, amateur clips Magozzi hadn't seen last night – civilians were already cashing in on shooting their happy kids building snowmen, and then the MPD knocking them down, looking for corpses. He pushed away his plate and dragged a napkin across his mouth.

He heard the rumble and scrape of the city plow and sand truck out on the street, and felt that old twinge of disappointment, still with him almost thirty years later. When he was a kid, a snowfall like yesterday's would have shut down the city for a day at least, maybe two – joyous, unexpected holidays that kept everyone home and turned back the clocks about a hundred years. Dads pulled their kids on sleds right down the middle of the street, moms stayed home and baked cookies and cooked up big pots of homemade soup, and every house smelled like wet woolen mittens drying on a radiator. But eventually you'd hear the dreaded sound of the big trucks pushing the plows, parents' faces would sag in relief that everything was getting back to normal, and kids would groan and grumble and scramble to complete the homework they'd cast aside.

The Department of Transportation had come a long way since then, and Minneapolis had learned to handle just about anything nature could dish out. This city cleared roads and sidewalks and parking lots faster than any other place in the country, and Magozzi couldn't remember the last time schools and businesses were closed for a whole day, let alone two in a row. Progress wasn't always such a good thing, he decided.

Gino called just as he was heading out the door. 'What are you doing?'

'I was just going outside to find some kids and pull them on a sled.'

'You'll kill them. It's icy out there. Come to work instead. Malcherson wants us both in his office as soon as you get in.'

'You're there already?'

'Just pulling into the lot now, which is pretty full for a Sunday morning, by the way.'

'I'll be there in twenty minutes.'

'Not in one piece, you won't. That stuff they put on the

roads to keep the ice melted isn't doing so hot this morning. I did a three-sixty on the freeway, sailed right through about four red lights on Washington, and I am not getting in a car again until the spring thaw. Wear your booties. There's more snow coming.'

Chief Malcherson was the perfect embodiment of Minnesota's stoic, Scandinavian sensibility – the man probably had actual emotions, but if he did, they weren't for public viewing. But this morning, the gravity of losing two men was strikingly evident on his hang-dog face. The loose skin around his mournful eyes and his remarkable bloodhound jowls seemed to have dropped a couple of inches since the press conference, as if he'd been dragging his hands down his face all night. He barely looked up from the papers on his desk when Magozzi and Gino walked into his office. 'Good morning, Detectives. Please have a seat.'

Even Gino, who rarely missed an opportunity to comment on the Chief's sartorial savvy, was subdued and respectful and got straight to the point. 'Morning, Chief. You did an excellent job with the press conference last night. That couldn't have been easy, just standing there looking composed while all those reporters kept busting your balls.'

Malcherson ignored him. If he ever thought too hard about Detective Rolseth's compliments, he would probably have to fire him.

'We need to move very quickly on this case, Detectives. The press has its teeth in the serial-killer scenario, and we are going to have to address that, and hopefully eliminate it as a possibility. Unfortunately, I didn't find anything in your reports last night that would do that.'

'Neither did we, Chief,' Gino said. 'But it could have been the ex-con with a grudge, like you said, or some nut-bag out of the asylum or who knows what. Serial killers aren't the only sickos out there. The press just gloms onto them 'cause they're ratings grabbers. And that's the difference between us and the press. They jump to conclusions; we have to wait for the facts.'

Malcherson nodded, closed the folder containing last night's reports, and filed it in a drawer. He never cluttered his pristine desk with anything he wasn't using at the moment, including photos of his family, which were neatly arranged in their own cubbyhole in a bookcase. 'Do you have anything new for me this morning?'

Magozzi nodded and laid a fat manila folder on his desk, feeling almost guilty for messing it up. 'Copies of the ME's and the BCA's preliminary reports.'

Malcherson looked wearily at the volume of paperwork. 'Can you summarize the new information for me?'

Magozzi opened his own folder and started ticking off points. 'All the slugs from the scene were .22s, and ballistics is working on them now. We should hear something by noon. There's some trace, but both scenes were so contaminated, Jimmy Grimm isn't optimistic it will yield anything. Also, the BCA found a blood trail after we left the scene yesterday that matched Toby Myerson's blood type, along with one of his gloves.'

'So we're thinking this is how it went down,' Gino continued. 'Tommy Deaton was ahead of Myerson on the trail, and the killer was waiting for him under the cover of trees and surprised him point-blank just as he was skiing out of the woods. Myerson sees his friend get shot, takes off a glove and goes for his gun. But the killer either gets lucky or is a dead-eye dick and hits him in his shooting arm, which explains the blood trail. Myerson skis all the way to the other side of the field, which is no mean feat, considering the arm shot shattered the tibia, then he caught one in the back of the neck, probably real close to where the snowman was built around him, because that slug most likely paralyzed him instantly.'

Malcherson took a moment to process the scene Gino had just laid out, his mask of Scandanavian ice still intact. 'Unfortunately, what bothers me most about this scene does absolutely nothing to dispel the serial-killer notion. In fact, it may support it.'

Magozzi asked, 'What's that, Chief?'

'The carrots.'

Magozzi smiled at him. Underneath the great suits and polished personna of the Chief, there was still an investigator, alive and well and still thinking like a cop. 'Good call, sir. A lot of people carry rope in their cars for emergencies, but the carrot's a dead giveaway. Whoever it was came prepared to build a snowman.'

Malcherson's phone lit up. 'Please excuse me a moment, gentlemen.'

Magozzi smiled a little at the Chief's pervasive politeness, then watched Malcherson answer the phone and reach for a fresh tablet. For what seemed like a long time he took fast and furious notes without saying much to the person on the other end. 'I'll call that up immediately, Sheriff,' he said at last. 'As it happens, Detectives Magozzi and Rolseth are in my office right now. If you'd stay on the line for just a moment, I'll put this on speaker.' He pushed hold, and Magozzi noticed the Chief was three shades paler than he'd been a few minutes earlier.

'This is Sheriff Iris Rikker from Dundas County.'

Gino nodded, recognizing the name from the papers a few months back. 'The green-as-grass deputy who skunked the sitting sheriff.'

'Correct. She may have a snowman of her own. You need to listen to what she has to say.' He pushed SPEAKER and nodded at Magozzi, who inched closer to the phone.

'Leo Magozzi here, Sheriff Rikker. The Chief tells us you've got another one of our snowmen up there.'

'As I told your chief, I'm not entirely certain, Detective. From what I saw on the news last night, it doesn't look precisely like the ones you discovered in Theodore Wirth Park yesterday, although it may have originally. It's difficult to assess that at this point.' Magozzi frowned, trying to sort the relevant from all the words she'd spewed out. It was like talking to an FBI agent. 'Explain, please.'

'Your snowmen looked very carefully crafted; almost artistic, in fact.'

'And yours?'

'Well, we've had freezing rain here this morning, then sleet, and now snow . . .'

'Same here.'

'. . . so even if this had started as a recognizable duplicate, the weather conditions would have altered it considerably. I've sent a photograph to your chief so you can make an assessment for yourself.'

Magozzi saw Chief Malcherson at his computer on the credenza behind the desk, downloading a file from online.

'In the meantime,' Sheriff Rikker went on, 'we are preserving the scene as well as we can under the circumstances, which of course means we haven't begun to dismantle the snowman yet, and without at least rudimentary examination of the deceased, we haven't yet determined with any degree of certainty that this was a homicide.'

Gino yawned noisily, and even Magozzi was getting a little impatient. 'You *are* sure there's a body in there, right?'

He could almost hear a backstep in the pause that followed, and then a snippiness in her speech. 'I'm very sure, Detective. His hands were exposed. You'll see that in the photograph.'

'Any chance it could just be someone who got caught out in the storm and then covered with snow?'

Another long pause, and Magozzi sensed a little temper in there somewhere. That was the trouble with a lot of woman cops, in his experience, especially women in power spots. They couldn't take a little good-natured ribbing like a man could. 'There is a very definite structure to this form, Detective. Whether or not it was perfectly executed, and in spite of the weather damage, it was obvious to all of us that someone constructed a snowman around this body. Whether or not it relates to your case remains to be seen. From our perspective at least, this was a courtesy call. After you've examined the photograph, you may be able to better determine the necessity of sending your people up here in these weather conditions.'

. . . better determine the necessity . . . ? Who the hell talked like that? Magozzi rubbed at his temple and saw Gino doing the same thing, a pained expression on his face. The woman was giving them both a headache.

'Fine, Sheriff Rikker. I see the Chief has your photo loaded now. Can you hold a moment while we take a look?'

'Certainly.'

Malcherson pushed the hold button, then stepped aside so Gino and Magozzi could see the computer screen.

'Jeez, she's touchy,' Gino grumbled. 'Like talking to a porcupine.' Then both he and Magozzi stared at the digital image for a long moment.

'Oh, man,' Gino said. 'We got another one.'

Magozzi leaned over and punched the speaker button on the Chief's phone. 'Sheriff Rikker? Sorry to keep you waiting. Detective Rolseth and I will be up there as soon as we can. You have any problem with BCA handling the scene?'

'The BCA was my next call.'

'Let us do that. I'd like the same guys who worked the park snowmen.'

'Certainly, sir.'

Magozzi raised his brows. First she was snippy, now she was calling him 'sir,' and then she made nice by giving them detailed driving directions and closed with thanks to all of them – at least that was what Magozzi thought she was doing. All very polite and proper and way too long, mentioning them each by name as if reading from her notes, which she probably was. If she was a cop, Magozzi was a bowl of cornflakes.

'Doesn't sound like any cop I ever met,' Gino remarked after the Chief had closed the call.

'In point of fact, she was an English teacher before she entered law enforcement,' Malcherson said.

'No kidding? Well, that explains it. Only an English teacher would take five hundred words to say what she could have summed up in four. I'd hate to get Mirandized by her – she's probably got her own ten-page version.'

Malcherson gave him a sour look. 'I happen to find her linguistic precision refreshing. And I'm certain I don't have to remind both of you to treat Sheriff Rikker with the same respect you would afford any other elected official and fellow law enforcement officer, elocution notwithstanding.'

'No problem, Chief. She has my respect until she screws up, and so far, she seems to be handling things okay. I just wish she'd get to the point a little faster. Most of the stuff we do on the job is time sensitive, you know?'

Up in Dundas County, Iris Rikker hung up the phone, closed her eyes so she couldn't see the office she was sitting in, and replayed the conversation in her mind, trying to shake the feeling that the Minneapolis detective thought she was a total idiot.

A cursory rap on the door frame interrupted her thoughts, and Lieutenant Sampson stomped in, throwing back the hood on his parka and scattering snow all over the place. 'MPD coming?'

Iris mentally added a verb and prepositional phrase so that she could understand the question. 'Detective Magozzi and Detective Rolseth are on their way. They're also sending the same BCA team that processed the Minneapolis scene.'

Sampson flopped down in a big leather recliner and jerked up the foot rest. 'Good deal.'

She got up and looked out the wall of windows over the lake, thinking how convenient it was to have a crime scene right outside the sheriff's window. She couldn't see much through the thickening snowfall, and was glad of that. 'We need to put up some sort of plastic sheeting to preserve as much of the scene as possible. Do we have such things in the building?'

Sampson didn't say anything for a second, so she turned around and looked at him. She didn't like him lying back in the recliner as if he were in his own living room. It was disrespectful, wasn't it? And if she ever intended to take charge of this office and do the job well, it was important that she establish the ground rules of respect right at the beginning, and now was as good a time as ever to start . . .

'That was good thinking about the plastic sheeting,' he said, messing up the mental speech she was planning about behavior modification, thoroughly confusing her because she thought he may have actually said something nice to her. 'But a little slow. I already had some boys pick up a tent from the rental shop. They're putting it up now. Christ, what a morning. You going to put lace curtains up in here or what?'

Iris just stared at him for a minute, finally deciding that she had a better chance of modifying the behavior of an earthworm. The truth was, a man like Sampson belonged in this office more than she did. He looked different with the hood pushed back. Dark hair, which seemed appropriate for some reason, squinty dark eyes, and the scruff of a weekend beard. Precisely the appearance of a man you'd expect to find in a wood-paneled office with a flat-screen television, leather recliners, and a stack of *Playboy*s on a table.

Sampson pushed himself up from the recliner, apparently weary of her silence. 'Well, I just wanted to see if the Minneapolis boys were going to show or if we had to start processing the scene ourselves. I've got to get back out there.' He stopped at the doorway. 'I suppose you want to interview the night janitor who found the body.'

Iris blinked. 'Yes, I do.'

'I'll send her in. Margie Jensen, in case you haven't met.'

'Thank you.'

Iris waited until he was well out of the office before she sagged back down into the stupid leather chair and started wishing she were dead, or at least home, with her cat throwing up on her foot.

She'd never even thought to ask who had found the body. She didn't know what the hell she was doing. And Sampson knew it.

You're not fooling anyone, Iris. You never walked the street or manned a patrol or processed a crime scene. You don't even speak the same language as these people.

A short older woman in coveralls rapped on the door frame with a broom handle and walked right in. 'I'm the janitor, Margie Jensen, and I don't know anything.'

Iris smiled at her. *That makes two of us.*

12

It was pushing nine a.m. and snowing hard by the time Magozzi and Gino finally got on the road in one of the department SUVs and headed north out of the city.

Magozzi was behind the wheel, Gino was rigid and still in the passenger seat, giving himself a gastric bypass with a too-tight seat belt, staring out the windshield as if he could prevent catastrophe by not blinking. 'I hate these damn SUVs,' he said. 'We're too damn high. Bet we tip over twenty times on the way up there.'

'Can't tip over,' Magozzi said. 'The ice ruts under the snow are too deep.'

The morning's icy pellets had turned to snow, the wind was gusting, and the plows were having trouble keeping up, even on the city freeways. Magozzi figured visibility was about two car-lengths, give or take. It got worse once they cleared the shelter of the downtown buildings; worse yet when they left the suburbs behind and hit open land.

'Starting to feel like we're driving off the edge of the world here, Leo. I can't see for shit.'

'We've got swampland on both sides, nothing to stop the wind. It'll get better once we hit some woods.' Magozzi was four-wheeling it through the new four inches that had accumulated since the last plow run.

'You sure there are woods up here?'

Magozzi was concentrating hard, trying to see the edges of the road. 'Hell, I don't know. We're heading north. There are woods in northern Minnesota, right? Lean back. You're fogging the windshield.'

Gino tried to sit back and relax, but within seconds he was canted forward again, squinting through the driving snow. 'You're going too fast.'

'Goddamnit, Gino, relax. You're driving me nuts, and you sound like an old woman. Back when we were on the street you used to drive like a maniac.'

'Yeah, but then I got married and had kids, and I'd like to make it to their graduations.'

Magozzi sighed and eased up on the accelerator. 'There. I'm going thirty. Can you live with that?'

'I'll let you know. Damnit, this trip better not be for nothing – it already took at least ten years off my life.'

'It's either the same guy or a copycat. Bad either way, and I'm not exactly clicking my heels about working a tandem with this particular sheriff.'

'Tell me about it. Chief said English teacher, and I had a high school flashback to Miss Kinney, smacking her ruler on the desk. Tall, sour-faced old biddy. Pursed her lips all the time like she was pissed off at the whole world. She talked just like this Rikker woman, and I could never understand her, either. Spewed words like they were old pennies she was dumping out of a jar all at once. Just because you know a lot of words doesn't mean you have to use them all in the same sentence, you know?'

'Maybe she was nervous.'

'Whatever. Just get ready to translate for me. When cops get more than one adjective going I think it's multiple choice and my brain stops dead ... Jeez, Leo, the damn snow's going sideways. Can you see the road?'

'Nope.'

It took them exactly two hours to travel sixty miles, and that was on the freeway. By the time they took the right exit and hit the secondary roads, Magozzi was wishing he'd brought a snowmobile instead of an SUV. They sailed sideways through the first turn, then kissed the ditch a couple of times plowing through the rutted snow on a puny two-lane road with no shoulders. Gino was not happy.

'Man, this is starting to look like Fargo. Don't they have snowplows up here?'

Magozzi's knuckles were white on the wheel, something that rarely happened. 'Open fields in this spot, nothing to stop the wind. They could have plowed this ten minutes ago, and you wouldn't be able to tell. Keep an eye out for road signs, we got another turn coming up.'

'Thanks for the great news. Are we gonna go through that one sideways, too?'

'You want to drive?'

'I don't even want to be in a car in this stuff. We pass any kind of a hotel, just drop me off, pick me up in April.'

Another twenty minutes and they were fishtailing through the left turn onto Kittering. Once the SUV straightened out, Magozzi hugged the right edge of the road, looking for some purchase on the snow-covered slope. Gino squinted through the snow, but couldn't see the top of the hill. 'Forget Fargo,' he grumbled. 'This is a mountain, and the way our luck is going, it's probably Donner Pass . . . Oh, man, that's a hell of a drop-off on the left, Leo, so you don't want to be doing any of that sideways stuff on this road, okay?'

'Spoilsport.'

Magozzi felt the back end begin to slide and eased up on the accelerator, hoping like hell they didn't start sliding backward down the hill. By the time they finally reached the top, it took a full five seconds for him to unclench his jaw. He pulled up between two county cars parked along the side of the sheriff's office and shut down the car. He and Gino just sat there for a moment, breathing.

Finally Gino stirred and released his seat belt. 'I kind of feel like we oughta get out and kiss the ground or something.'

Magozzi shook his head. 'Can't do it. The country boys could be watching from inside, and they drive that road all day long. We'd look like a couple of wusses.'

'We are a couple of wusses.'

'No need to lay that out right at the start.'

The female deputy behind the dispatch station eyed their badges and nodded. 'Good morning, Detectives. The sheriff's expecting you. She'll be right down. How bad was the drive?'

Gino grunted. 'I'll tell you one thing. The only way I'm going back down that hill is behind a salt truck.'

'They never salt that hill. The runoff pollutes the lake.'

'Oh, yeah? You'd think the dead bodies from all the people sliding off the drop-off into the lake would pollute it a hell of a lot more than a little salt, and we were nearly two of them.'

The deputy blinked at him. 'You're kidding me. You actually came up Kittering Hill?'

'Left on Kittering, up the hill to the sheriff's office. Those were the directions.'

She let out a silent whistle. 'Man, nobody drives that hill in this kind of weather. That's just plain suicide. You should have come the back way.'

Gino's face was getting red. 'There's a back way? A better way?'

'Well, sure, you just pass Kittering until you get to Cutter. That sort of loops around the hill, easier grade, and the trees pretty much protect it from the weather. What joker gave you those directions, anyway?'

Gino and Magozzi remained stone-faced, and the deputy's face reddened as she made the connection.

'Oh ... hey ... listen, just for the record, Sheriff Rikker probably doesn't know about the back way, either.'

'Seems like something the sheriff ought to know,' Magozzi said stiffly.

The woman shook her head. 'She's the new kid on the block. Somebody should have told her about it before she came in this morning, but I guess it's kind of a hazing thing for the newbies, you know?'

'Just how long has she been on the job?' Gino asked.

'Well ... she worked dispatch for a couple months before she was elected, but we didn't have a lick of snow back then, and today's pretty much her first day as sheriff. Heck of a way to get your feet wet, huh?' The switchboard started buzzing and she smiled apologetically. 'Excuse me, Detectives.'

Gino grabbed Magozzi by the arm and pulled him aside. 'Did I just step into an alternate universe or are my ears shot, because what I thought I just heard was that a couple months of dispatch is all the experience this broad has ...'

'I'm going to tell Angela you referred to a woman as a "broad."'

'... which means that the least qualified law enforcement officer in the whole state is now the sheriff of one of the largest counties in Minnesota and she's the lead on a homicide investigation we might have to piggyback.'

'She was just elected in November, Gino. You knew that much.'

'Sure I knew that. I just figured she already had a few years on the job, and now it turns out all she did was push a button on a dispatch desk. Jesus, Leo. How does shit like this happen?'

'I think it's called democracy.'

'If we end up having to work the case with her, it's gonna be called on-the-job training, and I'm not in the mood to babysit . . .'

'Detectives?'

Gino and Magozzi both winced at the sound of a voice behind them, the same voice they'd heard over the speaker in Malcherson's office. As he turned, Magozzi wondered how much she'd overheard.

The person who went with the voice was neither a sour-faced old biddy or a woman who looked tough enough to throw her hat in the ring for sheriff. Iris Rikker was a petite blond with a sweet face and wide blue eyes that probably wouldn't shelter a lie easily. She was about as unofficial-looking as you could get, right down to the absence of a uniform. She did have a gun, however, and Magozzi couldn't decide if that made him feel better or worse about the situation.

'Detectives Magozzi and Rolseth?' she asked again uncertainly.

'Yes . . . Sheriff?'

'Sheriff Iris Rikker. Pleased to meet you.' She smiled politely and shook their hands while Magozzi made quick introductions.

'I'm really sorry you had to drive up here in this weather. Were the roads horrible?'

'Nah, they were spotless,' Gino said, irritable as he always was after a brush with death, real or imagined.

'Is the BCA here yet?' Magozzi asked.

'Yes, they arrived a few minutes before you did. I had one of my deputies take them down to the site. Would you like some coffee?'

Magozzi blinked at her. They had a dead body and a BCA team waiting for them out in the middle of a snowstorm and she thought they should all sit down for coffee? He glanced over at Gino, who was doing a really good job of concealing his disdain, except for the big eye-rolling part, and then the sharp tone he used when he said, 'The BCA can't start their job until we get out there for a first look, and they're going to be really pissed if we keep them waiting.'

Iris Rikker looked a little startled, and then more than a little embarrassed. 'Oh, God. Of course. I'm sorry. I just thought . . .' She grabbed a heavy parka from a wall hook and hurried out the door ahead of them before she remembered to put it on.

Gino zipped up as he watched her through the glass door, shaking his head. She slipped and slid across the parking lot toward a big new SUV, then took a header just as she reached for the door handle. 'If this case belongs to us and we have to work with that woman, I'm going to kill myself.'

Magozzi pulled on his gloves. 'It's her first day, and definitely her first murder. Maybe you need to cut her a little slack.'

'Screw that. We've got two of our own down, and we don't have time to cut anybody any slack.'

'Bobby Windemeyer.'

'Huh?' Gino paused just before he pushed open the door.

'Bobby Windemeyer, your first DB, remember? You took one look at the kid and broke down and bawled like a baby. Moved the body, stepped in blood, pretty much trashed the whole scene.'

'Hmph. That was a long time ago.'

'Exactly. This is Iris Rikker's long time ago. We all get one of those.'

Gino acted like he hadn't heard him, glowering out at the SUV that had just pulled up to the door, a red-faced Iris Rikker behind the wheel. 'Oh, Christ, now she expects us to ride with her? I sure as hell hope she drives better than she walks.'

13

Detective Tinker Lewis was buried under the down comforter, listening to the sleet on the bedroom window, being coaxed awake by the aromas of brewing coffee and frying bacon wafting up the stairs.

It had to be Sunday, otherwise Janis wouldn't be anywhere near the stove. She could make coffee and fry a pound of bacon, and on a good day, three or four slices might be edible. Tinker was profoundly grateful that she attempted these things only one day a week. The kitchen belonged to him.

By the time he got downstairs she was standing with her hands on her hips, glaring down at a mass of greasy bacon languishing on a paper towel. 'I suck at this. What kind of an idiot can't fry bacon?'

Tinker sorted through the mess with a fork, looking for a piece that wasn't either raw or burned black. 'Maybe if you didn't waste your time doing those silly heart surgeries, you could stay home and practice cooking, become a better wife to your poor beleaguered husband. I could buy you an apron.'

'That's all I've been waiting for.' She looked up at him and frowned. 'Why are you dressed for work? It's Sunday.'

'Cops die, we all work.'

He took one look at her face and wished he were agile enough to kick himself. Janis was on one of the transplant teams at the U, and they'd had a marathon surgery scheduled yesterday, maybe eighteen straight hours in the rarefied, isolated atmosphere of the operating room. No TV, no radio, no news from the outside world. He'd been sound asleep by the time she got home, and she hadn't heard.

'I'm sorry.' He took her hands, sat down with her at the kitchen table, and told her one of the things that any cop's wife dreads hearing. Someone out there was killing cops, and suddenly her husband was in the line of fire.

When he finished, she sat quietly for a while, still holding his hands. 'So we're inside saving a life yesterday, and on the outside, someone took two away. Sometimes I don't even know why we try so hard to keep up.'

Tinker gave her one of his sad smiles. 'So you saved the kid. I'm glad.'

'He's ten years old.'

'I know. And now he'll live to see eleven. That's big time, Janis. It makes up for a lot.'

She closed her eyes for a moment, then got up and held out her hand, palm up. 'Give it to me. Then make us something decent to eat if you're going back out there.'

Tinker reluctantly unholstered his weapon and put it in her hand, then shook his head as she got the cleaning kit from a top cupboard and got to work. He'd taken care of that last night, but telling her that wouldn't do a bit a good. It was some kind of peculiar ritual with her – checking and rechecking his weapon anytime there was a hint of something going down, maybe because it was the only way she could actively participate in keeping him safe. He had no clue how she'd learned how to do such a thing – probably just from watching him during those years he'd been on the street – but she did it meticulously and well. The irony of seeing those million-dollar life-saving surgeon's hands ensuring the proper operation of an instrument of death had always disturbed him, and he'd learned long ago to turn away from the wrongness of it.

He was first to the phone when it rang. He saw Janis stiffen and stop working to listen, which she did whenever the phone rang during times like these. She relaxed a little when he said, 'Oh, hi, Sandy. Good to hear from you.' She started to tense up again a few minutes later, because Tinker wasn't talking, and he had his little notebook out.

It took Tinker half an hour to get to downtown Minneapolis, a drive that normally took ten minutes. The sleet had put down a layer of ice on roadways and sidewalks that had barely been cleared after the big snow, and the Highway Patrol had travel warnings over half the state. For once, most Minnesotans had decided to listen, hunkering down until either the sun or the sand trucks came out.

The downtown streets were surprisingly empty, even for a Sunday morning, and a good thing, too, since the little Honda was sliding all over the place. The hot Sunday brunch spots were all closed, their overhangs dripping icicles, and for the first time since he couldn't remember when, almost every church in the city had canceled Sunday services.

The sky was still raining ice when he slid to the curb in front of one of the old office buildings serving as temporary quarters, while the county sucked toxic mold out of parts of its new kazillion-dollar complex. Heads were still rolling over that one.

The uniform he had requested was waiting on the sidewalk, bundled up in winter gear, ice crystals sparkling on the fur of his cap. Tinker thought he looked like a Christmas decoration someone had forgotten to take down.

‘You Detective Lewis?’

‘Right.’

‘Chalmers, out of the Second. You want to give me the word on this before you make me break down the door of a government building?’

Tinker held up a key ring. ‘Turns out his wife had an extra set, so we’re legal. You weren’t briefed?’

‘I was just told to get my ass over here. Homicide calls, we’re there, especially after yesterday. Sarge figures anything you’re taking a look at might have something to do with what happened to our boys in the park.’

‘I don’t know about that, but anything a little off-kilter sets me on edge, and I want to look at it. And straight up, this guy’s a friend of mine. Steve Doyle. A parole officer. He had a meet set up with a new parolee yesterday afternoon, and hasn’t been seen since. His wife got caught down in Northfield by the storm, didn’t get back until late last night, and found him gone. No calls, no messages, no luck tracking him down. She called me at home first thing this morning.’

Chalmers took off his cap and banged it on his leg, releasing a shower of ice crystals. ‘Well, friend of yours or not, I gotta ask. Any chance this guy just checked into the No Tell Motel while the wife was out of town?’

‘No chance at all.’

Chalmers looked him in the eye for a moment, then nodded and moved toward the door. ‘Then let’s get out of this weather and see what we can see.’

The building was as deserted as the streets, and had that musty smell of crumbling brick and old plaster. Chances were the county would be one of the last tenants before some kind of remodel happened.

The parole office was straight ahead, and the door was wide open. Tinker took a look at the open door and felt the hairs on the back of his neck stand up. You could lose a pay grade for leaving a government office unlocked, especially a parole office. These places held a lot of information you couldn't find anywhere else in the system: confidential witness information, victim addresses, and a lot of sealed files, especially on juveniles.

He unholstered his weapon, then felt a little silly when Chalmers followed suit. For all he knew, maybe Steve had been working late, then decided to stay put once the freezing rain started to fall. Or maybe another parole officer was putting in some weekend time to catch up on his workload and they'd walk in with weapons drawn and scare the poor guy to death. Which served him right, Tinker thought, for not at least closing the door.

He looked at Chalmers, sensed that his thoughts were traveling the same road, then the two of them shrugged at each other and moved forward, stopping on either side of the open door, listening. They both flinched at the sudden scurrying sound of some small animal inside the wall, then grinned at each other a little sheepishly. Truth was, the most alarming thing here was them.

But then they stepped through the doorway into the empty office and saw the first of the blood.

There wasn't a lot of it; just a trail of drops and streaks that led straight to Steve Doyle's desk. Officer Chalmers looked at the blood trail and actually scratched his head. 'So, we got a crime scene here, or a really bad paper cut?'

'Damned if I know. Too much blood for a paper cut; not enough to send someone hightailing for ER.'

'Tough call.'

While Chalmers made a slow circuit of the office, Tinker walked over to Steve's desk and stood very still while his eyes moved to take it all in, and suddenly it wasn't a tough call at all. There were too many things wrong here. A coffee mug upended on the desk; a pool of liquid eating away at the wood finish. A muted television left on in one corner, its screen showing a raucous studio audience on its feet, shaking their fists, pointing at something or someone, yelling in complete silence. And, most telling of all, Steve's coat, still hanging on a tree near the desk, the limp, empty fingers of gloves poking out of the pockets.

Chalmers sidled up next to him and looked around at the TV, the spilled coffee on the desk, the abandoned coat. 'I don't like this.'

'Me either.' Tinker pushed a blinking light on the phone with the end of the pencil. There were seven messages. Four of them were from someone named Bill Stedman, asking for an immediate call-back. The other three were from Sandy, each one more worried than the last.

'That his wife?' Chalmers asked.

'Yeah.'

'You want me to give Stedman a call?'

Tinker lifted his head. 'You know him?'

'Sure. He runs the halfway house over on Livingston. First stop for a lot of Stillwater's bad apples when some asshole parole board decides it's time to turn them loose on the public again.' Chalmers pulled out his cell phone, pushed a number and handed over the phone.

'You know his number by heart?'

'Hell, we all do. Those places are top on our list when we're shopping for dirtbags. Bastards all repeat, every damn one of them.'

When Bill Stedman answered, Tinker identified himself and his purpose, took notes for five minutes, then closed the phone and looked at Chalmers. 'You have a roll of crime-scene tape?'

'In the squad.'

'I think we need to seal this place off.'

Less than half an hour later Bill Stedman blew into the lobby on a blast of cold air that dropped the temperature ten degrees in five seconds. He was a big man, more muscle than fat, and Tinker caught himself wondering if the man had spent some time on the prison weight benches. 'Wind's picking up, mercury's going down,' he said, peeling a knit cap that bristled with ice off a shaved skull. 'And it's going to dump on us again. How the hell are you, Chalmers? You guys took a real hit yesterday. Damn near broke my heart when I heard it was Deaton and Myerson. I liked them both.'

Chalmers nodded. 'Everybody did. Detective Lewis here was on scene.'

Stedman turned to Tinker. 'You think this has something to do with the dead snowmen?'

Tinker concentrated so he wouldn't wince. Simple truth, he was doing a favor for a missing friend's wife, but these men were going the extra mile because they thought he might be on the trail of whoever killed Tommy Deaton and Toby Myerson. Tinker was starting to feel guilty. It wasn't exactly a deception, but it was close. 'No way of knowing at this point. We aren't sure what exactly went down here yet, but some of what you told me on the phone gave me a bad feeling about it.'

Stedman eyed the yellow tape crisscrossed over the doorway to the parole office. 'I surely don't like the looks of that.' He walked over and looked into the office.

'So far, it's just a precaution. Like I told you, there's not a lot of blood. Might not even be a crime. Maybe an accident of some kind.'

'I don't think so.' Stedman looked grim. 'Let me tell you how this works. When these guys get out, we tag-team them pretty close for a while, especially the repeats running through the system for the second or third time. You never know what those guys are going to do, which means we do everything by the book, and then some. If he hadn't shown up for the meet yesterday, Doyle would have called me, right after he called out a warrant. Plus, Weinbeck never checked into the house by curfew last night – another automatic for a warrant, which was why I was trying to reach Doyle. Trust me, the man was here, he's running now, he's got a history of violence, and this doesn't look good.'

Tinker kept his face expressionless. He was just hearing what his gut had told him all along, but didn't much like hearing it out loud. He looked at the soft case Stedman was carrying. 'Thanks for bringing that over. Hell of a day to ask a man to come outside.'

'No sweat. I've been locked in a house for two days with sixteen stir-crazy ex-cons. I need to see your creds before I show you this.'

Tinker handed over his badge case and watched the man's eyes shift from the ID to his face, then back again. 'Okay, Detective. Did you get a chance to look around for Doyle's copy of the file?'

Tinker nodded. He'd spent the last twenty minutes in latex gloves going through every piece of paper and every file in and on Steve's desk, including the locked drawers. 'There's nothing here with Weinbeck's name on it, except a notation in Steve's day planner for yesterday's meet.'

Stedman sighed and headed for a padded bench on one wall. He sat down, put his case on the floor between his feet, and pulled out a fat file folder. 'Kurt Weinbeck, did three out of five in Stillwater. They cut him loose Friday on a conditional release – six months with me and my boys.'

Tinker asked, 'What was he in for?'

'This.' Stedman handed him a sheaf of photos.

Even Officer Chalmers recoiled when he saw the one on top. 'Jesus. What is that?'

'That,' Stedman replied, 'is what his wife looked like last time he was through with her. Seven and a half months pregnant.'

Tinker took a closer look at the photo. He could recognize it as a person now that he knew what he was looking at, but just barely. He glanced at the rest of the photos of a ruined face, then turned them upside down on the bench. 'Are you telling me he only did three for a double?'

Stedman sighed and started thumbing through the rest of the papers in the file until he found the wife's hospital records. 'Believe it or not, she and the kid lived through it. Six months in the hospital, and about a million surgeries over the next two years to put her back together again. She's the reason I wanted you to tear this place apart looking for Doyle's copy of this file. That's the one and only place you'll find this woman's address.'

'You don't have it in yours?'

'Nobody has access to the addresses of victims trying to stay out of sight, not even the court. Doyle had it because she had to be notified when her ex was released, and you can bet your ass he wouldn't let that file out of his sight.'

'So he wouldn't have left it at home.'

'I've worked with the man a long time. He wouldn't even

take that file home with information like that inside. He'd keep it here under lock and key with all the other confidential stuff. You sure you hit all the locked cabinets?'

Tinker held up a jangling key ring. 'Every one.'

'So we've got a missing parolee, a missing parole officer, and now a missing file with a victim's address in it.' Stedman pulled out a cigarette, leaned forward on the bench, and lit it. No one mentioned the laws against smoking in public buildings. 'I've got copies of the public court documents. She took back her maiden name after the divorce. Julie Albright. That's all I know, that's all I can give you, except a hell of a lot of experience with guys like Weinbeck.' He turned his head and looked Tinker in the eye. 'He's going after her, Detective.'

14

Sheriff Iris Rikker looked tiny behind the wheel of the big SUV, and Magozzi hoped she was tall enough to reach the pedals. He took the passenger's seat and let Gino slide into the back – that way, his view out the windshield would be obstructed, and he'd have less opportunity to anticipate the worst. His nonstop commentary on the way up here had nearly driven *him* crazy, and he was used to it. He figured the sheriff didn't need the extra stress this morning.

Gino poked his head between the front seats. 'You got the four-wheel engaged on this thing?'

Iris nodded. 'The four-wheel is always engaged.'

'Yeah? Are you sure? Because I think there should be a little light on the dashboard or something that tells you the four-wheel drive is on, right?'

'I suppose there is.' She put the truck into drive and eased forward out of the parking lot.

'I don't see it.'

'What?'

'The four-wheel-drive light.'

Iris glanced over at Magozzi, who was trying not to smile.

'It's right there, Gino.' Magozzi pointed to the center console.

Gino slumped back in his seat.

As they crawled down the hill toward the lake, the crime scene and surrounding activity materialized out of a blurry white mist of snow: there were county cars, state patrols, the BCA vans, and a few civilian vehicles that Magozzi hoped belonged to off-duty cops and not the general public. No media yet, thank God. But most notable was a garishly colorful tent with stripes and polka dots and smiling clown faces plastered all over it erected out on the frozen lake itself.

Gino leaned forward again. 'What the hell is that? Is the circus in town, or what?'

'That's the crime scene,' Iris replied.

'Nice tent,' Gino remarked. 'Really sets the mood. Are you handing out candy, too?'

As far as Iris knew, she didn't even have a temper. Cats threw up on her, men cheated on her, the high-schoolers she taught used to ignore her most of the time, and not once had she felt the compulsion to fire back an answering shot. Maybe it was because she placed cats, husbands, and high-schoolers on the same mental level – all creatures who were incapable of change, biologically mandated to behave a certain way. Or maybe it was because fighting back simply wasn't in her nature. She had the feeling that Detective Gino Rolseth was going to change all that, because she had to struggle to keep her tone even. 'Bob's Party Rental on Main Street was kind enough to donate it. It was all we could get on short notice.'

Gino grunted. 'Great. We're gonna have every kid in the county swarming the place, trying to buy tickets.'

'Perhaps we could leave you at the entrance and you could hold them off with your big gun,' Iris said sweetly, and then snapped her mouth shut, wondering where that had come from.

'Yeah, well I took a look, and your gun's bigger than

mine. Besides, from what I hear, dealing with kids is what you're trained for.'

Magozzi slid down in the passenger seat a little and covered his eyes.

Iris skidded into an empty space at the landing and slammed the truck into park. So that's what this was about. Not just the pompous city cop looking down his nose at the county cops. This was all about her, the English teacher wearing the sheriff's badge. The *woman* wearing the sheriff's badge. He probably hated all women. Sexist pig. Then again, he could just be a conscientious detective who didn't want an important investigation fumbled by someone as inexperienced as she was. Lord knows she couldn't blame him for that. If there was one thing Iris knew, it was the extent of her own incompetence.

She sighed and turned in her seat to face him. 'The only alternative to that tent would have been to drive stakes into the ice to support a tarp, but with the ice in such poor condition, we didn't want to risk it.'

Gino frowned at her. 'What do you mean the ice is in poor condition? It's the middle of January.'

'You might recall that we had a very mild winter until just last week, and the lakes around here are all spring fed, so there's still some open water and weak spots. Be careful.'

'Are you telling me this ice isn't safe?'

'Well, they told me it was. By the way, if you hear the ice cracking under you, don't panic. That happened a lot when I went out there earlier, but they said not to worry.'

When he reached the landing's edge, Gino stopped dead, his eyes wide and busy as he examined the ice. 'There's a crack – a big, zigzaggy crack right there.' He pointed it out to Iris. 'What's that mean?'

Iris looked at it worriedly. 'I didn't see that before. Try not to step on it.'

They watched her walk gingerly out onto the ice, careful to skirt the crack. 'Let's go,' Magozzi said.

'Just a minute. I want to see if she falls in.'

'Come on, Gino, look at all the fish shacks out there. If the ice can hold them, it can hold us.'

'So says you. When was the last time you were tromping around on a spring-fed lake after a warm snap?'

Magozzi shrugged. 'Never.'

'Goddamnit,' Gino muttered.

By the time they caught up with Iris, she was talking to the two deputies stationed in front of the tent's entrance. Both of them were starting to look like snowmen themselves as the heavy precipitation accumulated on their hats and parkas, and they didn't look particularly happy to be there, or to be talking to Sheriff Rikker, for that matter.

As they drew closer, Magozzi heard Sheriff Rikker ask one of deputies if he was keeping a sign-in sheet for everyone who entered the crime-scene area. 'What do you think?' the deputy snapped back, and then remarkably, unbelievably, Iris apologized to the man for asking the question in the first place.

Magozzi and Gino exchanged a look. Any sheriff they'd ever met would have had that man on the ground first, and in the unemployment line second.

So there was a little attitude flying around Dundas County, Magozzi thought, obviously directed at the new sheriff. How Iris Rikker posed a threat was beyond him – maybe it was just pure Neanderthal stuff and men up here didn't like women in charge. But more likely, it was because she seemed like the kind of woman who'd gone through life with DOORMAT stamped across her forehead. Nobody liked or trusted an authority figure who couldn't command respect; in fact, most people resented it, as if it were a betrayal of some kind. Her students probably threw spitballs at her, and that deputy was doing the adult equivalent right now. So how in the hell had she gotten elected?

Jimmy Grimm was standing inside, near the door of the crowded tent, when they walked in, giving space to the techs who were swarming around a snow-encrusted figure, shooting photos and video. Magozzi noticed Iris taking a quick step backward, looking a little shell-shocked by all the lights and activity.

'Jimmy. How goes it?'

'Well, I almost died five times on the drive up here, all so I could freeze my balls off in a circus tent, but other than that, I'm just peaches. But if it keeps snowing like this, we're all going to end up checking into the Bates Motel. You notice that place on the drive into town?'

'Yeah. The Dew Drop Inn or something like that. Put it this way – I wasn't surprised by the vacancy sign. Have you met Sheriff Rikker?' Magozzi gestured her closer.

Jimmy was all smiles as he took her hand. He was almost as good at assessing people as he was a crime scene, and he pegged the sheriff as a greenhorn the minute she walked into the tent. She had a lost, little-girl look about her, as much as she tried to hide it. Probably her first body; certainly her first murder investigation, if it turned out that way.

Jimmy was a nice guy in general, but he was especially kind to kids, animals, lost souls, and the uninitiated – he didn't have to know her history to figure out that she was out of her element and stumbling up a sharp learning curve, and he made the effort to put her at ease. 'If you have any questions, Sheriff, come to me – these two don't know anything – they're just a couple of pretty faces. We let 'em hang around so they can schmooze the media.'

Iris smiled, shaking his hand. 'Nice to meet you, Mr Grimm, and thank you so much for coming.'

Jesus, Magozzi thought. She's standing in a tent with a dead body and a bunch of crime-scene techs and she sounds like a hostess at a cocktail party. 'So what have you got so far, Jimmy?' he said, interrupting the nice-fest.

'Take a look for yourselves. Make a hole, boys,' Jimmy directed the techs with cameras, and they cleared a space for Gino and Magozzi to step in closer.

Gino looked at the thing, then his face crunched up like it did that time he took a bite of McLaren's anchovy pizza. Rikker had been right. If it had started out like one of the storybook snowmen in the park, the weather had made a mess of it. The big head was sleet-pitted and misshapen, with icy rivulets frozen on the fat cheeks, as if the damn thing had been crying. But the snowman shape was absolutely there, and the guy attached to those blue-white hands sure as hell hadn't built it around himself.

'Could be number three,' Magozzi said, standing next to him, and Gino nodded.

Iris stood rock-still a few paces back, feet, hands, and nose already numbed by the cold, trying to look somber and professional, although what she really wanted to do was jump up and down and clap her hands. Number three meant it was the Minneapolis killer, and that meant it was their case, and they'd snatch the investigation right away from her. Oh, darn. She kept her smile deep inside.

'Or it could be a copycat,' Magozzi said.

Iris's inside smile faltered.

'I don't like the posing thing,' Detective Rolseth was saying. 'Damn fishing pole freaks me out as much as the skis did. Almost worse if it is a copycat – that means there might be more than one out there this sick.'

'Maybe it's not posed,' someone said from behind them, introducing himself as Lieutenant Sampson when they turned around. 'Seems I heard the two you found in the park were skiing when they caught it. Maybe this guy was ice-fishing.'

'No way anybody's going fishing in this kind of weather,' Gino said.

Sampson shrugged. 'It's winter. It snows. Weather doesn't bother the fish, and it sure doesn't bother the fishermen. Every one of those shacks out there is pumping smoke right now.'

'Pumping smoke?'

'From the heaters.'

'They got heaters in those things?' Gino asked.

'Heaters, TVs, beer coolers. Standard equipment. But those are the players. The die-hards still sit outside in the weather, like this guy. Easier to move yourself than a shack when it's time to auger a new hole.'

'This is the damnedest way to have a good time I ever heard of.'

Sampson smiled at him. 'You ought to give it a try sometime.'

'No way. God made ice for hockey and scotch, and that's about it. But either way, posed or not, we've moved on to another winter sport here . . .'

'And another killing field,' Magozzi added. 'If it isn't a copycat, we got a traveler.'

Gino looked down at his boots. 'Shit.'

'All yours.' A tech carrying all the cameras passed Jimmy on his way out of the tent. 'I'm going to get these back in the van.'

Magozzi looked around at all the faces inside the tent. 'Where's Anant?'

Dr Anantanand Rambachan was chief medical examiner for Hennepin County; philosopher of the world, as far as Magozzi was concerned; and the one person he knew in the whole system who'd managed to retain every ounce of his humanity. More important, he'd examined Deaton's and Myerson's bodies in the park yesterday after Gino and Magozzi left, and Magozzi had really wanted him on this scene, too.

'He's back in the Cities with a five-year-old girl on the table,' Jimmy answered. 'Went through the ice on Cedar Lake last night, and you know how Anant feels about kids.'

Magozzi did. No matter what else he was working on, if a child came through the ugly swinging doors, Anant tended them before all others. *Always, Detective Magozzi, we put the babies to bed first. In life, and in death, this is the right thing.*

'So who do we have?' he asked Jimmy.

'Dr Dredlock.'

Magozzi gave him a disapproving head shake.

'Hey, I call him that to his face all the time. He thinks it's funny. Besides, his real name's Rowland, and it plain doesn't go with hair like that. Anyway, he's good, Anant likes him, I like him, and he assisted on Deaton and Myerson yesterday, so he's running with the book. He already did a prelim and pronounced our friend here, then hightailed it back to the van to warm up. He'll come back out for the finish once we get the snow peeled away.'

Jimmy watched the rest of his crew snugging a plastic tarp all around the ice-fishing snowman, and when they were satisfied, he rubbed his mittened hands together. 'Okay, just like yesterday at the park, boys and girls. Let's crack this snowman, see what we've got.'

Iris held her ground but closed her eyes and listened to the sound of snow chunks being laid carefully on the plastic tarp. She opened them when she heard a big piece fall to the plastic and someone hiss, 'Oh, shit.'

The snowman – what was left of it – looked bizarre. Although the head was relatively intact, all of the snow on the man's torso had fallen away at once. Probably, Iris thought in a detached, scientific part of her mind, because all the blood had kept it from sticking properly. The man's chest was a mess. So you had Frosty the Snowman's head stuck on top of a horror movie.

Iris felt herself start to tip over, and then she felt a strong, mittened hand on her upper arm, pushing against her, holding her steady.

'Deep, slow breaths,' a voice said very quietly. 'Move your eyes away, don't close them. Just breathe.'

If she made the tiniest movement, like turning her head to see the face, there wasn't a doubt in her mind that she would pass out in a dead faint. Or maybe throw up. But she recognized the voice. Rolseth, of all people, was saving the day, trying to make her look like an actual cop.

When they removed the snow from the head, Iris stared at the exposed bluish face; the closed, swollen eyes; the gaping mouth.

'Anybody know this guy?' Magozzi was asking.

Nobody did.

'And I don't suppose we have a chance in hell of printing those hands until he thaws.'

Jimmy Grimm shook his head. 'Not a full set. They're frozen tight to the pole. Try to move the fingers, they'll snap like pretzel sticks. Try to pull the pole out, we'll be ripping some serious skin.' He crouched down for a closer look. 'Might be able to give you something off that one thumb, though. It's sticking out a little.'

'Give it your best shot. The sooner we ID him, the sooner we'll be able to look for a connection with the other two.' Magozzi glanced back at Iris. 'You're hooked up to the database, right?'

Iris opened her mouth to speak, pretty excited to know the answer to at least one question, but Lieutenant Sampson beat her to the punch. 'You get a print, I can run it from my squad in about ten minutes. Faster if he's been printed by the state. We've got them all set up to run through the Minnesota database first. Saves a lot of time.'

That got Gino's attention. 'Wait a minute. I can't make a cell call out here and you got computers in every squad with that kind of muscle?'

Sampson shrugged. 'Sure. Wireless computers, satellite GPS. Just like downtown.'

Gino folded his arms over his chest and grunted. *His* car didn't have GPS.

Sampson was as good as his word. He slogged back from his squad in the lot within five minutes, holding a printout. 'Got a hit in about two seconds. The guy's a parole officer out of Hennepin County. Lives in Minneapolis. Name of Stephen P. Doyle. Ring any bells?'

Magozzi looked down at the sorry remains of one

Stephen P. Doyle and shook his head. The man was wearing a gold wedding band. 'It's going to ring a real sad bell with somebody.'

15

Johnny McLaren was alone in Homicide by the time Tinker finally made it to the office. He was standing by the coffee-maker, mug in hand, watching the drips come out as if there were a speed limit on the damn things. His red hair was sticking out as if he'd been electrocuted, and his narrow face was the unhealthy color of a vanilla milk shake.

'Sorry I'm late, Johnny.'

'Jeez, Tinker, I almost called the dogs out on you. Janis called three hours ago, said you were going to make a quick personal stop. I figured you were nose down in a ditch somewhere, and I couldn't get through to your cell.'

Tinker hung up his coat, straightened it on the hanger, then slumped into his chair. 'Yeah, I was working the cell pretty hard. The personal stop turned into what might be some bad business.'

McLaren held his breath. If he had any kind of a curse attached to his Irish heritage, it wasn't his weekend love affair with fine aged whiskey – that had nothing to do with being Irish, and everything to do with being a cop and a lonely man. His real curse was his morbid and fearful imagination. Ten seconds after Tinker said 'bad business,' his mind had leaped to the conclusion that the personal stop was a doctor appointment, and that Tinker was dying of some horrible terminal illness, would probably drop dead at his desk before the day was over.

'Jesus, Tinker, what is it? Are you okay?'

'I don't know. The whole thing feels wrong . . .' Tinker looked up at McLaren's face, falling by the second, and almost rolled his eyes. 'Oh, come on, Johnny. You're always doing this. One of us gets a hangnail, you're up all night worried we've got flesh-eating bacteria or something. You've got to stop or you'll drive yourself crazy. I'm fine. It's Steve I'm worried about.'

'Oh. Good. Steve who?'

So Tinker gave him a quick rundown, and Johnny listened quietly, trying not to look elated that it wasn't Tinker, it was only one of his friends who might be in trouble. When Tinker shoved the picture of the brutalized ex-wife under his nose, he caught his breath.

'Jesus. They let this guy out?'

'They did.'

'And right now the only person who knows where this woman is, is the guy that did this to her?'

'You got it.'

'Whose job is it to find her?'

Tinker shrugged. 'By the time I follow that trail he could be in Julie Albright's backyard. I put Tommy Espinoza on it. He's hacking into a bunch of secure websites as we speak, breaking all kinds of laws trying to find her. If he can't, he's going to call the Monkeewrench people.'

'So we wait on that one. What about your friend?'

'That's a waiting game, too. The scene's weird, but there's no place to go with it from what I saw. So I called in Crime Scene, hoping they might pull a rabbit out of the hat. Told them it was a possible, which is a hell of stretch from the physical evidence. I'm going to get called on the carpet for this one.' He jumped when the phone rang and grabbed it before McLaren even thought to move, hoping to hear

Espinoza's voice, or maybe even someone from the Crime Scene Unit, but it was only Evelyn on the switchboard. He spent a few minutes calming her down – funny, that he was so good at calming other people when he felt like jumping out of his own skin – then hung up. 'Snowman calls keep coming in,' he explained to McLaren. 'Evelyn's running out of Valium.'

McLaren shrugged it off. 'It's been like that all morning. A kid builds a snowman in his own front yard, ten seconds later the next door neighbor's dialing 9-1-1 trying to get a unit sent out to knock it down, see if there's a body inside. You know how many snowmen the kids in this city build after a storm?'

'Probably a lot . . .'

'You got no idea. And then you've got the do-it-yourselfer paranoiacs who bust up the neighbor kid's snowman themselves, the kids freak, the parents get pissed, want their neighbor arrested for trespassing and destruction of private property and traumatizing their kids, blah, blah, blah. They got a double shift running in the 911 center and they're still swamped, and God help the poor bastard who tries to call in a real emergency.'

Tinker took a breath and switched gears from Steve Doyle and Julie Albright back to the job he was supposed to be doing today. 'So where is everybody? I thought we were going to have a full house.'

McLaren headed back to the coffeemaker. 'We do. Everybody's in. A lot are out in the field, muscling informants or doing the last of the interviews on people who were at the park yesterday; others are locked in dark rooms all over the house, watching the newsvideo and a ton of out-of-focus home movies of red-cheeked kids with snot running out of their noses, which is a colossal waste of time, if you ask me. No way the doer hung around for family photos.'

'Some of the really sick ones do.' Tinker finally got around to hanging up his coat, pushing to the back of his mind the involuntary thought of Steve Doyle's coat hanging in the empty parole office.

'Yeah, I know. It's got to be done, but it's a pain.'

'Where are Magozzi and Gino?'

McLaren looked confused for a moment, then rolled his eyes up to the ceiling. 'Oh, man, of course you didn't hear . . .'

'Hear what?'

'We might have another snowman up in Dundas County.'

Roadrunner's face, feet, and hands were completely numb and his body was encased in what had to be a half-inch of icy snow, which made him think about the snowman murders yesterday. He shivered, but it had nothing to do with the temperature. If he made it to Harley's before he froze to the seat of his bike and turned into a snowman himself, he'd be lucky.

In spite of the nasty weather and impending hypothermia, he paused on the Hennepin Avenue Bridge to catch his breath, as he always did when he took this route, looking at the great, frozen Mississippi, the Stone Arch Bridge beyond, and the old brick riverfront mill buildings that had long since been renovated to store people instead of flour and grain. They looked like old postcards superimposed on the backdrop of downtown's sleek, modern high-rises. It was a pretty city, even in the snowy gloom of January, and it didn't seem right that such horrible murders could happen in a nice place like this.

He stayed there as long as he could stand it, then pedaled hard across the bridge, taking two bad falls on the ice before he realized there was no way he was going to make it to Harley's on his bicycle. He turned around and headed back to his house.

The path Roadrunner had shoveled down his driveway was a perfect fit for his mountain bike, but it wasn't nearly wide enough to accommodate even one of Harley's Hummer's oversized tires. But five-foot drifts were child's play for the massive vehicle, and Harley plowed straight up to the front door and leaned on the horn.

Roadrunner waved from the front window of his colorful Nicollet Island Victorian, closed the shades, and hurried out the front door, limping slightly. 'Thanks for the ride,' he said as he clambered into the huge truck and buckled himself in.

'I can't believe you were stupid enough to even try to bike over today. How's your knee?'

Roadrunner touched the throbbing goose egg he'd sustained on one of his falls and cringed. 'It's okay. I put ice on it. And I had to give it a try. Cabs and buses aren't running today.'

'You've gotta get yourself some wheels one of these days, you know that?' He patted the steering wheel tenderly. 'Get one of these little honeys and it'll change your life. Might even be able to score yourself a date.'

'This thing is obscene. I can't believe you bought it.'

'Lighten up. I'm a big man and I need big wheels. Besides, it's not like I live in L.A. and I'm shuttling kids to soccer practice in it. This is strictly a winter vehicle, and we live in Minnesota.'

'You could have bought a hybrid. They have some nice hybrid SUVs now.'

'Right. They're nice if you hate cars. I mean, do you see Arnold driving a hybrid? I don't think so.' Harley put the Hummer in reverse and stomped on the accelerator. It didn't even shimmy as it munched over an icy drift.

Roadrunner rolled his eyes and gave up on a losing battle. 'So why are you so hot on working today? I thought you were bored.'

'I was, until I started playing around on the Web last night and came across some pretty wild stuff about that whole snowman thing in the park yesterday.'

'Like what?'

'Well, just for the hell of it, I plugged the Monkeewrench crime stat software in to cruise the net before I went to bed last night, just to see if any twisted sister had ever put a body in a snowman before. When I got up and checked the run record this morning, the thing had worked six hours before it pulled one hit, some renegade thread from a chat room, and it didn't say much – just "Minneapolis snowmen" and a couple lines in all caps that said, "Kill him while there's still time. Put him in a snowman."'

Roadrunner shrugged. 'So what? There's a million crazies on the Web saying sick crap like that.'

'I'm with you a hundred percent on that, but the thing is, that message was posted at nine a.m. Central Standard Time, yesterday morning.'

'Uh . . . okay. Is that supposed to mean something?'

Harley scowled at him. 'Hell, yes, it means something! Think, Roadrunner – Magozzi and Gino didn't find the bodies until noon Saturday. Three hours *after* the original post. Somebody knew about those bodies in the snowmen a long time before they were discovered.'

Roadrunner's mouth dropped open. 'Holy shit, Harley.

Did you go into the chat room? Did you trace the thread?'

'I sure as hell tried. I couldn't hack that site to save my life.'

'Come on . . .'

'I'm serious. This thing'll drive you nuts. The URLs keep shifting, the codes keep changing, and I'm thinking they've got this thing programmed to reroute on some kind of a weird loop. You know the last time I couldn't hack into any site?'

'Never.'

'Exactly.'

Roadrunner's eyes started jerking back and forth the way they did when he got upset. 'We've got to find a way, Harley. We've got to trace that thread, and then we've got to call Magozzi.'

'Now you know why we're all working today.'

Grace was trying to coax magic out of one of the several Monkeewrench computers when Harley and Roadrunner got up to the third-floor office in Harley's Summit Avenue mansion. Annie Belinsky was hovering behind her, all her glorious excess poundage decked out in a red velvet dress with white ermine trim and matching knee-high stiletto boots.

'Any luck yet?' Harley asked as he shrugged out of his jacket and tossed it on the floor.

Annie shook her head in disgust. 'We've been going at it from separate angles, and a few minutes ago Grace managed to break through a firewall. In the time it took me to walk from my desk to hers, it kicked her off.'

Grace pushed herself away from the desk and rubbed her eyes. 'And I just figured out why. There was another firewall behind the first one; probably another one behind that. We did what? Seven corporate security jobs in the past three months? And this is as good as anything we did. Maybe better, and it's just a stupid chat room.'

Annie click-clacked back to her own desk and cleared her screen. 'Lord, I hate it when people try to keep me out of a conversation. Forward the path you took, Grace. I don't care how many firewalls there are, I'm going to knock them down one by one until I get in there.'

'I put the path on the network so we could all work it, but this is going to take a while ...' The phone interrupted her. She picked up when she saw Minneapolis Police come up on the caller ID. She listened for a minute, then said, 'Give me the name, and then give us five minutes.' She ended the call quickly, then spun her chair to look at the rest of them. 'Forget the chat room for now. That was Tommy Espinoza from MPD. He needs some help in a hurry.'

'Something to do with the snowman murders?' Annie asked.

'No. It's a different case. We have to find a woman before her ex-husband does.'

'Is it bad?'

'It sounds like it might be real bad.'

Harley brought his screen to life with the jiggle of his mouse. 'What do we have to go on?'

'Just a name. Julie Albright.'

'Great. Do we even know what state she's in?'

'We'll start with Minnesota.'

'Why are the cops having such trouble finding her?' Roadrunner asked.

'She's in hiding.'

'But if the cops can't find her, how's the ex-husband going to?'

'He stole some files. He knows where she is.'

'So does the IRS,' Harley said, his fingers flying over his keyboard. 'Why didn't Espinoza try that?'

'He did. It's a sealed file.'

Harley's hands dropped to his lap. 'Jeez, Grace, the confidentials are a bitch to break into. This is going to take a hell of a lot longer than five minutes.'

'Then we'd better get started.'

Ten minutes later, while the rest of them were still clattering on their keyboards, Annie clapped her hands and said, 'Found her . . . oh, for heaven's sake, would you look at that. Her address is Bitterroot.'

'Our Bitterroot?' Grace asked.

'The very same. Dundas County.'

Harley made a face. 'That place up in the sticks where we tweaked all that high-tech security last fall? Who the hell lives at a corporation?'

Grace picked up the phone and started to dial Tommy Espinoza. 'She probably uses her place of work as a mailing address. She's in hiding, remember?'

16

By the time Gino and Magozzi started to head back to the Cities, the snow had stopped and the clouds had moved east into Wisconsin. As far as Gino was concerned, the view had been a whole lot better when snow was obliterating the landscape. He eyed the snow-drifted fields and scattered farms with the deep suspicion of a man who has found himself in a foreign country.

'I don't know, Leo. You ask me, farmland is just plain butt-ugly. Too many empty fields with nothing to look at.'

Magozzi smiled, mostly because he was in a warm car on his way back to the city, and the snowplows had managed to swipe the roads since the harrowing drive out here. 'In the summer those so-called empty fields produce a lot of what makes you the corn-fed beauty you are.'

'Well, they ought to scrap some of the cornfields and grow a few restaurants. I swear to God, when we passed those cows a minute ago, I started salivating.'

'Five miles to Dundas City and that place Sampson recommended.'

Gino snorted. 'Yeah, right. The Swedish Grill, which has got to be a local joke. You ever see a Swedish chef with his own cooking show? There's a reason for that, aside from the fact that all their food is white. They've got no cuisine, no palates, and no business grilling stuff.'

'You want me to drive right by?'

'Hell no. We could starve to death before we hit the next place.'

They blinked their way past a cluster of buildings that called itself a town. It had a weird name Gino couldn't pronounce, and even weirder letters, like *o*'s with umlauts and slashes through them. A large sign trumpeted some auspicious connection to a sister town in the old country. Gino couldn't pronounce that one, either.

A little farther down the road Gino eyed a highway sign and read aloud: '"Carl Moberg slept here." Who's Carl Moberg and why do we care where he slept?'

'He was a famous Swedish writer.'

'Yeah, so what did he write?'

'*The Emigrants.* It was about the hardships of settling Minnesota.'

'Oh, yeah. Hey, I think I saw the movie. Isn't that the one where they get caught in a blizzard and have to cut their horse open and put their kid inside so he doesn't freeze to death?'

'I think it was an ox.'

'Whatever. Christ, I had nightmares for a year after I saw that. Kind of makes you wonder why anybody settled here in the first place.'

'Brilliant marketing. The governor needed settlers for his brand-new state, so he started giving away free land to anybody who'd take it. He glossed over the Siberian winters and the mosquitoes and focused on the rich cropland and fjordlike surroundings. He sold it as kind of a home away from home, and it worked like a dream in the old country. They came in droves from Scandinavia.'

Gino looked skeptically out at the barren landscape of snowdrifts, frozen lakes, and skeletal trees and thought about the dead horse or ox or whatever it was. 'They must have been really pissed off when they got here. How the hell do you know all this stuff, anyhow? You sound like an encyclopedia entry.'

'I paid attention in history class. Why don't you know this stuff? Isn't Rolseth a Scandinavian name?'

'I always thought it was German, but what do I know? Hell, when you think about the history of the Vikings, you gotta figure pretty much everybody has a little Scandinavian blood in them one way or the other.'

'Good point.'

Bars and gas stations and unidentifiable pole buildings started cropping up along the roadside as they approached another dot on the map. Gino was staring intently out the windshield and made a funny snuffling sound.

'What?'

Gino gave him a goofy smile and pointed. 'There's a teapot in the sky.'

Magozzi looked up through the windshield at a water tower that was, incredibly, shaped like an old-fashioned teapot, covered in rosemaled flowers and emblazoned with the message: VÄLKOMMEN TO AMERICA'S LITTLE SWEDEN. He couldn't help but smile. 'By God, there is.'

'Gotta be the only one like it in the world.'

'I hope so.'

'Come on, don't be such a killjoy. There's probably some deep meaning behind it.'

'Or not.'

'Yeah, or not. But it's unique, you gotta give it that. And how often do you see flowers on a water tower? Makes you feel better about drinking the water, right? I mean, White Bear has a bear on their water tower and you can't help but think about the whole bear in the woods thing.' Gino heard a muted beep and pulled out his cell phone. 'Well, glory hallelujah. This piece of crap finally picked up a signal.'

'Weather's clearing up. Either that, or we're close to what might be the only tower for miles. Better talk fast.'

Gino nodded and pushed speed dial. 'Got a pile of messages from the office while this thing was in a coma. Maybe Tinker and McLaren solved the case while we were gone and we can go on vacation. Hey, Tinker, we're on our way back. What's the word? What do you mean, turn around? We just left, and let me tell you, this place is like a third-world country. Instead of cell towers, they got teapots in the sky and houses in the middle of lakes . . . all right, all right, hang on.' Gino pulled out his notebook and a pen and started scribbling while he listened.

The phone call was taking a long time, and Gino was silent for most of it, which was a good sign, as far as Magozzi was concerned – it probably meant that something had broken on the case in Minneapolis. By the time he pulled into the lot of the Swedish Grill, Gino was in the middle of telling Tinker about the snowman on the lake.

'. . . still can't tell if it's the same doer. This guy's chest was blown wide open, so it wasn't a twenty-two, like Deaton and Myerson, and the victim wasn't a cop, but he was law enforcement. A parole officer out of Minneapolis, name of Steve Doyle. Tinker? Hey, Tinker. You still there?' Then Gino went silent again and just listened, his expression grim. 'We'll take care of it on this end,' he said at last. 'In the meantime, find out where Weinbeck was Friday night, when Deaton and Myerson got hit. I'll call you back.' He flipped the phone closed and looked at Magozzi. 'We've got to go back to the sheriff's office.'

Magozzi raised his brows. 'You don't want to eat first?'

'We don't have time.'

'You drive, I'll talk.' Gino turned on the roof lights while Magozzi fishtailed out of the parking lot and pushed it as fast as he could on the road back toward Lake Kittering.

'Steve Doyle's been missing since yesterday. His last appointment was with an asshole named Kurt Weinbeck, who just checked out of Stillwater for damn near killing his pregnant wife. Weinbeck is a no-show at his halfway house, Doyle's office is trashed and there's some blood, and his car is missing from the ramp. The wife's files and contact info are missing, too, so Tinker figures Weinbeck's going after his wife, and guess what? She lives up here in Dundas County – someplace called Bitterroot.'

'So Weinbeck is probably Doyle's shooter.'

'He looks good for it.'

'No way a twenty-two put a hole like that in Doyle's chest.'

'Yeah, I know. Which means he probably isn't our snowman killer. Tinker said the TV was still on in Doyle's office when they got there. At the time of Weinbeck's appointment yesterday the channel was doing wall-to-wall coverage of the park fiasco, so he could have seen it, maybe figured he could pin Doyle's killing on our killer if he just built a snowman around him.'

'Maybe. Or maybe he switched guns. Maybe he's good for them all.'

'Not likely, but wouldn't that be roses? All tied up in one neat package. I could be home by six eating Angela's spaghetti.'

'We're dreaming.'

'Tell me about it. Domestics are the only things on

Weinbeck's sheet. Those yellow-bellied bastards don't usually go around popping cops, but Tinker and McLaren will look at it anyway. Anyhow, back to Weinbeck's ex-wife – calls herself Julie Albright now – Tinker gets her on the horn to warn her, and she blows him off, says she's not worried, if you can believe that.'

'Maybe she'll change her mind when we tell her her ex killed his parole officer to get to her.'

'That would change my mind. So the upshot is he wants us to talk to her in person, try to get her into protective custody, either with the locals or with us. This Weinbeck character isn't messing around.'

'She might be harboring him. It wouldn't be the first time that happened.'

'That crossed my mind.'

17

Iris was sitting in the oversized leather chair in the sheriff's office – her office, now – stuffing another bite of a peanut-butter-and-pickle sandwich in her mouth, feeling strangely guilty for eating at all while there was a BCA team on the lake outside her window, addressing the messy aftermath of the violent death of a human being. Every time she closed her eyes she saw the frozen horror of Steve Doyle's dead face, and still she ate the damn sandwich. There was something wrong with her.

The paper in front of her was filled with the scribbled notes she'd taken during Detective Rolseth's call. Just looking at them gave her a headache.

The upside was that if this Kurt Weinbeck character really was Steve Doyle's murderer – and by all accounts, it sounded like he was – her first homicide was already solved. The bad news was, he was still loose, probably somewhere in her county, stalking one of her citizens, and it was ultimately her responsibility to catch him before he could murder anybody else.

Her butt sank so far into the cushy chair that she felt like she was being swallowed, and her feet didn't touch the floor. Surely a sign from on high if ever there was one. She didn't fit in the chair, she didn't fit in the office, she didn't fit in the job. The last bite went down like a dry brick, peanut butter sticking to her throat.

By the time she got downstairs Sampson was already

in the lobby, and the Minneapolis detectives were coming through the front door. Magozzi gave her a nod of recognition, and Iris nodded back. That, she decided, was the secret to communicating with men. Whenever possible, use signals instead of words. Words just confused them.

Magozzi was thinking that Iris Rikker was looking a little worn around the edges, and small wonder. First day as sheriff of a peaceful rural county, and already she had one body, and maybe a murderer hanging around, trying to raise the count to two. No way she could have bargained for that when she put her name on the ticket.

Sampson, on the other hand, seemed surprisingly nonchalant. He looked up from retying his boots. 'I called Julie Albright, let her know we were coming.'

Gino was stamping his boots on a doormat that was already soaking wet. 'Our guy talked to her, said we might have a tough time talking her into protective custody.'

'You got that right. She thinks she's safe in Bitterroot.'

Gino's thoughts went back to the airport parking lot two days ago, when they were pulling a half-dead woman out of a trunk. She'd thought she was safe, too. 'No place is safe when you've got one of these bastards going after a woman, and this one's worse than most, because he's willing to kill other people to get to her. We all need to be on the same page when we talk to Julie Albright or we're never going to get her under the wing.'

Sampson straightened and shifted his utility belt under his parka. 'The thing is, I'm not so sure we've got anyplace half as secure as where she is right now. Take a look at Bitterroot first; see what you think. You ever been out there, Sheriff?'

Iris shook her head, sticking to her new signaling plan.

'I'll drive, then. You might want to ride with us,

Detectives. It's kind of tricky to find unless you know the back roads.'

'Fine by me,' Magozzi said. 'How far away is this town?'

'It isn't a town, it's a corporation.' Sheriff Rikker was having trouble with the zipper on her parka, and it was frustrating her. 'According to Lieutenant Sampson, some of the employees live on site. Julie Albright is one of them.'

'Ten minutes as the crow flies,' Sampson said. 'Twenty in a car.'

'You know, I never got that.' Gino was eyeing a bakery bag sitting on the dispatch counter. 'If a crow always gets someplace faster, why didn't they just follow the crows when they were building the roads?' His stomach growled noisily, making Sampson smile.

'Too many lakes, too many swamps. Roads up here twist like crazy going around them. Half the time even the locals need a compass to know which way they're going. Grab that bag, will you, Detective? Sounds like we all missed lunch.'

Gino actually put his hand over his heart, a gesture only food could inspire.

Ten minutes later Sampson was powering the big county SUV down a narrow, curving road with ten-foot snowbanks towering on either side. Sheriff Rikker was next to him, clutching her pocketbook as if it were an airbag; Magozzi and Gino were in the backseat, which was just the way Gino liked it. Way he figured, the people in the front would get it first when they ran smack-dab into one of those snowbanks. He leaned forward and breathed jelly bismarck into the front seat.

'This is supposed to be a road? What happens if we meet a car going the other way?'

'Plenty of room.' Sampson braked hard just before a

sharp curve and they fishtailed for a second. 'Looks narrower than it is because the snow's so high.'

Gino snorted, not believing that for a minute. To a pair of eyes used to a six-lane city freeway, it looked like they were driving down the white throat of some enormous monster.

'And it's a good road,' Sampson added. 'Gross-weight standards up for eighteen-wheelers, what with all the shipping they do out of here.'

'You're telling me we could meet a semi on this cow path?'

'Probably not on a Sunday.'

'Seems like a pretty out-of-the-way location for a business. You'd think they'd locate on a major road, instead of back here in the toolies. Anybody want to split the last bismarck?'

Ten minutes later the road uncoiled a little and Magozzi and Gino could see a tall cyclone fence that stretched as far as they could see in either direction. It was even more interesting when they got closer.

Magozzi nudged Gino with his elbow. 'Look at the top of that fence.'

Gino leaned over his partner and peered out the window. 'Huh? What are those thingamajigees?'

'Looks like the cameras Grace has mounted all around her place.'

'Oh, great. A whole corporation as paranoid as Grace MacBride. What the hell do they make here, Sheriff?'

Iris was staring out at the fence and the cameras mounted every twenty feet or so, mystified by all the security. 'As far as I know, organic products. Food, cosmetics, things like that. I've ordered a few things from their website.'

'Looks more like a military installation, if you ask me. Or

maybe a prison . . . Jesus, look at that.' They were pulling up to an enormous pair of gates with a brick guardhouse on the left. A small woman in boots and a big parka exited the little building and headed for the car. 'That woman's carrying, Leo.'

'I see that.'

'They've got their own security force.' Sampson rolled down his window. 'All of them have permits to carry.'

The female guard pushed back the hood on her parka and bent toward the car window, looking past Sampson as if he weren't there. 'Sheriff Rikker?'

'That's right.'

The woman grinned. 'Congratulations on the election, Sheriff. Great pleasure to meet you.'

Magozzi thought Iris looked a little flummoxed by the greeting. Or maybe it was the congratulations.

'Thank you very much.'

'And will you vouch for your passengers?'

'Yes, this is Lieutenant Sampson –'

'Aw, come on, Liz,' Sampson interrupted. 'Don't give me a hard time. The two guys in the back are Minneapolis PD, and they won't give you their weapons, either. I'll let you frisk me, though, if you want.'

'Tempting, but I'll pass. Straight to the office,' she reminded him.

'I know the drill.' He closed the window, waited while one of the electronic gates swung open, then pulled through.

Gino was puzzled. 'I don't get it. They knew we were coming, they could see it was a county car, and they stopped us anyway.'

'They stop everybody. Drives me nuts, but they're pretty

strict about it. Except for Liz. I think she does it just to piss me off.'

'So every time you get an emergency call out here you've got to stop while they check the car? That's just plain crazy.'

'Well, the thing is, we never get called out here. Not one call as long as I've been on the job, and that's fifteen years. Only reason I'm a familiar face is that I've got a friend who lives here in the residential neighborhood around the back of the complex.'

As they drove inside the gates, all that could be seen in any direction were woods and fields, all buried under snow. 'What complex?'

'Over the next hill.'

And indeed it was. A cluster of modern buildings with a courtyard and landscaped parking lot. It looked like a dozen other corporate complexes that grew like weeds all over the Minneapolis suburbs. Except this one was out in the middle of nowhere, surrounded by a ten-foot-high cyclone fence with armed guards at the gate. It wasn't the first time Magozzi had seen elaborate corporate security, but this seemed a little over the top for a place that made jelly and face powder. So did the metal detector and second armed guard at the building entrance.

A woman Sampson introduced as Maggie Holland was waiting for them in a large office just off the lobby. She could have been anywhere from forty-five to sixty-five years old – Magozzi was finding it harder and harder to tell these days – but it was an age span that made him a little uneasy, probably because a lot of women in that group were long past the time when they expected anything extraordinary from men. *Fractured fairy tales,* he thought. *We all take the rap for that.*

Ms Holland greeted them all cordially enough, but made a particular fuss over the new sheriff, just as the guard at the gate had. Iris Rikker apparently had a fan club out here she didn't know about.

After the pleasantries, she slipped straight into no-nonsense mode. 'Julie Albright will not go with you.'

Gino nodded. 'That's what she told our detective on the phone. We might need your help talking her into it.'

'I'm afraid I couldn't possibly do that. She's much safer here than she would be with you. Perfectly safe, in fact.'

Gino got a little impatient when he still had a long drive to make it to Angela's spaghetti. 'Listen, we saw the security you've got out here, and let me tell you, a fence, a couple of guards, and a metal detector might put a damper on corporate espionage or whatever the hell you're worried about, but it's not going to stop a man like Kurt Weinbeck. He already killed a man to get to her. Your little fence isn't even going to slow him down.'

'There's a little more to it than a fence and a couple of guards, Detective Rolseth.' Ms Holland pressed a button on her desk computer and a portion of a wall parted to reveal an enormous computer screen. She pressed a few more keys and a mosaic of live video feeds appeared.

Magozzi recognized the guardhouse at the entrance, the parking lot, and the lobby they'd just passed through, but there were at least twenty other views displayed, some outside, some showing various offices and labs he assumed were somewhere in this building. He examined them all carefully.

'This screen is displaying views from all the security cameras in what we call Quadrant One. Bitterroot is divided into twenty quadrants, all monitored with cameras and motion detectors and analyzed in real time by our security staff in the media room, twenty-four hours a day. It's based on the surveillance the casinos in Las Vegas use.'

'Impressive. How many cameras?'

'Hundreds of them. But we can't possibly monitor every square inch of a thousand-acre compound, so we had a local software company integrate the motion detectors and the cameras. Now when something moves out of camera view, the detectors direct the nearest camera to adjust the view to follow it.'

Gino was jabbing Magozzi with his elbow, jerking his head toward the screen, but Magozzi had already seen it: a tiny Monkeewrench logo at the bottom of the screen.

'We also have security around the clock patrolling the compound and particularly the perimeter. And there are more layers of security, but I think you get the picture. Nothing you have on the outside can offer this level of protection to Julie.'

Magozzi looked straight at her while his thoughts moved fast, racing through the details his cop's eyes had recorded for the brain to sort through later. 'So just exactly how many Julie Albrights do you have living here?'

He'd surprised her with that one, and Maggie Holland didn't look like the kind of woman who surprised easily. 'Very good, Detective. Quite a leap, actually, in view of the little you've seen . . .' She glanced at Sampson. 'Or were you told in advance?'

Magozzi caught the look. 'No. And it wasn't that much of a leap. The only people I've seen here so far are all women, including the ones on your camera screens up there. Now that probably isn't so unusual for a cosmetics company, but your security guards are all women, too, and you don't see a lot of that. Add Julie Albright and the security to the mix and it makes you wonder. Plus, you've got a real faint scar across your throat that looks a little ragged for surgery, and your nose has been broken and healed a couple of times. Way I figure, that makes two of you, at least.'

Gino had been frowning hard, trying to follow the underpinnings of the conversation. Suddenly his face cleared. 'Oh, man, it was right there in front of my nose and still I was about ten steps behind on that one. And there are at least three, by the way. The guard at the metal detector had some broken fingers on her left hand, never set. Twist injury, from the way they healed. So how many more?'

Ms Holland looked at him calmly. 'All of them.' She glanced over at Sampson, who was looking down at the floor, but of course he had always known; and then over at poor Sheriff Rikker, who was struggling to put it all together.

Iris had been staring at the scar on Maggie Holland's neck ever since Magozzi mentioned it. It was unforgivably rude, which was totally unlike her, and yet she couldn't pull her eyes away. It was one thing to watch the news stories and learn the statistics in class; even listening to all the domestic calls that came over dispatch still kept her one step removed. But to see evidence of the reality was like a hard slap across the face. She felt like she'd been sucked up from her world and abruptly dropped into a new one, where men didn't leave their wives, they beat the crap out of them.

'Every woman who lives here came because she wasn't safe on the outside,' Ms Holland was saying.

'Same thing with the men?' Gino asked.

'There are no men. That's what keeps the women safe.'

Gino was frowning. 'Wait a minute. How many people live here?'

'Almost four hundred.'

'And not one of them is a man.'

'That's correct. No man ever enters this property without a day pass and an escort.' She smiled at Sampson. 'Not even police officers.'

Gino looked at Magozzi. 'Is that even legal?'

'Probably. It's private property. We keep men out of the safe houses in the city, and basically, that's what this place is starting to look like. One big, permanent safe house.'

Maggie shook her head. 'It's not a safe house. It's a town that happens to be safe. That's all any of us wanted, a place we could be safe from rape, murder, assaults against our children . . . It didn't take long for the founders of Bitterroot to figure out that all they had to do to eliminate those dangers was one thing: eliminate the men.'

Eliminate the men. Magozzi's brain ran into the brick wall of those three words and revved there like a useless, speeding engine. He tried to remember that his real job was back in the Cities, trying to find the murderer of two cops, that Kurt Weinbeck probably didn't have a thing to do with his real case, that he had a job and a sort-of life and a woman he cherished who wouldn't talk to him – but he was having trouble focusing. He kept hearing those same three disturbing words over and over in his head, and the worst part was the brain tickle that told him he'd heard those words before, or something like them. 'That's a pretty damn extreme solution,' he finally managed to say.

Maggie Holland nodded. 'But it *is* a solution. We haven't had one violent crime in Bitterroot in the sixty years of its existence. Can you think of one other town in the entire country that can make that claim?'

Magozzi didn't reply.

'And when you really think about it, it isn't that extreme at all.' Maggie's eyes shifted to Iris. 'You live alone, do you not, Sheriff Rikker?'

Iris nodded.

'Well, in a sense, is what we do here so very different from what you do in your own home? You lock your car doors, you lock the doors to your house when you come home, your ground-floor windows when you go to bed, and you probably don't admit strangers readily. These are sensible precautions women everywhere employ to keep themselves safe. Bitterroot does the same thing, only on a larger, even more secure scale, because our residents are higher risk.'

'So you built yourself a prison and put the innocents inside,' Magozzi commented, sounding much more judgmental than he'd ever intended.

Maggie smiled, but the smile had a real hard edge to it. 'We may have prison-style security, Detective, but it's not to keep the innocents inside, it's to keep the monsters out, and we do that very well.'

And you couldn't argue with that, Magozzi thought. If Bitterroot really hadn't had a single violent crime in sixty years, they were doing a hell of a job protecting people he and Gino and Sampson and Sheriff Rikker couldn't. That kind of failure was a tough admission for any cop, and probably a big part of the reason he was finding it hard not to be defensive. It just all seemed so wrong – the law was supposed to provide refuge, not inspire mass exodus to a high-security facility that probably put San Quentin to shame.

Apparently his thoughts were printed in big type across his forehead, because Maggie Holland was looking straight at him with one of those little smiles people reserve for idiots who just don't get it. 'I think it's time you saw the real Bitterroot,' she said quietly, but Magozzi wasn't going for the carrot.

'We need to speak with Julie Albright. That's why we're here.'

'Of course. But Julie's daughter has a cold today, so we'll go to her house instead of having her come here. It isn't far, and you can see a bit of the village on the way.' And then her demeanor shifted abruptly from all-business to all-roses, and she looked at each of them with one of those kindly, grandmotherly expressions Magozzi imagined the Big Bad Wolf had used on Little Red Riding Hood. Damn woman was a shape-shifter.

18

Magozzi, Gino, Sampson, and Iris followed Maggie Holland down a hallway and out a side door into an enclosed parking lot. The only vehicles parked there looked like something Walt Disney dreamed up.

'What the hell are those things?' Gino asked. 'They look like golf carts on growth hormones.'

Maggie laughed politely. 'You're very close, Detective Rolseth. They're electric, like golf carts, but with the large tires and high clearance of ATVs. Enclosed, of course, to allow for our weather, and large enough to accommodate all of us if you don't mind close quarters for a few moments. They're the only vehicles allowed in the village.'

She opened one with a key card and settled behind the wheel while the rest of them piled in behind her. There were three rows of two seats, one to a side. Gino and Magozzi took the ones at the rear and automatically looked for seat belts.

'You won't need them, Detectives,' Maggie called back. 'Top speed on these is fifteen miles an hour, and the streets curve a bit too much to ever go that fast.'

The heaters kicked in immediately – the one and only good thing about electric vehicles, Gino thought, his eyes busy as he watched Maggie open the lot gate with a remote, then head out onto a narrow strip of tar that curved sharply to the right and nowhere else.

'This is the one and only way into the village,' he heard

Maggie explaining to Iris, who was riding next to her. He felt like he was on a tour bus with one of those annoying, chatty guides. 'Through the corporate complex with all its security, then the locked parking lot and onto this road. And as you can see, the road is much too narrow to accommodate a standard-sized car.'

Gino was scowling out at the thick stands of mature trees crowding the road that looked more like a bike path. 'The people who live here can't drive their own cars to their own houses?'

'That's correct. There is no road that connects to this one. It begins and ends at the enclosed parking lot we just left.'

'So you come back from town with a buttload of groceries and do what? Hoof it all the way through the building to get to the carts? Sounds pretty damn inconvenient, if you ask me.'

Maggie smiled at him in the rearview mirror, a little wickedly, he thought. 'Not as inconvenient as having your nose broken.'

Gino shut up and looked out the window. They were moving into a residential area that looked like any small town in America about a hundred fifty years ago, before they widened the streets for traffic. It was an idyllic scene of uniform, well-kept homes that could have been transplanted right off the set of *Leave It to Beaver,* complete with tidy shrubs, charming lampposts, and an ensemble cast of smiling, red-faced children playing in the fresh snow. Without exception, every single one of them stopped what they were doing and waved at the cart as it passed.

Gino nudged Magozzi and said under his breath, 'When was the last time some kid on the street waved to you for absolutely no reason?'

'Five years ago. He waved, then chucked a rock at my back window.'

'That's what I thought. Does the word *Stepford* ring any bells?'

Magozzi sighed and watched the scenery roll by: an open, parklike area with a gazebo and playground equipment, and adjacent to that, a larger brick building that looked very much like a school.

'That looks like a school,' he heard Iris echoing his thoughts from the far front seat.

'It is indeed. Multiple grades and fully accredited, for any children who might be at risk on the outside. But just as many attend public school.'

And the school and the houses and the park were just the tip of the iceberg, Magozzi realized as they drove farther into the village. There were businesses, too – a mom-and-pop grocery store, presumably without the pop, a beauty salon, a little coffee shop, even a health clinic. It was the perfect reproduction of a perfect little town; a tranquil snapshot of traditional Americana, at least at first glance. But if you looked a little closer, it was anything but traditional, because this town belonged exclusively to women. For some reason, that made Magozzi very sad.

Julie Albright greeted them at the front door of her little house, and every one of them except Maggie Holland had to concentrate furiously not to wince at the woman's face, which looked like a jigsaw puzzle put together very badly. It wasn't as though Magozzi hadn't seen it a hundred times before, but it always set him back on his heels. She was such a tiny thing – a full foot shorter than he was, at least, with watchful, wary eyes, still haunted by the lingering remnants of terror. He wondered if that look ever went away.

Her eyes finally found his and stayed there. It was a funny thing about abused women, he thought. No matter how many female officers they took on a call, the victims ultimately always sought solace in the very gender that had treated them so badly.

'Won't you all please come into the living room and sit down?'

All five of them were crowded onto a small section of tiled floor by the entrance, their boots dripping melted snow.

'Thank you, no,' Magozzi smiled at her. 'We won't take that much of your time. We just needed to confirm personally that you're aware of the situation, and prefer to stay where you are.'

Julie Albright's smile might have been pretty once. It wasn't anymore. 'You've seen the security?'

'It's impressive. But we do need to remind you that your ex-husband still hasn't been apprehended, and that we're presuming he kidnapped and murdered his parole officer for one reason: to get to you.'

Julie nodded. 'Maggie told me.'

'Did she tell you the officer was murdered here in Dundas County, not so far from Bitterroot? He knows where to find you, Ms Albright.'

One of her hands crept up to finger a rope of scar tissue near her mouth. 'He's always been able to find me, Detective. No matter how far I ran, or how well I hid, he's always found me. He's very good at that.'

Gino was looking over a planter into a cozy living room with toys on the floor and a playpen in the corner and windows on every wall. Sure, the front door had a deadbolt, but that didn't do a hell of a lot of good in a glass house.

'Listen, Ms Albright, you gotta understand. He could still be in the area, the guy's a killer, and I don't care how good the security is out there on the perimeter. If he finds a way into this town, you're an open target in this place. You ask me, you'd be a whole lot safer under guard someplace in the Cities, out of the area.'

'How many guards?' she asked abruptly.

'Excuse me?'

'How many guards will there be at this place in the Cities you're talking about?'

'Well, I don't know. A couple, maybe. Police officers. One inside, one out, whatever we need to secure the place.'

Julie tried to smile again. 'No offense, Detective, but I have a whole town protecting me out here.'

Gino was getting frustrated. 'No offense back at you, but you've got four hundred untrained *women* out here and a hell of a lot of space to cover, and I don't care how good their intentions are, they can't protect you like a couple of highly trained cops in close quarters –'

'It didn't do me a lot of good the last time,' she interrupted quietly, and Gino's mouth closed slowly. 'I know you mean well; I know there are good men who would do anything to stop this from happening. I had two of them guarding my house the night Kurt broke in and cut me. They meant well, too.'

Gino's eyes screwed up. 'Yeah, but were they cops?'

She looked at him for a minute as if she felt sorry for him, and Gino didn't get that until she answered. 'Yes, they were. MPD.'

There wasn't a lot more to say after that. Just Sheriff Rikker's assurances that the county would keep a heavy patrol schedule around Bitterroot until Weinbeck was caught; Magozzi's feeble, paternalistic reminder to Julie Albright that she lock her doors, keep a phone close, and avoid trips out of the complex until further notice. She nodded politely, as if everything they said had meaning, even though they were part of the system that hadn't been able to protect her in the first place.

Gino shook her hand as he went out the door, which was an unusual thing for him to do. 'Be safe,' he said, and she would have had to be blind not to see how deeply he meant that.

They were halfway down the front walk when Julie called out to Iris. 'I forgot to congratulate you on the election, Sheriff Rikker. I voted for you. We all did.'

The ride away from Bitterroot and back toward the sheriff's office was silent for a time, then Gino started spewing words like a volcano that just blew the cork off. 'Jesus Christ, Magozzi, MPD right there on duty when Weinbeck did that to her face? How the hell does that make you feel?'

'Like shit.'

'Tell me about it. And I'd like a word or two with the sergeant of the two assholes that pulled that duty, because there's no way you can justify it. No way that animal should've gotten to her. And why the hell didn't we ever hear about it? Hell, Kristen Keller should've been all over it, abysmal failure of MPD to protect its citizens, shit like that, man, somebody's sleeping with somebody or we never would have dodged a bullet like that one.'

'It happens,' Sampson said quietly, ending Gino's rant. 'No matter what you do, no matter how hard you try, you get somebody dead-set on getting to somebody else to do them harm, they'll find a way.'

Magozzi looked at the slice of the man's profile he could see from the backseat. 'You speaking from personal experience? I'm only asking, because you said you had a friend in Bitterroot.'

'Actually, it's my sister. Another one who did everything right. Got restraining orders, went to a bunch of different shelters, but the son of a bitch kept coming after her. I'm a cop and I couldn't even protect my own sister. Not without going down for murder, anyhow.'

Iris was turned sideways in the passenger seat, watching his face. 'So you knew about this place all along.'

'For a few years now.'

'Why didn't you tell us?'

He shrugged. 'I guess I figured it was the kind of place you had to see for yourselves. I could have told you that Julie Albright is safer here than anywhere; I could have told you what Bitterroot was all about, and that they haven't had a single incident in sixty years; but that doesn't mean much until you see the kind of security they have.'

Gino was shaking his head. 'I still can't believe this place has been around for that long and nobody's ever heard of it. Why's it a secret?'

'It's not a secret, exactly, they just don't advertise. Adds another layer of security.'

'Then how do the women find out about it?' Iris asked. 'How did your sister?'

'There's kind of an underground network – and I hear there's a website you can access if you know the right people to ask.'

'A lot of their security is pretty high-tech,' Magozzi pointed out. 'Stuff that hasn't been on the market for sixty years, like the motion detectors and the cameras. So what did they do for security before?'

Sampson shrugged. 'They always had their guns. Maggie said we'd be surprised at how many of the bastards turn tail and run when they see women holding weapons, instead of cowering in a corner, like they're supposed to.'

Magozzi wasn't surprised by that at all. Most of the men who beat women were instantly docile when they faced someone who could fight back. But there were always a few exceptions: the ones so crazed by rage that even an armed cop couldn't stop them from making one last desperate lunge at the woman.

He'd been on half a dozen domestic calls like that back when he still rode a squad, and he couldn't imagine a single one of those men turning tail and running at the sight of a gun.

19

Magozzi and Gino rode in comfortable silence for the first half hour of their trip back to the Cities from Dundas County, which was exactly what they both needed. Magozzi thought that if the discrimination police would let you get away with it, it should be written into department policy. Men partnered with men, women with women.

In his early days on the force, he'd been paired with a savvy female officer as good at the job as anyone he'd known then or since. She could control the bad guys, hysterical victims, her weapon, her career – anything but her mouth, as if silence were some fearful thing she had to keep at bay with constant conversation. There wasn't anyone he would have rather had watching his back, and still, after about two weeks with her in a closed patrol unit he started to have fantasies about running the car into a tree – on her side.

Sometimes you had to have quiet, to think about things, or stop thinking about them. Women didn't get that. It was one of the ten million things he'd simply accepted and stopped trying to understand a long time ago. Women's and men's minds worked differently. It didn't make one method better than the other; it just made working with the opposite sex – on the job or in a relationship – a whole lot tougher.

'Ah, shit,' Gino said suddenly, and Magozzi smiled. Typical male conversation starter.

'What?'

'Damn watch stopped. You know I hate these things. My dad's watch stopped, he wound it back up. Nowadays you have to make a trip to the store, wait in line for some gum-cracking kid to sell you a battery, wait again while they try to figure out what battery fits and how the hell to get the case apart . . . crap. How come the dash clock doesn't work?'

'Probably because no one had time to read the two-hundred-page manual and learn how to set the thing.'

'New cars, new watches, and we still can't make anything work. The world is going to hell.'

'In many ways.'

Gino let out a noisy sigh, as if he'd been holding his breath for thirty minutes. 'I gotta tell you, Leo, Bitterroot kind of messed me up. Left me conflicted. I looked at Julie Albright's face, thought to myself, we're spitting in the ocean here. A couple days ago we're all on top of ourselves 'cause we got that woman out of the trunk before she died, and then . . . Christ, I can't even remember her name . . .'

'Betty Ekman.'

'Yeah, damnit, and then we find out there's a whole god-damned town filled with Betty Ekmans and Julie Albrights, and why the hell couldn't we get to them *before* they got stuffed in trunks or cut to pieces?'

Magozzi closed his eyes. 'We do what we can, Gino.'

'Oh, yeah? Then how come four hundred women had to build a whole damn town to keep themselves safe? Shit. How am I supposed to go home and tell Angela about that? She'll give me a drink and a plate of pasta to die for, pat my head because I feel bad, but all the time she'll be giving me that doe-eyed look, the sad one, like I should be able to fix it.'

'She does not think that, and you know it.'

'Maybe not, but the thing is, you feel personally responsible for one woman, you start feeling personally responsible for all of them, and Bitterroot was an in-your-face reminder of how goddamned short we fall.'

'So maybe you skip Bitterroot when you tell Angela about your day.'

'You're kidding. Whaddya think? You get to keep this stuff to yourself when you're married?' Gino looked immediately contrite. It was getting harder and harder to remember that Magozzi had been married once, and that Heather hadn't given a shit about Leo's job. 'Sorry, buddy. I keep forgetting about Heather.'

'I wish I could.'

It was barely after five, and already full dark by the time they got back to City Hall. It wasn't the worst thing about winters in the Midwest, but it came close. Dark when you left for work in the morning, dark when you came home at night. Magozzi wondered if he'd remember what color his house was come spring.

Homicide had cleared out for supper, with the exception of Johnny McLaren, who was barely visible behind the towering piles of paperwork on his desk. The whole place reeked like microwave popcorn and scorched coffee, and trash cans were overflowing with empty soda cans and take-out containers.

'Did we miss the party?' Gino asked, poking around for leftovers.

McLaren was bleary-eyed and about as messy looking as his desk, but he was genuinely happy to see them. 'Yeah. The dancing girls just left.'

'If Gloria sees this pigsty, she's going to have your hide, Johnny.'

'That's what I'm hoping for.' He pushed back from his desk and stifled a yawn. 'Hey, did you guys do a drive-by out front? Is the building still under siege?'

Magozzi was at his desk, leafing through message slips. Half of them were from reporters, the other half from garden-variety crazies who claimed they'd seen alien spacecraft, the Loch Ness monster, a yeti, and the ghost of Karl Marx building snowmen in Theodore Wirth Park Friday night. Nothing from Grace. Not that she'd ever leave a paper trail. 'We parked in the underground lot and snuck in that way. There were still satellite vans on Fourth, though. They'll probably camp out until the ten o'clock news.'

McLaren shook his head in disgust. 'I watched the early news – you should hear all the talking heads playing profiler. I didn't know whether to laugh or puke. They've got their hearts set on some diabolical serial killer who was beaten and tortured as a child in front of Christmas cartoons.'

'Sounds plausible,' Gino said, sampling a half-eaten lemon bar.

'Any mention of the Dundas snowman?' Magozzi asked, dragging a chair up to McLaren's desk and sagging into it.

'No. Kind of a miracle, isn't it? I don't know how you guys managed to keep that under wraps for this long, but whatever you did, it worked.'

'Simple – nobody lives in Dundas County,' Gino said. 'You could test nukes up there and it would take a month before anybody noticed the tap water was glowing ... Johnny, you shouldn't eat this microwave popcorn.' He pointed to a stainless-steel bowl brimming with unnaturally yellow puffs. 'They use that fake butter that stays in your bloodstream for the rest of your life.'

'No kidding?'

'That's what I heard. Hey, where's Tinker?'

McLaren winced, suddenly remembering that Magozzi and Gino hadn't gotten the full story when they were up in Dundas. 'He went to notify Steve Doyle's wife. He didn't mention this to you on the phone, but I guess he was a pretty close friend. That's how he got wind of it in the first place – Doyle's wife called him at home early this morning in a panic.'

Gino's hand had stopped halfway to the bowl of poison popcorn. 'Damnit. I knew he sounded funny on the phone when I told him Steve Doyle was the Dundas snowman. How's he doing?'

'He's taking it hard, and, man, does he want Weinbeck. BCA called in a prelim on the Dundas scene, and so far they've got zilch for forensics. Same thing with the body. Nothing that would really point a legal finger at Weinbeck.'

Magozzi frowned. 'I thought everything pointed a finger at Weinbeck. He had an appointment with Doyle, there's blood and signs of a struggle in the parole office . . .'

'Yeah, yeah, we even got some partials of Weinbeck's on the remote for the TV up there, but the only tune he has to sing is that he showed for the appointment, he and Doyle talked, watched a little TV, that Doyle was alive and well when he left, and as of now, we can't prove him wrong.'

'The file with his ex-wife's address is missing.'

McLaren shrugged. 'So Doyle took the file with him, maybe headed up to Bitterroot to talk to Julie Albright, and on the way the psycho snowman serial killer mugged him.'

Gino blew a raspberry. 'That's a crock of shit.'

'I know that. You know that. We just can't prove it. Hell, we've got a prosecutor who thinks circumstantial evidence against jaywalkers should get them the chair, and even he wouldn't touch this one.'

'We need to place Weinbeck in Dundas County.'

'That would help. Finding Doyle's car up there with Weinbeck's prints all over it, something like that.'

Gino started fishing for popcorn again. 'Dundas is looking. At least I hope they are. That new sheriff's got less experience in the field than my two-year-old. I don't know what her idea of a dragnet is, but it probably involves setting out a plate of cookies with a net over it.'

Magozzi winced. 'Ouch.'

'Come on, Leo, the woman doesn't have a clue and you know it. She's probably at home right now watching reruns of *NYPD Blue* trying to figure out what the hell she's supposed to do next.'

McLaren looked at Magozzi for confirmation. 'Is it really that bad?'

Magozzi sighed. 'She's brand new, right off the dispatch desk. No field experience. But I don't know. She might do okay.'

'Might do okay?' Gino rolled his eyes. 'Tell me this man isn't a total sucker for a pretty face.'

Magozzi glared at him. 'I didn't see any pretty face. I saw a sheriff.'

'Yeah, right,' Gino grunted. 'Anyway, you ask me, I'm having a hard time connecting the snowman up in Dundas to the two we had in the park, which means we got two cases, and we just wasted a whole damn day on the wrong one. You know, the minute things started to look good for Kurt Weinbeck murdering Doyle, I got this really cool dream scenario that we'd find him up there with Doyle's blood all over him and Deaton's and Myerson's sidearms in his pockets, but I gotta tell you, it just doesn't fit. The snowmen didn't match, the weapons didn't match, and the truth is, yellow-bellied wife beaters don't go around offing cops. I'm betting Weinbeck saw the thing in the park on TV and decided to make it look like our killer did it by sticking Doyle into a snowman of his own.'

'I'm with you.' Magozzi was leaning back in his chair, arms folded across his chest, eyes closed. He didn't open them when he talked. 'Two cases. Weinbeck killed Doyle, and Dundas is the lucky winner of that one; somebody else killed Deaton and Myerson, and we better get our asses in gear on that one, or Sheriff Iris Rikker is going to solve her case before we solve ours.' He opened one eye at Gino. 'Who would be the yokels, then?'

'Don't give me that crap. *We* solved her case. *We* told her who did it. All she has to do is catch the guy.'

McLaren talked down to the doodle he was creating on a well-used paper napkin. 'Or . . . maybe your dream scenario wasn't such a bad call, Gino. Maybe Kurt Weinbeck is a little more than your average yellow-bellied wife beater.'

Magozzi opened both eyes and looked at him. 'You got something?'

McLaren looked uncomfortable. 'Hell, I don't know. I don't like Weinbeck for killing two cops, either, but stuff keeps cropping up.' He kept scribbling on the napkin and Gino leaned forward to see what he was writing. Turned out it was an alligator in a dentist's chair, having a tooth pulled. Christ. Sometimes he thought McLaren was a hell of a lot scarier than most of the guys they yanked off the street. He flopped back and gave his bruised stomach a rest while McLaren kept talking.

'So this afternoon I get a call from Narc about a drug

dealer about to go down to the deep cells for three counts of attempted murder. Trial's next week, and Prosecution's got four star witnesses that should get them a slam-dunk. Two of them are the dirtbags he tried to kill along with the guy who's still in a coma. They cut a deal on the drug charges in exchange for testifying against the big guy. You want to take a stab at who the other two witnesses were?'

Gino threw up his hands. Getting information out of an Irishman was never easy. 'Christ, I don't know, Mr Mustard and Miss Scarlett.'

McLaren was grinning. 'I'll give you a hint. Two guys in blue outfits, first on the scene, caught the dealer reloading for a killing shot, a-a-nd . . . they liked to ski.'

'Deaton and Myerson?'

'Bingo. You win the canned ham. Now guess the street name of the sleazebucket going to trial.'

Gino glared at him. 'How about you guess how long it'll take me to strangle you if you don't spit out whatever the hell you're trying to tell us.'

McLaren didn't look a bit worried. 'They call him the Snowman.'

Gino and Magozzi just stared at him for a minute while they thought it through. It always made Johnny uncomfortable when they did that, and they did it a lot when they were working a case hard, and somebody said something that shot their minds off in a different direction.

Gino finally looked away, scrubbing at his blond brush cut, hoping to coax some more brain cells to life. 'Okay. So this Snowman character is up for trial, and suddenly two of the witnesses against him end up dead.'

'Packed in snowmen,' Johnny reminded him, as if he could forget such a thing. 'And the other two bailed on the testifying deal about ten seconds after the Chief went public with Deaton's and Myerson's names today. Said even if the cops didn't get the Snowman's message, they sure as hell did, and the way they figured, getting fitted for a prison jumpsuit was a hell of a lot better than getting fitted for a coffin.'

Magozzi was trying hard not to swallow the bait right off the bat, just in case there might be a hook inside. 'Okay, so I'm guessing you've either got the Snowman locked in a holding cell somewhere, or else there's a wrinkle.'

Johnny nodded. 'A little one. The guy's in Stillwater serving five on the drug charges while he waits for the attempted murder trial.'

'Kind of a big wrinkle.'

'Wouldn't be the first time a doer called for a hit from prison.'

'Risky stuff. Somebody always talks, and those guys go down like bowling pins. Unless they've got some kind of a family network working the outside. How big is this guy?'

'Not that big. Kind of new on the Minneapolis scene when they nailed him, but he's Russian, and a lot of them think *The Godfather* was a documentary, and that putting out a hit in America is cake. So I was checking with Stillwater just before you came in, asking about the Snowman's prison buddies, visitors, like that. Turns out he had the same cellmate for the past two years, your friend and mine, Kurt Weinbeck.'

Gino didn't like the coincidence, but he didn't like the leaps McLaren was taking, either. 'Your threads are getting down to gossamer, McLaren.'

'You gotta think outside the box. Sure, Weinbeck might not be your first choice to hit a couple cops, but the trial's coming right up and maybe the Snowman's desperate. So he offers his buddy the amateur some fast dough to take care of two of his witnesses and send a warning to the other two. Weinbeck takes care of the Snowman's business, then forces Doyle to drive him up to Dundas so he can take care of his own. I know it's all paper-thin, but we got too many threads here. I think we got to take a look at it. Only thing I can't figure out is why Julie Albright is still alive. He had plenty of time to get to her after taking care of Doyle.'

Gino and Magozzi looked at one another. 'The storm might have stopped him, or maybe Bitterroot,' Magozzi said. 'He wasn't counting on the security.'

'What security?'

Gino got up out of his chair. 'You tell him. I'm going to call Dundas and give them a few pointers.'

'*What?*'

'She doesn't know what she's doing, Leo, and you know it. And we're going to just sit here while one case for sure and maybe two hang on whether or not she can figure it out?'

'You can't do that, Gino.'

'I'll be tactful.'

'You for sure can't do that. Sit down. I'll call.'

'Fine by me. Tell her to slap Weinbeck's photo on every cow.'

Magozzi walked over to his desk and picked up the phone.

'. . . and to get every unit she's got on the road looking for Doyle's car, and not to touch the damn thing if they find it . . .'

Sheriff Iris Rikker was tired. Magozzi could tell, because it only took her one word to say hello.

'Hi, Sheriff. Leo Magozzi here. Listen, a couple things

came to light today on the investigation into the two snowmen in Theodore Wirth Park that we thought you should know. We're still at the coincidence stage, nothing solid, but there's a real slim possibility Kurt Weinbeck might be involved.'

'I see.'

Wow. All he got for that was two more words. Gino wasn't going to believe this. 'So a couple of points: First, Weinbeck may be a lot more dangerous than we thought, to anyone, not just his ex-wife.'

'He's probably killed at least once, Detective; he's most certainly on the run, and he's armed. We already thought he was pretty dangerous.'

Magozzi closed his eyes. Either he was duller than he thought, or she was sharper than Gino thought. 'I know that. Just an extra take-care for your men.'

'Thank you.'

'The other thing is, we really want to talk to this guy about our snowmen, so if you get a handle on him, we'd appreciate a heads-up.'

'Of course.'

Magozzi hunched over the phone and frowned. Now came the hard part. How the hell did you tactfully ask if she was doing all the things that any cop was supposed to do? 'Uh . . . any luck finding Doyle's car?'

A low chuckle came over the wires, and Magozzi's frown deepened into a scowl. What was so funny about that?

'I would have called you if we'd found Mr Doyle's car, Detective Magozzi. We've called in all the shifts, and we're covering the roads mile by mile, but we've got a lot of them, and it's going to take some time. We also ran copies of Kurt Weinbeck's mug shot and put them up on every vertical surface in the county – the local city p.d.'s are helping with that – plus we have four units doing continuous-circle patrols on the road around Bitterroot, and officers calling personally on all the adjacent landowners. Does that answer your question?'

'I just asked if you found the car.'

'That's what you asked out loud. It isn't why you called.'

He could hear the smile in her voice, and for some reason it pissed him off. It also made him feel like a jerk.

20

When Magozzi got home at nine o'clock, he found lasagna warming in the oven and some kind of elaborate salad in the refrigerator. He searched the house without pulling his gun, foolishly imagining that Grace would be hiding somewhere, hopefully dressed in her black flannel pajamas.

She answered her cell on the first ring. 'Magozzi. It's about time you got home.'

'Where are you? You left me supper. I figured that meant you expected me to sleep with you.'

Grace never laughed out loud, but he could hear the smile in her voice. 'We've been trying to reach you all day, finally called the office. McLaren told me you were on the road, and that you had another snowman. I figured you could use a bright spot in your day.'

'This is the nicest thing you've ever done for me. Also very out of character.'

'It's just leftovers. We had it here for supper. Listen, Magozzi . . .'

'Next thing I know, you'll be waiting at the door holding a martini dressed in plastic wrap.'

'Magozzi, listen. This is important. We may have something on the snowmen in the park.'

He set down his plate and got serious. 'I'm listening.'

'We pulled a thread from a chat room off the Web that said "Minneapolis snowmen, kill him while there's still time.

Put him in a snowman." The thread was posted at least three hours before you found the bodies.'

'Jesus.' Magozzi pulled up a chair and sank into it. 'Our killer might be at the end of that thread. Did you trace it?'

'We can't hack into it. The security is like nothing we've ever come across. We've been trying all day, and we'll keep trying. We're pulling an all-nighter over at Harley's, and I've got to get back to it, but keep your cell on all night, all day tomorrow. I'll call as soon as we have something.'

Magozzi had time for one bite of lasagna before Gino called.

'I got a bedtime story for you, Leo,' he said without preamble. 'I just talked to McLaren. Pittsburgh's got a body in a snowman just like ours.'

Magozzi finished chewing and swallowed. The lasagna was amazing, but it went down hard. 'Damnit. What are they thinking?'

'They're guessing copycat. This was just a courtesy call because of all the news coverage on our boys.'

Magozzi told him about what the Monkeewrench crew had found on the Internet.

'Goddamnit, Leo, I knew this was going to happen when the media climbed all over it. We're going to have bodies in snowmen all over the country. Close your peepers, tomorrow's going to be a nightmare.'

After he hung up with Magozzi, Gino leaned against the back of the sofa and let the silence of the sleeping house wrap itself around him like a protective cloak. The Christmas tree had been down for over a week, but Angela was still finding clusters of needles with the vacuum, and the fragrance of pine lingered.

Gino smiled when he heard the telltale creak of a stair riser, followed by the soft padding of his daughter's feet as she crept downstairs. It was a ritual she'd started a couple years ago, just after the Accident, a.k.a. baby brother, had been born. Whenever long hours, a particularly troubling case, or just plain insomnia kept him up after the rest of the house finally went silent, Helen would sneak downstairs to steal time alone with him. In Gino's book, that was just about as close to winning an Oscar for parenting as you could get – if your fifteen-year-old daughter still thought spending quality time with her old dad was worthwhile, then you'd probably done something right.

She appeared at the bottom of the stairs, bundled up in her warm winter robe, and gave him a rosy-cheeked, two-dimple smile. 'Hi, Daddy.' She plopped down on the sofa next to him and pecked him on the cheek.

'Hi, sweet pea. I didn't think I'd see you tonight. When I got home, your mother said you were already sound asleep, snoring like a lumberjack.'

She gave him a playful slug on the arm. 'I don't snore. So, did you find the killer yet?'

Helen had never been one to waste time with transitional conversation, but her bluntness always took Gino by surprise. Of course, it shouldn't have – she'd inherited her looks from her mother, fortunately, but her personality came from him, for better or for worse. 'Not yet.'

'Do you have any leads?'

'We're working on it.'

'I'll bet it's a serial killer,' she said with great certainty. 'They pose their trophies, you know.'

Gino squeezed his eyes shut and rubbed them. There was too much information loose in the world today, just laid out there on the TV or the Web for any kid to see, long before they had the good sense to be repelled by the real horror of it. He wished his daughter wasn't so fascinated with his job, and he was terrified that someday she might want to follow in his footsteps.

'So what did he use to tie them to the trail markers?'

'How do you know about that?'

Helen gave him the eye-roll, the classic teenage admonition for being so dense. 'Daddy, it was all over the TV.'

'Fifteen-year-olds shouldn't watch TV.'

She gave him a mischievous smile. 'The entire school saw you and Uncle Leo on the news yesterday. Ashley thinks Uncle Leo is totally hot.'

Gino winced at the adjective. She was too young for that kind of thinking, wasn't she?

'You looked nice, too, Daddy.'

'Gee, thanks. And tell Ashley Leo's old enough to be her grandfather.'

'He is not.'

'Well, father, at least.'

Helen tipped her head and regarded him with one of those scary wise-woman smiles that he saw on her face more and more these days. 'Young women our age are always attracted to older men, Daddy, don't you know that?'

Oh, dear Lord, Gino thought as he stared at the strange, wonderful creature sitting next to him in her fuzzy red robe with white reindeer cavorting all over it. Kid's robe, woman's face. He couldn't keep up.

21

It was almost eight p.m. when Sampson walked into Iris's office unannounced and plopped a Styrofoam take-out container on her desk. There was something about the way he did it that reminded her of old Puck's glory days as a hunter, when the cat used to deposit gifts of dead rodents on her pillow in the middle of the night.

'This isn't a mouse, is it?' she asked, prodding the container with her pen.

Sampson gave her a puzzled look. 'Nope, it's the best cheesecake in town, from Trapper's on Highway Eight. But if you prefer mice, I saw a couple down in the filing room earlier.'

Iris had been forcing false, polite smiles all day, so it was a little startling when she felt herself genuinely smiling from the inside out for the first time since she'd crawled out of bed this morning. 'Thank you, Lieutenant Sampson.'

'You're welcome, Sheriff.'

'And thanks for . . . well, thanks for not making me feel like an idiot today.'

'You weren't an idiot today. Otherwise, I would have let you know. Why are you still here? It's been a hell of a long day.'

'I'm just finishing up. I authorized overtime for anybody who wants to work extra shifts until we apprehend Weinbeck. I can do that, can't I?'

'Hell, Sheriff Bulardo used to authorize overtime for late-night poker games, so I think you're safe.'

'Did he really?'

'Sure he did. Bulardo and his cronies did a lot of things below the board, but they were good at covering their tracks. Just for the record, I never took part in any of it.' He made himself at home on the recliner and kicked up his feet. This was definitely a bad habit Iris was going to have to address at some point very soon, cheesecake or not. 'Hell, as long as we're on the subject, I might as well tell you something I think you need to know.'

This didn't sound promising. It was the kind of statement that usually prefaced bad news, like, 'Iris, there's something I think you need to know. Mark has been taking two-hour lunches with his secretary for the past month.' 'Oh? Like what?'

'Well, I'm sure it's not a newsflash that he's plenty pissed about losing his seat, but he's even more pissed that it was a woman who pushed him out. Double the humiliation for a man like that.'

Iris grimaced. 'I figured as much. He seems like a good ol' boy.'

Sampson nodded. 'He is, with a network of good ol' boys, and a lot of them are still on the force.'

Iris recalled her earlier encounter with the rude deputy at the Lake Kittering crime scene. 'I think I've met one of them already.'

'You have, and there's more where he came from. Bulardo's still got a lot of friends, and you're going to have to figure out who they are and do a little house cleaning. But in the meantime, you might want to watch your back.'

Iris suddenly had the unsettling feeling that Sampson was holding out on her, telling her just what he thought she needed to hear, but not everything she needed to know. 'What are you saying? Is Bulardo dangerous?'

'That depends on your definition of dangerous.'

'Dangerous is an angry, bitter, humiliated ex-sheriff who is plotting to kill off his successor.'

Sampson actually considered that for a moment, which scared the hell out of Iris. 'I don't think he'd ever go that far. But he can and will make your life a living hell if you give him half a chance.'

Iris sagged back in her big chair. In *Bulardo*'s big chair – a hand-me-down from the former regime, chosen to accommodate a six-foot-four, two-hundred-and-fifty-pound frame. And apparently, Bulardo's shadow was even bigger than the man himself, and it was positioned directly over her head. 'Great. And I thought the criminals were the only ones I had to worry about.'

'Politicians are some of the worst criminals around. Current company excepted.'

Iris gave him a weak smile, then decided to change the subject before she did something intelligent, like tender her resignation.

'Detective Magozzi called earlier. He said there's a chance that Kurt Weinbeck might be connected to the Minneapolis snowmen, too.'

'"Might" being the operative word, or we'd have half the MPD up here already stomping the county flat.'

'They want to talk to Weinbeck badly enough to check on how we're handling it.'

Sampson's eyes got smaller. 'He actually asked that?'

'Not in so many words. He wants a call if anything breaks.'

Sampson sighed and crooked his arms behind his head. 'If I were Weinbeck, I'd be a thousand miles away by now. And even if he isn't, we've got the county covered up and locked down. I think we can sleep easy tonight.'

'Speak for yourself. I'm going to see Steve Doyle's face in my nightmares for the next ten years.'

'I hear you,' he said quietly, turning to gaze out the window, at the sprinkling of lights from the fish shacks on the lake below. 'You know, when I first started out, I used to think that crime scenes and dead bodies and violence were all things you'd get used to eventually, because they were part of the job, and if you didn't get used to them, you'd drive yourself crazy.'

Iris followed his gaze out the window and thought about a good man she'd never met named Steve Doyle, dying out there on Lake Kittering, a few hundred yards from where she sat. 'Do you ever get used to it?'

'Some do, I suppose. I never did.' He turned away from the window and looked at the stack of papers on her desk. 'Field reports?'

'No. I already went through those. I was reading through the dispatch log for last night and today, just to make sure there wasn't something we missed.'

Sampson raised his brows slightly and nodded.

In man-speak, Iris supposed that was a baby kudo for thinking of another rock that needed turning over, so she gave him a small smile. 'The truth is, it doesn't feel right just going home when there's still a killer out there.'

'There's always a killer out there.'

That single short sentence, more than anything else Iris had seen or heard today, shook her to the core. And yet it was probably the way all cops had to think; a sad, hopeless reality that English teachers never had to consider when they put their heads on their pillows every night.

Sampson pushed himself up from the recliner with a weary sigh. 'They're talking about an ice storm later. Don't stay too late.'

'I won't.'

He was on his feet and heading for the door when Iris suddenly realized she didn't want him to leave. It felt good to have the company, and it would probably feel really good to wind down and let the day go with somebody who understood. And besides, she wasn't quite ready to go home to her dark, empty house just yet.

'Would you like to split this cheesecake with me?' she blurted out, probably sounding desperate and pathetic, like the kid nobody would play with at school.

'No, thanks. I already had a piece.' He paused at the door, looked at her for a moment, then shrugged. 'But I wouldn't mind a cup of coffee, if there's any made.'

Maybe he'd recognized something in her eyes, or maybe he just felt sorry for her, but Iris didn't particularly care what his reason was for staying – she wasn't above accepting charity at this point. 'It's a half-hour old. Will that do?'

'That'll do just fine.' Sampson added powdered creamer and a few packets of sugar for good measure, then took his place on the recliner again. 'So how does the city girl like living in an old farmhouse?'

'Well, it's creaky, drafty, the ceiling leaks, and I just got a notice from the EPA that says I have to update my septic system by next September to the tune of about fifteen thousand dollars. Other than that, it's charming.'

'The place sat vacant for a couple years before you

bought it. A lot can happen to a house when nobody's living in it.'

'I'm surprised it took so long to sell. It's a beautiful piece of property and the price was right. All it needs is a little TLC.'

Sampson tipped his head to one side. 'Superstition still runs pretty high out here. Not a lot of people are all that eager to buy a haunted house.'

Iris rolled her eyes.

'Hey. Don't make fun. That place used to scare the crap out of us when we were kids.'

Iris frowned. 'When you were kids? But the lady just died a couple years ago.'

Sampson chuckled. 'Emily isn't your ghost. It's her husband, Lars, and he's been haunting that place for almost thirty years.'

'How'd he die?'

Sampson shrugged. 'Nobody knows for sure. The way the old folks tell it, he was a mean, lazy, drunken son of a bitch and a whoremonger to boot.'

Iris frowned, trying to remember if a whoremonger was a pimp or a john. Who used words like that in this century?

'Let the cows starve and the few crops he planted rot in the fields,' Sampson continued. 'Just kept selling off the land piece by piece to pay for his habits – and that was Emily's land, by the way, not his. One day he just up and disappeared. Some folks figured he'd just wandered off drunk into the woods one night and died of his own stupidity; others figured Emily finally got fed up, killed the bastard, and buried him somewhere on the land. That's when the ghost stories started.'

Iris gave him a rueful look. 'He left her, that's all.

Sometimes men do that.' She colored a little then, because this was a small place in a big county and of course Sampson knew her history. And now he was looking at her hard.

'Not all men.'

'Hmph. Speak for yourself.'

He smiled a little and got up to leave. 'I always do, Sheriff.'

When Iris left the office a half an hour later, a wicked combination of sleet and snow had already begun to lacquer the roads, and snow-laden tree limbs were sagging perilously close to breaking point under the additional burden of ice. Judging by the fast-deteriorating conditions, Dundas County was going to be one giant hockey rink by sunrise. Sampson hadn't been kidding about the ice storm.

By the time Iris turned onto the winding county road that would take her home, her speedometer was barely registering, and her palms were slick with sweat inside her gloves. She hadn't seen another pair of headlights in fifteen minutes, and the absolute blackness peculiar to this alien world without streetlamps seemed to swallow her up. It was always on dark, lonely drives like this when she wondered if she'd ever get used to life in the country.

The one person in this world she counted as a friend had been horrified that she had agreed to move this far north, or as she had put it, 'to the world center of cultural nowhere and about as far from help as you can get in an emergency. I've seen the country, and let me tell you, it's dark, dangerous, and no one lives there.'

She smiled at that particular memory until it was clouded by the reminder of what a sheep she'd been then, following a soon-to-be unfaithful husband who had childish dreams a whole lot bigger than any other part of his anatomy, including his brain. And her friend had been right about most of it, especially the dark.

In the first weeks after her husband had moved out, it had spooked her whenever she pulled into her driveway at night, saw that creepy old barn jump out at her from the dark, and the shadows of countless trees and bushes that could conceal an army of intruders with imagined, evil intentions. It had taken a while for her to realize that as a rule, there weren't any intruders out here, and the country was a whole lot safer for a single woman alone than the nicest neighborhood in the Twin Cities, for all their glorious streetlights. But despite all the sound logic that told her this was true, she still looked at simple things – an open barn door, for instance – as vaguely malevolent.

Iris finally pulled into her tree-lined driveway, past the looming hulk of the barn, with its now blessedly closed door, and up to the house. She let out a deep sigh, gathered her things, and marveled that she had made two death-defying trips in one day without a single detour into the ditch.

She was halfway to the house when she noticed the footprints. They were partially filled in with fresh snow, but undeniably footprints – two sets of them – one heading toward the house and up onto the porch, the other heading away, toward the drive.

22

Iris was having trouble moving her feet, and wondered if she could literally freeze in her tracks after a few seconds of immobility. Still, she just stood there while icy pellets spattered against the hood of her parka, staring down at the footprints in the yellow glow of the light from the porch.

Already the weather was starting to distort them, but it was plain that they were larger than hers. Much larger. A man's print.

She closed her eyes and took a breath. *Great, Iris. This morning you were afraid of the dark, tonight you're afraid of footprints. How silly is that?*

Well, maybe not so silly, she decided, because today she'd seen a bloody corpse stuffed in a snowman, heard a ghost story, and learned there was a killer roaming the county. Little things like that could make footprints look pretty darn sinister.

She opened her eyes and squared her shoulders, breathing fast and hard, as if oxygen were courage she could suck right in.

Smart cops call for backup. Stupid cops die. Her instructor in procedures had drummed that mantra into her head for weeks. For a woman suddenly alone in life, she'd found it strangely reassuring to know that she'd never be alone on the job. The tricky part was learning when to apply the lesson. *Hello, this is Sheriff Rikker, and I have footprints here. Send backup.*

She had a little brain giggle at that, and reversed her earlier decision. Damnit, she was being silly after all. Close to paranoid, actually. So she had footprints in the yard. So what? Sure, she was really off the few beaten paths they had out here and hadn't had a single drop-in all year, but that didn't mean it couldn't happen. Maybe someone was looking for directions; maybe Mark had come by to pick up some of the winter things he'd stored in the basement and she'd missed a chance to shoot him with her new big gun; maybe the Jehovah's Witnesses were out proselytizing in a snowstorm.

She got disgusted and cold at the same time, and truly weary of being afraid. What would her constituency think if they ever found out their new sheriff had been scared out of her wits by a couple of sets of footprints? She hadn't counted on this job, but now she was stuck with it, and it was time she started thinking and acting like a cop instead of a timid, apologetic woman who got nervous every time she drove home after dark.

She pulled out her flashlight and moved her feet at last, following the set of prints that led away from the porch and around the side of the house.

It was breathless and silent, except for the hiss of sleet and the intermittent creaks of tree branches complaining under the new weight of accumulating ice. Every few steps, she'd stop and sweep the cone of light on the yard around her, but the snowy surface was pristine except for the set of prints she followed.

The ugly, tubular shape of the five-hundred-gallon propane tank came into view on the far side of the house, its metal sides flashing back her light. The trail of footprints turned into a jumble around the tank.

'Oh, for God's sake,' Iris mumbled, and felt her shoulders drop a full inch as the tension drained out of them.

The propane man. Her one and only regular visitor, and she'd forgotten all about him. A tall, round teddy bear of a nice guy with big feet and a big laugh and enough black magic to know when her tank was getting low and needed a refill. So he came to make a delivery, stopped at the house to say hello as he always did, and went about his business when he found she wasn't home.

She shook her head at her own foolishness and turned around to slog back to the porch. *Nice going, Iris. You almost called the cops on the propane man.*

She never saw the prints behind the tank, close to the house. Never noticed the narrow basement window that was almost closed, but not quite.

In spite of the pokey water heater, the laboring furnace, and the windows that leaked warm air like a sieve, magic happened whenever Iris walked into the old house. No matter how badly the day had gone, the minute she walked into her cozy kitchen, it all simply fell away, almost as if the house itself refused to admit bad things. She didn't know what it was about the place – a homeyness that came with old-fashioned woodwork and arched doorways and big fireplaces, maybe – but she did know that she'd never felt it before.

Puck was sitting in front of the refrigerator, blinking big green eyes in silent greeting. Even before taking off her coat Iris picked up Puck, stroked her silky black fur, and felt the rumbling hum of her purr against her cheek. It wasn't much of a warm body to come home to, but tonight it felt like enough. Puck meowed a complaint when Iris set her down, and Iris knew just how she felt. Every living creature needed a hug now and then.

She shrugged out of her coat, then hung her car keys on a handmade pegboard that made it look like a janitor lived here. There were five pegs, all jammed with loaded key rings, most of which had been here when they bought the place. A hundred keys at least, and Iris had no idea what they were for. She was afraid to throw them out, thinking that eventually she'd find the secret doors they all belonged to.

Yes, she'd been a brave little soul, following the scary footprints until they proved her a fool, but she still felt compelled to make a pass through the house before she did anything else, flipping on each and every light until the place was glowing like a centenarian's birthday cake. Once she was satisfied that she and Puck were the only two inhabitants, she dumped out a plate of tuna for the cat and poured herself a glass of wine. 'Cheers, Puck.'

Puck sniffed the plate, bolted down an enormous mouthful, then blinked up at her mistress, seemingly confused by the rare gift of human food.

'We're celebrating my first day on the job, so you get albacore, I get chardonnay.'

Puck seemed satisfied with the answer, and went back to the work of eating.

What coming home to this house started, the wine finished. By her third sip, Iris felt the last of the tension seep out of her body, letting the exhaustion move in. The simple act of locking the back door seemed monumentally difficult. It was so hard to turn the ancient deadbolt, so draining to move through the house, flipping out the lights one by one, focusing on the window locks, trying to remember if they had to be turned to the right or to the left.

Great, she thought, *on top of everything else, turns out you're a cheap drunk. Three sips of wine and you're over the moon.*

She forced weary legs up the full flight of stairs to her bedroom, feeling like an Everest climber without a flag to plant in the summit. She marveled that she didn't drown in the shower, remembered to brush her teeth and hang her holster on the front bedpost, and then she didn't remember anything else, except how to pull the covers up to her chin.

A good night's sleep, she thought, remembering Sampson's words as she closed her eyes.

But there were other eyes in the basement that had looked up at the creaking floorboards as Iris had moved through the house, waiting for the floors to go silent.

23

Iris was never certain what awakened her in the middle of the night – not in this house. Squirrels in the attic bowling with their winter cache of nuts; mice in the walls, shredding what was left of the hundred-year-old newspapers they used for insulation in the old days; branches from an overgrown tree scraping the siding; and once, a black bear coming out of hibernation long enough to poke around her barbecue grill for summer leftovers. You never knew.

And tonight she revisited her day in her dreams, from the slow grinding of her almost-dead battery in the morning to the crunch of snow under her feet as she followed the propane man's footprints at night. Once again she saw Steve Doyle's dead face and Julie Albright's ruined one, which didn't do a lot for a restful sleep, either.

She rolled her head to the right to read the digital clock. Three a.m. Plenty of time to snuggle back under the down comforter for a few more hours before her bare feet hit the cold floor, to start another day. She closed her eyes and started to drift off, thinking that she had to stop turning the heat down so low at night, because, damn, it was cold.

Some noises disturbed your sleep; some yanked you up out of blackness like you were a hooked fish on a line, snapping open your eyes and making your heart pound. Was it a real noise, or one you dreamed? You never knew that, either, so you lay there holding your breath, listening hard, waiting for it to happen again, afraid that it would, because the noise that Iris had heard sounded like a wild animal screaming.

She counted her breaths, thinking they were way too fast, trying to keep up with her heart. She got all the way to fifteen before she heard it again and sat straight up in bed.

Was that Puck? It sounded a little like the old cat, and then again it didn't. It was incredibly loud, the kind of long, complaining yowl that made your blood run cold, and Puck never so much as meowed during the night. The only time she'd ever heard her make a sound like that was the time Mark had accidentally slammed her tail in the door . . .

She was out of bed before another second passed, racing down the stairs, flipping on lights as she went, her thoughts faster than her feet or heart, wondering what horrible thing had happened to the old cat, if she had the vet's emergency number written down, if she could start the damn truck to get the beast to the vet's office before she died of whatever injury she'd managed to sustain . . . and then Iris hit the kitchen and stopped dead.

The back door was wide open, a frigid wind was blowing through the screen door, filling the house with winter, and Puck was outside on the porch, yowling like a banshee.

It turned out that Iris was more cat owner than cop, because she jerked open the screen door to let Puck in before she ever thought of leaving prints on the handle. It was only after the streak of black, angry fur barreled into the kitchen and off to God knew where to warm up that she realized she shouldn't have touched the handle. What that realization implied hit a second later.

Someone had been here. Inside the house. And maybe they still were.

Iris thought she had already felt fear this day – of the

dark, the barn, and then the footprints – but how pathetic those silly little fears seemed now, in the face of genuine terror. There were biological reactions she'd never experienced, happening so fast she could barely catalog them. Muscles tensing to run or fight, adrenaline shooting through her veins, flooding her with heat while the shrapnel of a million shattered thoughts started ricocheting through her brain: *Where is it safe, outside, inside, I have to get my weapon, should I search the house, was this in the handbook, how many electricians does it take to screw in a lightbulb, and isn't adrenaline supposed to make you focus, goddamnit?*

She took a deep breath and willed her heart to slow down and her knees to lock, willed all that pesky, mind-scrambling adrenaline to break down into its original, benign components and leave her alone, because she obviously didn't have the kind of thrill-seeking personality that thrived on endorphins.

Nice career choice, Rikker.

For endless seconds she just stood there, frozen like a wild rabbit, hoping she'd blend into the landscape and the big bad wolf wouldn't see her, but it was pretty likely that if the big bad wolf was in the house, or outside, for that matter, he'd be able to see her just fine with all the lights she'd turned on.

Now, Iris. This is when you call for backup. Right now.

Five minutes later a squad came roaring into the driveway, siren wailing, light bar flashing, the side spots busy on her yard. It slammed to a halt behind her SUV and Lieutenant Sampson ran for the house.

'Inside or outside?' he demanded in a harsh whisper when he came through the door. He was unshaven, barely dressed, with his boots untied and his jacket flapping open, but his eyes were sharp and busy.

'I don't know.' She breathed it, more than said it, feeling what every other person in trouble probably felt when the cops showed up and took charge. Saved, protected, grateful. She wondered what it would be like to be on the other end of that feeling, and realized for the first time that this was why good cops became cops in the first place, and that this absolutely, positively was what she wanted to do with her life.

He looked at where she was, backed into a corner; a little pajama-clad woman in bare feet holding a butcher knife. 'Where's your weapon?'

'Upstairs.'

'Jesus.'

He made her follow right behind him, his body blocking hers. While he searched the bedroom and the closet, Iris pulled jeans and a sweater on over her pajamas, strapped on her belt holster and drew her weapon. They searched the rest of the house top to bottom, and found the open basement window last. 'In this way, out through the door you found open,' Sampson said.

Iris was frowning at a pile of scattered boxes near the old furnace. Clothing had spilled out of them onto the cement floor.

Sampson followed her eyes. 'Fire hazard there. Too close to the pilot light.'

'They weren't there before. They were stacked against the wall over there, taped shut.'

'Anything missing?'

'I can't tell. They're boxes my ex-husband left behind, some tools and winter clothes, mostly.'

Sampson put the extra light from his flash on the pile, frowned at something, and started toeing clothes aside. 'Looks like your ex left his wallet behind.'

Iris looked at the square of leather he'd picked up with a gloved hand. 'That's not Mark's.'

Sampson opened the wallet, looked at the license through the plastic window, then up at Iris with a strange expression. 'Stephen P. Doyle. Jesus, Iris. Kurt Weinbeck was down here.'

24

Sampson used his shoulder unit to call for backup while they were running up the basement stairs.

Fast, Iris thought. *It's all so fast. Something happens and there's no time to think first, you just have to move and hope your thoughts can catch up with you.*

She grabbed her parka from the kitchen chair and jerked on her boots while Sampson was still talking. 'The house is clear, we'll be outside, two of us. Tell the guys not to shoot us.'

Good idea. Remember to always instruct your officers not to shoot you. But then there was that backup thing . . . you called for backup and then, class, you goddamned wait for it to get there before you make a move, because making a move without it is how you get killed. So why wasn't Sampson waiting? Because he has backup, silly. You.

The weight of that realization landed on her hard and almost buckled her knees. Being responsible for her own life was one kind of terror – she'd felt that for those minutes she'd been backed into a corner holding a butcher knife. But being responsible for someone else's was so much worse.

She closed her eyes for the millisecond that was all they could afford before they went outside to look for Kurt Weinbeck, and when she opened them she was looking at the pegboard with its rows of keys. One of the pegs was empty.

'Sampson.' Her voice stopped him just as he was about to jerk open the door. 'My keys are gone.'

'Maybe you left them in the truck.'

'No.'

'It happens. You have a hard day, a lot on your mind, you forget sometimes –'

'No.'

Something in her voice convinced him, and he went immediately still, except for his eyes. They moved slightly to the window, to the SUV that was sitting dark in the driveway, and then nodded once, silently, before easing open the door.

They stepped out onto the porch quietly, cautiously, their eyes and guns and flashlights trained on her SUV. They had a slight advantage because the porch was higher than the truck and they could partially see the interior, but there were still plenty of dark spaces their lights couldn't reach. Plenty of space for Weinbeck to hide.

The only sounds were the hiss and chatter of ice pellets hitting the house, the windows, and the glazed trees. Iris thought she heard a beleaguered branch groan and creak under the weight of ice, but there was nothing more, not even a breath of wind.

She noticed a set of footprints leading from the porch out to her SUV. There was no telling how fresh they were, but they were already encased in ice, and for the moment, perfectly preserved. It gave her some comfort, knowing that if Kurt Weinbeck popped up out her very own truck and shot them dead, the BCA would be able to make perfect casts of those prints and put him away forever. The wires would pick up the story and *CSI* would write an episode in posthumous honor of Lieutenant Sampson and his trusty sidekick, Iris Rikker – sheriff for a day.

Slowly, excruciatingly, they moved down the stairs and

began covering the short distance from porch to truck that seemed so very vast to Iris right now. In fact, all of her senses were distorted, not just her spatial perception – the light from her flash was vividly bright, the hushed crunch of icy snow beneath her boots was almost deafening, and the wool of her sweater felt like sandpaper against her skin.

They were close now, circling the vehicle, front to back, lights and guns raised as they swept the interior, and for the first time ever, Iris wondered what a bullet would feel like slamming into her chest at the speed of sound. Her light found the keys dangling from the ignition; otherwise the truck was empty.

'He's not in there,' Iris said.

'Never thought he would be.'

'You might have told me that before I spent the last two minutes scared out of my mind.'

One his shoulders lifted slightly. 'Figured you knew. If he had the keys and he had the vehicle, he would've been gone. Are you sure you didn't leave the keys in the truck?'

'Sampson.' She jerked her light to the line of prints they'd avoided stepping in. 'Those are not mine, and they're not yours.'

'Okay. Then why is the truck still here?'

Iris thought of her jumbled dreams, of imagining she was trying to start the SUV, grinding the battery down to its death. She opened the driver's door and turned the key. Silence.

Sampson almost smiled. 'Man, you gotta love that. Weinbeck breaks into your house, steals your keys, thinks he's home free, and then the vehicle won't start. Just beautiful.' He swept his light around the truck, and found another set of prints heading away from the driver's side. 'Those tracks are going to fill in fast if this keeps up. We've got to move.'

It was the first time Iris noticed that the icy mix had changed over to full snow. Funny what your mind shut out when you were totally focused on a simple thing, like trying to stay alive.

They followed the prints down the drive, almost to the barn, and that's where Sampson stopped. His light followed the trail up to the barn door, then he moved the flash up and down the enormous length of the building. 'What's in there?'

Iris knew exactly what he was asking. 'A lot of empty space, and a lot of places to hide.'

Halfway through Sampson's nod, the old barn made one of those old barn noises it was always making. He stiffened like a dog on point, then started making funny stabbing gestures all over the place. Iris had a momentary brain freeze. One hour in class, another studying the illustrations, and she'd had all the signals down, but they looked a lot different coming from a real cop instead of a cartoonish drawing in a textbook.

She was to go to the right around the building; he would go left. No noise.

Iris didn't stop to think about it; she didn't dare. She just started to move the way she'd been taught, and the second she took her first step through the knee-deep, ice-crusted snow that had drifted up against the building, her brain seemed to close the door on everything except the information her senses were feeding it. The animal-like focus lasted for two more steps, until she heard the sirens and saw the reflection of red and blue lights against the weathered siding as squads started to pull into the driveway.

'Go!' Sampson yelled at her, because the sirens had stolen the advantage of silence, and now they had to move faster.

By the time they met on the back side of the barn, there were five other officers slogging as fast as possible through the deep snow to join them.

Sampson and Iris both had their flashlights on a trail of bizarre-looking tracks that started at one of the barn's back doors and headed straight across the snowy field into the night.

'What the hell kind of tracks are those?' someone asked.

'Snowshoe,' Iris said, remembering Mark's notion to embrace winter sports once they had moved out to the country. He'd abandoned that idea after five minutes on the netted paddles last November, almost as fast as he'd abandoned his marriage. 'My ex-husband had a pair hanging in the barn.'

Deputy Neville, the blue-eyed, baby-faced officer who'd stood near Steve Doyle's body and wished her a pleasant good morning, moved next to Iris, playing his flashlight over the rolling field that grew corn in the summer and snow in the winter. 'What's on the other side of the field?'

'Sarley Game Preserve,' Iris said. 'Five thousand acres of trees and swamps.'

Sampson stared hard at nothing, seeing the Dundas County plat map in his mind. 'Damnit. Lake Kittering backs up to the far side of that preserve. Courthouse on the east side of the lake, Bitterroot land on the west. He's got a straight shot and big head start.' He jerked his head toward Iris. 'You have a sled?'

Iris shook her head.

'Kendall, get on the horn, get the snowmobiles over here fast, as many as they've got, then all the rest of you head for

Bitterroot, double up on the perimeter patrols. Neville, stick around, we're going to have to take a look in that barn, just in case . . .' He looked down at where Iris was digging under his jacket, around his belt line. He didn't know what to make of that.

'Cell phone!' Iris said, and snatched it away the second he had it out of the holster. While Sampson continued to bark out orders, she called dispatch, pulled all the patrols in tight around Lake Kittering and the game preserve, and then called Maggie Holland at Bitterroot and got her out of bed. When she finished, Sampson took the phone and made one last call to Detective Magozzi's cell.

Son of a bitch, it was cold, even with all the heavy winter gear he'd found in the basement. If it hadn't been for that lucky little score, he'd probably be as dead as a doornail by now, laying out here in the field, turning into a snowman himself. Now, there would be some irony.

The snowshoes had been another stroke of luck. They sure as hell took some getting used to, and they were a pain in the ass, collecting snow and bogging him down every couple hundred yards, but he couldn't have gotten this far, this fast, without them.

And come to think of it, that whole basement thing could have ended badly if the owner of the house had decided to come down to clean the litter box or throw in a load of dirty laundry while he was snoring away by the furnace. But it hadn't gone down like that, and Kurt Weinbeck was starting to believe that his fortune was finally turning for the first time in his life. Things happened for a reason. Maybe this whole plan of his was destiny, and that fate or the gods or whoever was running the show was on his side, smiling down on him, making sure he had his chance to make things right.

The only problem was, he still wasn't sure how he wanted his plan to end, or how to make things right. Part of him – the weak part of him – wanted to give Julie another chance, take her and the kid down to Mexico with him and start over, build a new life together. Maybe buy a little place by the beach, get a small trawler, and set up a fishing charter business or something. He wasn't a wealthy man by any stretch, but he had done pretty well for himself selling insurance and bartending part-time ... His thoughts ground to a halt.

Had done pretty well. Past tense. *Had* done pretty well for himself until that goddamned fucking bitch had sent him to prison. And he just wasn't sure if he could live with her after that. She couldn't even begin to imagine what kind of torture she'd put him through; what it was like in hell day after day, month after month, year after year, and know you'd never be able to erase those memories, no matter how hard you tried. No way she'd ever felt that kind of pain.

He felt a white-hot rage building and boiling inside as he thought about the injustice of it all, and his anger, so pure and perfect, gave him the moment of clarity he'd been seeking, just like it always did. Suddenly, he knew exactly what to do. He needed to show her the pain, needed to make her understand what she'd done to him. That was the only way justice would be served. It was payback time.

And then he'd probably have to kill her, because odds were, she wouldn't survive the road trip south once he was finished teaching her a lesson.

The snow was coming down hard now, and visibility was so bad, he almost ran smack into the fence before he saw it.

With a little friendly persuasion, Steve Doyle had been kind enough to warn him about all of Bitterroot's security, so he'd come prepared to deal with the fence – the bolt cutter he'd found on the basement tool bench would make short work of it.

He examined the fence a little more carefully, looking for the security cameras Doyle had told him about – there was something that could have been a camera perched on a metal stalk about three feet to his right, but it was so crusted with ice and snow, there was no way it was picking up anything but white. Yes indeed, luck was on his side today.

He went down on his knees and put the bolt cutter to work.

25

There was a row of overheads in the peak of the thirty-foot roof, but they didn't do much to light up the interior of the barn. Not one of them believed that Weinbeck was still in there, but the place itself was enough to spook anyone, with or without an armed killer hiding behind a post or molding hay bale. The intermittent creaks and groans of the old barn that always seemed to shift and complain, even on the stillest of nights, made it sound like the building was about to come down around their heads.

'Nice bed,' Sampson said, training his light on the big four-poster. 'You sleep out here, or what?'

Iris saw the tarp coverings thrown aside and piled on the dirt floor. There was the indentation of someone's body in the old feather mattress, and she remembered running her hands over that tarp just this morning. Had he been under there then? 'Not me,' she tried to say, but her voice cracked and her legs felt rubbery. *Who's been sleeping in my bed?* Fairy-tale lines screamed in her head.

Neville was over on the far side of the barn, his neck scarf pressed over his nose and mouth as he moved through a maze of haphazardly stacked hay bales that spewed decades-old mold whenever he brushed against them. 'Clear over here!' he shouted as he started to weave his way out, then Iris heard him grunt and fall, and then mutter, 'Goddamnit.'

He appeared a few seconds later, took the scarf off

his face, and coughed hard. 'What's under the trapdoor?'

Iris frowned. 'What trapdoor?'

'Haven't you ever been back there?'

'Not a chance. Mark had allergies, and I wouldn't go near that hay. It smells, and it's filled with mold.'

'Tell me about it.' Then he shrugged and tied the scarf around his face again. 'Gotta take a look, I suppose.'

Iris and Sampson snugged their parka collars over the lower half of their faces, tried not to breathe, and followed Deputy Neville through the maze. The odor of years of mold cementing hay bales together wasn't offensive in itself, but the minute you took the dustiness into your lungs, you knew it was noxious.

From the outside, the bales looked as if they'd been stacked haphazardly, but the deeper they went in, the more purposeful they seemed, like the boxwood maze at the botanical gardens.

The trapdoor was all the way back, set into the wooden floor near the outside wall. Their lights picked up the metal ring Neville had tripped on, poking up through a layer of hay dust, and then the long, heavy metal slide that snugged deep into a rusty hasp, locking it from the outside. It took some effort to kick the slide free of the hasp. It hadn't been moved in a long time.

Neville lifted the door and aimed his flash down into the hole. 'Deep,' he said. 'Ten, maybe twelve feet.' He went down on his knees, and then on his belly, poking his head into the space and moving his light around. Suddenly the light stopped moving and Iris heard him hiss, 'Oh, Jesus . . .' He scrambled back from the hole on his hands and knees, blue eyes big in a very white face.

'Weinbeck?' Sampson whispered.

'Hell, no.'

A few seconds with his light and Sampson found what he was looking for: a handmade wooden ladder buried nearby under some loose hay.

'How'd you know that was there?' Iris asked as he carried it over and he and Neville maneuvered it down through the trapdoor. She was looking for a diversion, anything to take her mind off what Neville had said was in the room under the floor.

'A lot of these old barns have root cellars like this, built deep enough to go beneath the frost line. Had to be a way to get in and out of it.'

They went down the ladder one by one, Iris last. She wasn't really afraid, and that surprised her. She was climbing down into a dark hole in the ground to see something horrible, and all she really felt was a sense of dread.

The room was crisscrossed with cobwebs that almost made a curtain, they'd been undisturbed for so long. Little white beads were stuck to the webs and squeaked underfoot on the floor when Iris stepped down from the ladder. 'What is this stuff?' Iris wondered aloud.

'Styrofoam.' Neville pointed to the walls and toed up the edge of a rug remnant. Panels of it on the floors, walls, ceiling. Pretty good insulation in a pinch, but you've gotta keep it up. Deteriorates in a hurry.' Then he directed his light to what he'd seen from above, lying on an old metal bed with a rotting mattress, and Iris caught her breath.

There wasn't much left of whoever it had been – exposed bones that gleamed white in the reflection of their lights, draped with the tattered remnants of clothing. Iris saw thin clumps of hair on the top of the skull and what looked like a few pieces of dessicated flesh that the rats and the insects had missed. More than anything else, it looked like one of the Halloween props from a haunted house.

Iris squeezed her eyes shut for a second, trying to make sense of it. They were looking for a killer and found a rotting, dead person in her barn. It didn't fit, it didn't compute. It was like looking for car keys in a drawer and finding an elephant instead. Curious, maybe, but the elephant sure as hell wasn't going to start the car.

'Lars,' Sampson said.

Neville looked at him. 'You think?'

'Maybe.' Sampson brushed aside some of the cobwebs and moved around the room that was only a little larger than Iris's kitchen. There was an ancient space heater in one corner; a shelf of moldering books that rats had made a mess of; and oddly, a sink and a flush toilet. 'Damn place is plumbed,' he murmured.

'And wired,' Iris said, pointing her light at a single bulb in a protective cage on the ceiling. She looked around the windowless room, at the rust-stained toilet and sink, the pathetic remains on the bed, at the only exit that couldn't be reached from the floor without a ladder, and saw the place for the prison it had been.

She didn't know what had happened in this room, or why; she only knew that she didn't want to be here any longer. She went up the ladder a lot faster than she'd come down.

And how was your day, Iris? Well, just peachy. There was this bloody corpse in a snowman, then a killer hiding in my house WHILE I WAS SLEEPING, and then big surprise, the skeletal remains of a human being in my barn . . .

Sampson and Neville had followed her up, closed the trapdoor behind them, and now Sampson was on his cell, listening. He flipped it closed with a snap. 'They've got a break in the fence at Bitterroot, and they don't know when it happened. Apparently the ice storm shut down all their cameras and motion detectors. We're moving in.'

26

Iris Rikker had called Magozzi back on the way to Bitterroot, giving him a quick update on the break in the fence and frozen cameras. By that time he and Gino were already in the car, heading north.

'Can you believe the balls of that bastard?' Gino shook his head after she hung up. 'He has to know every cop in the county is looking for him, and what does he do? Hangs around and breaks into the one place they're looking for him hardest.'

'Not balls,' Magozzi grunted. 'Blind, stupid rage.'

'Whatever. Christ. I can't believe it's five-thirty in the morning and we're on our way to Cow Patch again.' Gino was in the passenger seat, slurping coffee from a jumbo travel mug while Magozzi concentrated hard on the road. The freeway was plowed and sanded and they were making good time to Dundas, but the puffy bags under his eyes were partially obstructing his vision.

'Let's just hope Kurt Weinbeck is the end of the road and we can tie this thing off and be back in bed by noon.'

'Jeez, are you listening to motivational tapes or something? It never goes down that easy and you know it. None of us ever really liked Weinbeck for killing Deaton and Myerson. The way I look at it, we got called out of bed to freeze our asses off stomping through some snowy nowhere just so we can talk to the guy long enough to cross him off the suspect list for sure. Meanwhile, Iris Rikker catches a murderer on her first day in office, and you and I get hammered for making a bunch of road trips on somebody else's case while our own Minneapolis cop killer runs around loose. We are not getting a happy ending out of this.'

'You want to turn around and go home?'

'Nah. The puke killed Doyle for sure. Maybe we'll get lucky and corner Weinbeck in the woods by our lonesome, slap him around a little just for fun. That'd make me feel better. You hear anything new on the Pittsburgh snowman this morning?'

Magozzi kicked the speed up a few notches while Gino wasn't looking. 'I called again before I left the house, talked to their night guy. They're still thinking copycat.'

Gino nodded. 'That's what I figure. Our case just gave every sociopath in the contiguous forty-eight plus Alaska a cool, new way to pose bodies. Mark my words, snowmen will start cropping up all over the place, then somebody'll write a book, and then they'll make a TV movie of the week. *Minneapolis – Ground Zero for Every Lunatic in the Country.* The Chief will just love that. The poor guy still hasn't gotten over "Murderapolis," and that was over a decade ago.' Gino sighed and squinted ahead into the beams of the headlights. 'Oh, shit. Is that snow?'

The southernmost edge of the storm front seemed to end right at the Dundas County line. Once they made the turn off the freeway, the county roads deteriorated fast, and there were an alarming number of cars in the ditch for a place that was so sparsely populated.

'Jesus,' Gino muttered under his breath. 'It looks like a used-car lot out here.'

Magozzi pointed to sagging, ice-coated power lines that

looked like silver filament when they caught the light. 'Looks like they got an ice storm.'

'Yeah, yeah, I see that, just keep your eyes on the road. Man, that little track into Bitterroot is going to be a bitch.'

Maggie didn't often leave her little house at night, and certainly not alone. As the longtime manager of Bitterroot, she knew better than anyone that the complex was as safe as technology, caution, and human ingenuity could make it. There probably wasn't a safer place in the entire world for a woman to walk alone after dark. The reasoning part of her brain knew that. The other part – the one that stored the memory she'd been trying to forget for fifteen years – that was what kept her inside after the sun went down.

The chase had lasted a long time, starting in the house, leaving a wreckage of furniture behind as Maggie had dodged from one hiding place to another, finally making it out the door and into the front yard, screaming, bleeding, crying. She knew the neighbors would hear; she also knew it would be too late, because Roy was right behind her, still swinging the crowbar, and by then he didn't even look like her husband anymore, just a horror-movie package of blind, red-faced rage because Maggie had done the unthinkable by trying to fight back for the very first time in her life. There had been no moon, just stars stitching a lacy pattern in a dark, dark sky. Even in her terror she had noticed that, just before the crowbar came down one last time on the back of her skull.

There was still a definite depression where bone had finally knitted itself together – a ledge, really, that made her look like a Neanderthal with his face on backwards – but she covered that by fluffing her hair. Only a few people knew it was there. Laura was one of them, and Laura's house was where Maggie belonged in times of trouble.

A victim of abuse herself, she'd founded Bitterroot with her sister Ruth sixty years ago, and had devoted every year since to creating a haven where women could live without fear. As far as Maggie was concerned, the old woman had saved the lives of every single resident in Bitterroot – her own included – and that gave her the strength to face her night demons and hurry through the ice and snow to Laura's old farmhouse as soon as Iris had called.

Not that she believed Kurt Weinbeck or any other uninvited man would actually make it into the complex. The cameras would be on him the moment he touched the fence, the monitors would notify perimeter patrol, and a team of very well-trained and well-armed women would be on-site before he made it to the other side. No one ever made it past the perimeter patrol. Not anymore.

The farmhouse wasn't far from the main residential section, but it was far enough, and isolated enough to make the trip a harrowing one for a woman afraid to go out after dark. Maggie had been inordinately proud of herself for making the journey, thinking that after all this time, perhaps she was finally getting a little better.

She'd found Laura sitting in her favorite chair by the fireplace, bundled in a worn terry robe several sizes too large for her fragile frame. It was faded from years of washing, and frayed past mending around the cuffs, but the robe had belonged to her sister, Ruth, gone these many years, and she refused to give it up. Maggie hadn't been surprised to find the old woman out of bed at such an hour. More and more lately, Laura had been getting day and night confused.

'We have to lock the doors tonight, Laura,' Maggie had told her, and at that moment Laura's eyes had narrowed and sharpened, and, in them, Maggie saw the stalwart, intelligent woman she had been before her good brain had started to deteriorate.

'What happened?'

'Julie Albright's ex-husband is on his way here. The sheriff thinks he'll try to get to her.'

A little of her old fire had flashed in Laura's eyes. 'Let him try. He'll never get past the perimeter.'

But less than half an hour later Maggie got the call from Security, telling her that the ice had frozen the cameras and motion detectors and that the fence had been cut. She knew the news would devastate Laura, send her quickly back down that gray hole of mindlessness that overcame her when she was tired or stressed, but Laura surprised her.

'Where's Julie?' she demanded, as alert and acute as Maggie had seen her in some time.

'In her house, under guard. By our people and several deputies. We had to open the gates for them, Laura. They're coming in force, to search the whole property. They'll be going door to door, checking on everyone.'

Laura closed her eyes, and seemed to shrink in on herself as Maggie watched. 'My poor girls,' she whispered. 'Strange men in the compound, banging on doors . . . they'll be so frightened.'

'The call system is notifying everyone. They'll know they're policemen, here to help. Some of them will be women.'

Laura was shaking her head strongly, because she knew that wouldn't make a difference. The walls had been breached, the strangers were inside, and the sense of safety would evaporate with the first man who walked their streets unescorted. 'Sixty years, Maggie. A lifetime to build this place, to make it safe, and it's gone in a second . . .'

'No, Laura, that's not true,' Maggie insisted. 'You made a utopia here. You saved our lives, every one of us.'

'So we build Utopia, and all it takes is one crazed man to bring it down? That's not right, is it?' Laura looked up at her, and Maggie saw the eyes clouding, wandering, following the erratic path of thoughts that had already started to scatter and lose focus. 'Did you drink my tea? I can't find my tea. Someone took my tea. Do you have it in your pocket?'

Maggie looked away quickly and brushed at her eyes. It always broke her heart a little to watch Laura's quick shifts from apparent lucidity to muddled confusion. It was like watching a normal mind suddenly blink out like an old lightbulb. 'I must have taken it into the kitchen by mistake. I'll make more, Laura. And I'll bring you a cookie.'

'Really? That would be so nice.'

Maggie went to the kitchen and set the tea kettle on to boil. She was slicing a lemon when she heard the soft thud from the back porch that stopped her heart.

Stop it, Maggie. It's just a clump of snow falling off the roof. Nothing more than that. You did so well tonight. Don't lose it now just because of a little noise. Move, damnit. Don't just stand here like a frozen rabbit. Slice the lemon. Prepare the tray. Get the cookies, because there's nothing out there . . . except maybe a deputy. Remember? Now, don't you feel silly? It's probably just a deputy coming up the back steps. And all you have to do is turn around and look and you'll see that, and everything will be all right.

But Maggie couldn't turn around. Her mind was already fifteen years back in time, right after she'd stumbled for the last time in the darkened yard. She'd known then that if she didn't move fast, Roy would catch her and kill her with the crowbar. And yet then, as now, terror paralyzed her. A single tear rolled down her cheek.

Stupid then, and stupid now, Maggie told herself just as the glass pane in the back door shattered behind her.

By the time they pulled up to the corporate building, the snow was really coming down, every light in the complex was blazing, and Dundas County cars were all over the lot.

Iris Rikker was standing in the middle of a cluster of newly arrived deputies, and although she didn't look like much of a sheriff in her puffy parka and little moonboots, she seemed to be acting like one.

When Gino and Magozzi walked up, they heard her speaking tight, short and fast, not one extra word, just like a real cop, directing the officers in pairs wherever they were needed. Gino kept silent, brows raised, probably wondering how she'd learned to do that in the space of a day.

'Where do you want us?' he asked her, treating her like any other cop in command. Magozzi wondered if she knew what a compliment that was.

'The fence was cut around the back of the property. I've got men tracking from that end, but they lost the trail about an acre in. Snowshoe tracks fill in fast, so now they're just coursing. I put a contingent around Julie Albright's place, the rest of us are doing house-to-house checks as fast as we can, but it's a lot of houses.'

'Point us in the right direction,' Magozzi said.

'I was on my way back anyway.'

She led them around the huge corporate building instead of through it. There was no road, but a path had already been beaten through the snow by the deputies who had come before them. Iris was moving fast.

'He's on snowshoes,' she said as they hurried. 'Easy to

track, but we don't know what kind of a head start he had. The ice froze the cameras so they can't move and put the motion detectors out of business, so the communication center is blind. He could be anywhere.'

'How tight is the cover on Julie Albright?'

'Four outside, two in. We have Julie and her daughter in an interior room.'

Just saying Julie Albright's name aloud hit Iris hard, and stopped the straight line of her thoughts, if not her feet. What the hell was she doing, and when had she become so arrogant? She'd run against a sitting sheriff who at least knew how to do the job, damnit, and her reasons hadn't been one bit noble. And now it had all boiled down to this: a ruined woman and a beautiful child huddled in a house not too far from here, and whether or not they lived through this night depended on a pretend sheriff doing everything absolutely right.

She turned her head to look at Magozzi and Gino. 'What else?' she asked in a voice that sounded like a plea. 'What else needs to be done? What did I forget? Sampson had to run to check on his sister . . .'

She looked scared to death, totally unlike the assured woman he'd seen directing deputies like a pro, and now Magozzi got it. Sampson had been her crutch all day, her teacher, probably, but he hadn't been around for the big one. She'd done this on her own, and now she wasn't sure it was enough. It would take years on the job before she realized you always felt like you hadn't done enough.

'It sounds good,' he said, because that was the bare-bones truth, and Magozzi wasn't big on head-patting.

'Just like downtown,' Gino added. 'As long as you've got one of the outside guys at Julie's pulled back for an overview, cause sometimes guys working a building get so focused they forget to look around . . .'

She didn't even wait for him to finish; just started talking into a shoulder unit she had tucked under her jacket. 'Thank you,' she said to Gino when she'd finished. 'I didn't know to do that.'

Gino shrugged. 'You will next time.'

In the daylight, the village had looked idyllic; at night, it looked like a beautiful Christmas card gone wrong. A lot of the little houses still sported holiday lights, their colors softened and muted by the snow, and every tree branch glistened with a brand-new coating of ice. But there were armed men and women patrolling the narrow street now, approaching the cheery front doors like malevolent trick-or-treaters, and occasionally a fearful, cautious face peered from a lighted window.

'You need to get those people away from the windows,' Magozzi said, and Iris nodded.

'We just started on this block. I had them cover the ones that backed up to open land first, the ones that were in a direct line from where the fence was cut.'

'Let's cover it, then.'

The three of them split up, moving fast, and after ten minutes and four houses, Magozzi thought that if he never saw that haunted look in a woman's eyes again, it would be too soon. God. Every single face behind every single door looked the same.

He and Gino finished their last houses on the block at the same time, and met up in the middle of the narrow street. They saw Sheriff Rikker standing under a streetlight just ahead, making marks on a damp, wrinkled piece of paper, snow accumulating on her head and shoulders.

‘She stands still much longer in this, we’re gonna have to dig her out,’ Gino observed as they approached.

It was quiet on the block now, with all the houses searched. A few officers remained behind, assigned to patrol, but the snow deadened the sound of their movements. They could hear the shushing noise of their own boots pushing through the white stuff, even the scratch of Iris’s pen on the paper; but that was all.

‘This block next,’ Iris stabbed at a map of the village layout, then started leading the way.

They barely had a chance to move before they heard the shot. It was off to their left, down a continuation of the narrow street that cut into open land.

The sound had been muffled, Magozzi thought as all three of them started running; but you could tell it had started out big; maybe as big as the sound of the gun Kurt Weinbeck had used to blow a hole in Steve Doyle’s chest.

27

The mansion was silent except for the regular clicking of Grace's keyboard. Harley, Annie, and Roadrunner were grabbing catnaps after working most of the night. She was exhausted herself, and sometimes, while she waited for a new line of programming to run, she'd feel her eyes start to flutter closed. But then she'd remind herself of what Magozzi had said about a killer being at the end of that chat room thread, and that woke her right up. There were three dead men in snowmen already, but maybe they could make sure there wouldn't be a fourth.

The firewalls were getting harder and harder to break through. They'd found a second, then a third, and now Grace was beginning to wonder how many more there were, and how much time they had.

She pushed herself away from the desk and glared at the monitor. 'I can't keep doing this,' she said aloud, and then suddenly realized how true that was; that of course she couldn't keep doing this – and she didn't have to. It was like when she used to keep Charlie's big bag of food underneath the overhanging shelf in the pantry, just because that's where she'd always kept it. Every morning she'd bend to retrieve it, and a lot of mornings she'd stand too quickly, forgetting the overhanging shelf, and bang her head. How many times had she bumped her head before it occurred to her to move the dog food? It didn't matter how intelligent you were; sometimes routine and procedure blinded you to the obvious solution.

She heard Harley's footfalls coming up the stairs just when she was about to go down and wake him. An unappetizing, vegetal miasma preceded him into the room, and Grace recognized the odor of his latest obsession – some hideous herbal tea he brewed secretly every morning and tried to push on all of them. God knew what was in it, but Grace hoped it was legal.

'I'm not drinking that tea, Harley,' she said without turning around.

'You need more green stuff in your diet.'

'Not in liquid form, I don't.'

Harley set a mug of the stuff on her desk anyway. 'I had on the tube while I was brewing this. They've got another snowman.'

Grace closed her eyes. They were already too late.

'Don't look like that, Grace. It wasn't here. It was in Pittsburgh. So maybe our killer isn't even in the state anymore. Maybe he's on the move. Or maybe it's a copycat. They don't know much yet. Either way, we've got to get into that chat room.'

'I was just about to come downstairs. I have something new to try, but I need you and Roadrunner.'

'And Annie.'

'Actually, we can let her sleep. You and Roadrunner can handle it.'

'Are you shitting me? If I don't wake her up and we crack into this thing, she'll have my balls on a skewer. Be right back.'

Five minutes later Roadrunner stumbled in behind Harley, screwing his fists into his eyes like a kid trying to wake up. He found his way to the coffee machines, pushed the button on the one that held his Jamaican Blue, then stood there, watching it drip. It didn't pay to talk to Roadrunner until he was well into his first cup. He wouldn't hear anyway.

He was wearing a new Lycra suit this morning – lilac in color – and once Grace looked at him, she had a hard time pulling her eyes away. She'd never seen him in pastels before. He looked like a long, tall Easter egg.

Annie hadn't even bothered to get dressed – she was wearing her silk kimono robe and a pair of bedroom slippers with marabou puffs. 'Thanks a lot, Grace,' she grumbled as she shuffled over.

Grace smiled. 'I take it Harley broke down your bedroom door.'

'Oh, hell, that would have been a kindness. Damn bastard sneaked in. Guess what it's like to wake up and see that big hulking brute standing over your bed, watching you sleep.'

Harley sighed. 'It was a Sleeping Beauty moment. I think my heart stopped.'

'Pig.' Annie flounced down at her computer in a flutter of shedding marabou.

'Hey, Gracie thinks we're going to bust this thing wide open. She wanted to let you sleep, but I'd thought you'd want to be here.'

'Thank you, Harley. That was very thoughtful. But you're still a pig.' She turned to Grace. 'So there's a new snowman in Pittsburgh. Something real bad is going on out there, Grace. What's your new plan?'

'We've been going at this thing all backward. I thought we'd stop trying to break down the steel door and go to an open window.'

'Oh, honey, do not talk in metaphors. The sun isn't up yet.'

Grace swiveled her chair to look at them. 'We've been trying to crack into a chat room with the best security we've ever seen. We'll get there eventually, but it's taking too long. I thought we could try piggybacking Harley's and Roadrunner's virus on the specific chat threads that caught our attention in the first place, let the virus lead us into the thread, if not the site itself.'

'Goddamn,' Harley murmured, then there was the sound of his knuckles cracking as he flexed his fingers over the keyboard. 'This is going to work.'

Annie said, 'Then why didn't *you* think of it, genius? It's your stupid virus.'

'Because, Sleeping Beauty, I am a bull of a man. Charging right in, breaking things down, that's what I do. This subtle stuff is for girls.'

'Smart girls.'

'I'll give you that.' He shoved the disk containing the virus program into his drive.

'Way to go, Grace,' Roadrunner gave her a sleepy smile as he set an extra mug of his precious Jamaican Blue on her desk. 'That's pretty far outside the box for someone who said we weren't allowed to use that virus for anything except shutting down kiddy porn sites.'

Grace nodded. 'Viruses bad,' she reiterated their mantra, then grinned at him. 'Except when they do good.'

'It's pretty good at shutting down the porn sites.'

'And it was pretty good saving a thousand lives back in Wisconsin last summer.'

Roadrunner's smile broadened at the memory. 'You like my new suit?'

'I love your new suit.'

'Roadrunner, get your skinny ass over here. I can't get the damn thing to launch.'

It took exactly ten minutes for Roadrunner to pull up the entire chat thread on his monitor. 'I think I've got it.'

The others were behind his chair in an instant, reading over his shoulder in absolute silence.

Harley finally straightened. 'Oh, man. This is all bad.'

'And sad,' Annie added.

Grace's eyes had been busy while the text had been scrolling by, but when it stopped, she glanced up at the top of the monitor and frowned. 'Look at the subject line of this thread,' she pointed.

Harley squinted at it. 'Bitterroot. Wow, that's the second time in two days that name's come up. How weird is that, and what the hell does it mean?'

28

It was an old house – one of those massive boxy numbers they built in farm country when the state was new, and couples prayed for many sons to help work the land. Probably the original farmstead, Magozzi thought, but someone had taken a lot of care with it. The paint was fresh, the big front porch was new, and a modern air-conditioning unit was squatting between some bushes on one side. Funny, the things you noticed when you didn't even think you were looking.

They hadn't run far from the clustered houses of the village – maybe a hundred yards – but they all were breathing hard, and Magozzi felt the burn in his thighs from lifting his legs over the snow. Now they were crouched behind the last cluster of trees near the house, weapons drawn, senses screaming, catching their breath before they moved in.

Suddenly the front door opened wide, to show a woman-shape with light behind it. Magozzi squinted through the driving snow, but couldn't see clearly enough to be sure there was no one behind her.

'Officers?' the woman called out, and he recognized Maggie Holland's voice. 'Officers, are you out there? It's Maggie Holland, and it's all right for you to come in now.'

Iris, Magozzi, and Gino exchanged wary glances, then Gino stabbed a forefinger at Iris's chest.

Iris nodded, then called back. 'Ms Holland, it's Sheriff Rikker. Are you alone in there?'

'Not exactly. This is Laura's house. She's here . . . and Julie Albright's husband, but he's dead.'

Gino and Magozzi looked at each other, then started to move toward the house, bent over in a crouching run, dodging between the scant cover of single tree trunks, just as if Kurt Weinbeck were alive and well and waiting behind the door with a gun on Maggie Holland. You never knew.

Iris mimicked their movements, cursing her short legs because she couldn't move as fast through the snow. She fell twice, took a closer look at Maggie Holland smiling, waiting patiently in the doorway, then said the hell with it, stood up straight, and walked toward the porch.

'Goddamnit, Rikker, get down!' Gino whispered at her, but she was already at the porch and not dead yet. She poked her head in the doorway, then turned back and motioned them in.

It was like walking into a Freddy Krueger Disneyland. A fire crackled in the fireplace, cozy armchairs and old photos, even a little old white-haired lady sitting in a rocking chair with knitting in her lap, smiling in greeting, as if they'd dropped in for some holiday cheer. The only thing that didn't quite fit was the body bleeding all over a faded area rug with roses on it. Sheriff Iris Rikker stood over it, looking like a bewildered child who'd walked into the wrong house by mistake.

Gino bent next to what was left of Kurt Weinbeck, checked the carotid, the huge hole in his chest, then looked up at Magozzi and shook his head.

'This is Laura.' Maggie Holland closed the door and gestured toward the woman in the rocking chair.

She was old, but unbelievably spry, and shot up from her seat, extending a bony hand with a lot of years on it. Magozzi was still standing with his knees bent and his weapon out front, and suddenly the posture felt a little foolish. He straightened reluctantly, shifted the nine to his left hand, and felt the old woman's chilly flesh in his right. 'Detective Magozzi. Minneapolis Police.'

She had new teeth in a face that looked like his not-permanent-press shirts when they came out of the dryer. Too new. Hollywood white. On a young woman, the smile would have been drop-dead. On her, it just looked weird. 'I know who you are, Detective. Maggie told me all about you, and of course I see you on the television every now and then.' She folded her hands under a sagging bosom and looked around, seeming distressed for the first time. 'Sorry about the mess.'

Magozzi felt like he was in the Twilight Zone. This was an old woman who'd just witnessed a killing. There was a man bleeding on the rug in her living room. She was supposed to be horrified, frightened, trembling, in shock.

'But you see, he had the gun on Maggie, and I really didn't have any choice. None at all.' Her blue eyes moved back to him, and Magozzi noticed that they looked faded, like an old photograph about to disappear. 'You look upset, Detective. I'll bet you've had a heck of a time. All of you. Perhaps you should sit down by the fire, I'll have Maggie bring you some tea . . .'

Maggie Holland tried to talk her out of it; tried to send her off to bed, in fact, which seemed a sensible suggestion for an old woman who'd had such a night; but Laura would have none of it. Up until this point, she seemed remarkably sharp and self-possessed – almost abnormally so, considering the circumstances – but now Magozzi saw the first sign of petulance in her silent, head-shaking refusal. He thought first about shock, then dismissed it. None of the signs were there. More than likely, she'd started to make that slow slide backward into childish behavior that happens to many elderly when the mind starts to falter.

'I will not be sent to bed like a child!' she shouted suddenly, startling them all. 'And I will serve these officers tea, and I will answer their questions!' The outburst had been fast and unexpected; so was the sweet smile she instantly turned on Iris Rikker, as if there had been no outburst at all. 'You do have questions for me, don't you, Sheriff Rikker? I do love company.'

Creepy, Magozzi thought. *Around the bend, or at least moving toward it in a big hurry.*

Iris smiled right back at her, which Magozzi racked up as a point in her favor. Quick on the uptake, good instincts. 'It might be nice to chat a bit, if you're not too tired.'

Laura reached over to pat Iris's arm. 'Not at all, child.'

'She's very old,' Maggie Holland whispered to Gino when he followed her into the kitchen. She busied herself with boiling water and porcelain cups on a tray. They rattled when she set them down because her hands were trembling. 'And her memory is going. She gets confused. Remembers things the way she wished they had happened, instead of the way they actually did.'

'Is that right?'

'Yes.'

Gino pursed his lips and nodded. 'Pretty quick on the trigger for a confused old lady.'

Maggie shot him a cold glare. 'It wasn't the first time I had a gun pressed to my head, Detective, and I think I'm pretty much of an expert on whether the man holding that gun is prepared to use it. She probably saved my life.'

Gino had the decency to feel bad, which didn't mean he had the motivation to show it. Something wasn't right, and it was eating at a part of his brain like a termite.

'She tells some tall tales sometimes, but she's a dear woman. Founded Bitterroot with her sister, over half a century ago. This was their land; this is her town.'

'Gotcha. So she shot Weinbeck?'

Maggie Holland's lips were pressed tightly together, bleeding all the color out. 'She thought he was going to kill me. And he would have. He was crazed when he broke in. Crazed.'

'Uh-huh. You want me to carry that in?'

'Please.' She hurried to follow him, and moved immediately to stand behind Laura's chair. Her posture was rigid, protective, almost like that of a bodyguard, which Gino thought was pretty strange, considering the old lady had just saved *her* life.

Iris and Magozzi were sitting on a sofa opposite the rocker, both with notebooks propped on their knees, when Gino carried in the tray like a college waiter. He set it down on the coffee table between them and listened.

'So he broke in, grabbed Maggie, pointed a gun at her head, and asked where he could find Julie, is that about right?'

Laura was nodding emphatically. 'Exactly right. So I did my little-old-lady act, told him I'd get a map, and toddled out to the kitchen.' She looked at Iris and smiled. 'I don't usually toddle, you know. I do stretching exercises every morning to keep myself limber. That was just an act.'

Iris smiled back. 'That was very clever.'

'I thought so. And I do have a map of the village in the

kitchen drawer. But that's also where I keep the gun.'

'Ah.' Iris nodded. 'The .357 on the table over there.'

Gino sat down in an armchair and actually started pouring tea. Christ, this was weird.

'Yes, indeed. Maggie said I couldn't put it back in the drawer, although that's where it belongs. She said I had to put it down and leave it so you people could check it. For what, I just don't know.'

'It's just procedure, Miss Laura.'

Funny how she knew to call her that, Gino thought.

'So you came back into the living room, what? Holding the gun under the map?'

Laura beamed at her. 'Now, you're the clever one, because that's exactly what I did. Toddled back in, pretending to study the map, then when he reached for it, I shot him.' She looked over at Kurt Weinbeck's body and shook her head. 'I just hate doing that.'

Magozzi felt a chill run up his spine. 'You hate to shoot people?' he asked conversationally.

'Well, of course I do, Detective. Don't you?'

'Yes, I do.'

'Then you understand. It's dreadfully distasteful, but ... we do what we have to do. We take care of our own. Not that I've shot that many, of course. Not personally.'

Not that many? Not personally? Whoa.

He glanced at Maggie Holland, whose features suddenly looked paralyzed. When she caught him looking, she rolled her eyes and actually tapped a forefinger on the side of her head.

Iris was still bent over her little notebook, continuing to write, as if Laura hadn't said anything unusual. Magozzi had to bite his tongue to keep from firing questions. Batty or not, you couldn't just let a statement like that hang there without a token follow-up, at least.

Iris stopped writing and looked up a second later, her expression blandly pleasant. 'How many, do you think?' she asked Laura.

Way to go, Iris Rikker.

The old woman blinked, then her eyes wandered to follow her brain. 'Oh, my. All together?'

'Yes, if you please.'

'Goodness. I guess ... I'm not quite sure ...' She was blinking faster now, and her eyes were starting to water. 'Well ... I guess we could look in the lake. Is it important?'

Maggie Holland closed her eyes.

'Not really,' Iris said. 'Is that Lake Kittering?'

'That's the one. You live on Lake Kittering, don't you, dear?'

Iris stopped writing, but she kept looking down at her notebook. 'Close to it. I didn't realize you knew that.'

Laura chuckled a little. 'Of course I know that. We all do. You bought Emily's place.'

'That's right.'

'Well, just so you know, Edgar isn't in the lake.'

Iris started writing again, but the script was a little shaky. 'He isn't?'

'No. We buried him. Of course we were much younger, then. Ruth – she was my sister, did I tell you that? – at any rate, she was even younger than I was, and Emily was just a little swell in her tummy ...' Her eyes wandered and seemed to lose focus until her gaze found Maggie, standing right next to her. 'Oh, Maggie. Hello, dear.'

Gino and Magozzi exchanged a knowing glance. This sure as hell wasn't going to go much further. The old woman was losing it, if she ever had it in the first place.

'Are Alice and Bill coming?'

Magozzi's mind twitched a little at the names, but he let it go when Maggie answered her.

'They're on their way. I called them before the officers came in, remember?'

'Oh. Should I go to the bathroom first?'

'Would you like to?'

'Oh, yes, very much.'

It took her a while to get out of the rocker this time, as if the muddle in her mind could no longer manage to control the still-limber body.

The moment they heard the bathroom door close behind her, Iris looked at Maggie Holland. 'Who was Edgar, Maggie? The one they buried?'

Maggie looked disgusted. 'Don't be silly. Nobody buried anybody.'

'And I don't suppose there are any bodies in the lake, either?'

'Of course not.'

For some reason, Magozzi believed her.

'Quickly, before she comes back,' Iris said, and Maggie sighed.

'Edgar was Laura's husband. That's according to Laura's grand-niece – she's the woman on her way here now, and certainly in a position to know since Laura and her sister raised her right here at Bitterroot. Apparently he was an abusive, hateful man. He kept both sisters virtual prisoners on the original farm, which happened to include your land in those days, Sheriff. He beat them, treated them both like chattel, impregnated Laura's sister, and then simply disappeared. God knows where he went.'

Just like Lars, Iris was thinking, but she didn't say anything.

'There was no outside help for mistreated women in those days. Not that there's all that much these days,' she added bitterly, touching the scar on her neck. 'Laura and Ruth suffered under that reality, and after Edgar left, they were determined to create a sanctuary where things like that never happened to women. That was the beginning of Bitterroot.'

'So they didn't kill anybody,' Gino said, and Maggie glared at him.

'You don't understand, Detective. You can't possibly. You suffer under abuse long enough, you start to fantasize about killing your abuser. You don't act on it, of course, because that's the nature of your own psychology. You love your abuser, or at least convince yourself you do. Except in a very few cases, all of which make the national news, killing him would be utterly impossible.'

Gino nodded reluctantly at a truth he'd seen a thousand times.

'But you dream about it, especially afterward, and maybe when you get very old and the mind and the memory dim, the dreams become reality, and reality becomes the dream. That's the place where Laura is living now. I did warn you that she wasn't quite –' She stopped talking abruptly when Laura came back into the room, looking bewildered to find it full of strangers.

'We have company?' she asked in a small, timid voice. 'At this hour?'

Gino cleared his throat. 'We just stopped in to use your phone, ma'am, if that's all right.'

'Oh. Well, Maggie, I think I'd like to go to bed now.' She

left the room without once looking at the body of the man she'd killed, lying on the rug.

Iris touched Magozzi's shoulder as he got up to leave. 'I have to stay until the others come.'

'You have some kind of crime unit?'

Iris shrugged. 'Such as it is. I radioed Lieutenant Sampson when I came in. He'll take care of it.' She gestured vaguely toward Kurt Weinbeck's body. 'This seemed pretty cut and dried. I don't think we'll need the BCA.'

'Probably not.'

'But I'd like to ask your advice on something else. Will you wait?'

Magozzi nodded. 'No problem. We'll be in the car.'

29

Gino was shaking his head, clucking his tongue, as they walked back to the car. 'Man, was that goddamned weird or what? Walking into that house, listening to the old lady talk about shooting people, pouring tea while Kurt Weinbeck is getting stiff on the living room floor . . . Jesus. I felt like I just walked through the looking glass or fell down the rabbit hole or whatever the hell it was.'

'It was pretty weird.'

'Pretty weird? Are you kidding me? I feel like I just dropped acid or something.'

Magozzi smiled as they moved through the rapidly accumulating snow. 'Nobody drops acid anymore, Gino.'

'Whatever. I hope Rikker hurries it up. I just want to get the hell out of here and never come back. This place is freaking me out.'

'So you think there's any truth to it?'

'What?'

'The "bodies in the lake" business.'

'Hell, I don't know. The old gal showed her chops pretty good tonight. I can see her popping her husband way back when, especially after he knocked up her own sister, but I sure as hell can't see her as a frequent flyer. Either way, it's not our problem. We've got our own case to worry about, and this mess really burned us for time.'

A few of the Dundas County cars were leaving the parking lot by the time they made it back, but most of them were still in place. The deputies not working the scene clustered around idling squads, rehashing, embellishing, doing what cops did while they waited for the last of the adrenaline to burn away. An ambulance was pulling in, and one of the officers broke away from a group to direct the driver.

When they got to their own SUV, Gino flipped open his cell. 'I'm going to call McLaren and fill him in. Maybe he has some news. At least we can make Tinker's day, telling him a ninety-year-old lady plugged Weinbeck with the same caliber he used to kill Steve Doyle.'

There was definitely poetic justice in that, Magozzi thought sadly; it was just a damn shame Doyle wasn't around to appreciate it. He climbed into the car, started the engine, and turned the heater on full blast. Gino opted for staying outside and pacing figure eights in the fresh snow while he talked to McLaren. Gino hated the cold, but he hated making calls sitting down even more.

'So what's up?' Magozzi asked when Gino had finally finished and climbed into the passenger seat.

Gino sighed. 'The end of a dream. Bona fide proof that we wasted a day and a half's worth of golden hours on finding Deaton's and Myerson's killer. McLaren just confirmed a Friday-night alibi for Weinbeck. No way he could have done it.'

Magozzi sighed. 'Well, that's what we kind of figured all along. Is it tight?'

'Totally. His sister and about forty of his hair-ball friends threw a party for him.'

Magozzi frowned. 'So why didn't that turn up right away?'

'It's classic, stupid, drowning-in-a-shallow-gene-pool

stuff,' Gino muttered, rubbing his hands together in front of a heat vent. 'They picked Weinbeck up from prison, took him straight to a bar, and got him skunk-drunk. Stayed there until closing time, then took it back to her house and went all night. Major parole violation for Weinbeck, obviously, and she knew it, so she got real paranoid when McLaren called her up, sniffing around for info about her brother. So she did what comes naturally to people like that – she played stupid. Her loyalty lasted about as long as it took McLaren to threaten to book her as an accessory for Deaton and Myerson, then she spilled her guts. What a pisser. And usually the dumb factor works in our favor. Go figure.'

'Shit.' Magozzi let out a frustrated sigh and pushed on the steering wheel, suddenly feeling claustrophobic in this car, in this place, in this county. 'So now what? Head to Stillwater, put the screws to the Snowman?'

Gino lifted a shoulder noncommittally. 'I suppose that makes sense. Just because he didn't hire Weinbeck to kill Deaton and Myerson doesn't mean he didn't hire somebody else, right?'

'Right.'

'It's the strongest lead we've got.'

'It's the only lead we've got.'

They were both quiet for a long moment. 'So why do neither one of us like it?' Magozzi finally asked.

'I don't know. It's more like a weird feeling than anything else. Kinda like diet pop.'

Magozzi lifted a brow at him and braced himself for another Gino metaphor. 'Diet pop.'

'Yeah, you know, you take a sip and it tastes just great, just like the real thing. Then a couple seconds later it gets a little thin on the palate and you can start tasting the artificial sweetener. It's just not right, and you know it, but it's hard to peg.'

'Well, whether or not it sits right, we've got to look at it anyhow.'

'I know.' Gino's leg was starting to jiggle impatiently. 'Where the hell is Rikker, anyhow?'

A few minutes later, a black sedan pulled into an empty parking space across and kitty-corner from them, under one of the big sodium vapor lamps. Magozzi and Gino watched as a man and a woman got out, and then both their jaws dropped simultaneously.

'Jesus, Leo, are you seeing who I'm seeing? That's Mary Deaton's parents.'

Magozzi nodded, finally understanding why his brain had stumbled a little when he heard Laura ask if Alice and Bill were coming. 'Alice and Bill Warner. Which makes Alice the grand-niece that Laura and her sister raised right here.'

Gino blinked a lot of times at the overload of coincidences. 'Goddamnit, Leo, I'm sinking down into that dark place, 'cause this stuff is really getting to me. I mean, as far as I'm concerned, we just figured out that we've been working on two totally unrelated cases, and yet every single goddamned thread to both of them leads us straight to Bitterroot every time. What's that about?'

Magozzi was just shaking his head, trying to clear his mind, trying to focus. Bitterroot. Gino was right – it felt like it had to be central to both cases, because it just kept popping up, but when you looked at it close, there was nothing here to connect it to the Deaton and Myerson murders. Except the two people he was watching as they hurried through the snow, around the corporate building to the village in back. 'I don't know, Gino, but there can't be anything to it. Weinbeck was up here for his wife. He saw the news about Deaton and Myerson and put Doyle in a snowman to buy himself time. And Alice Warner just happens to be related to somebody who lives here. With four hundred residents and six degrees of separation, maybe that's not such a coincidence.'

Gino pressed both hands to his forehead. 'You know those smoothies when they put a bunch of different fruit in a blender and turn it on high? That's what my brain feels like right now. A big pink-and-gray smoothie. And I got that diet soda feeling again.'

Magozzi's eyes followed Alice and Bill Warner until they moved out of sight. He totally missed Iris walking up to the car.

'Thank God,' Gino said, jumping out of the car and opening the back door for her, eager to keep things moving and get the hell out of here. 'It's cold, Sheriff. Hop on in.'

She nodded her thanks and climbed in the back on a gust of cold wind and a faint hint of orange.

Soap? Shampoo? Cough drop? Magozzi wondered, searching for a mystery he might solve before they started piling dirt on him.

'Thank you for waiting, Detectives. I know you're probably anxious to get back to your own case. Is there still a chance that Weinbeck is your killer?'

'Not a chance,' Magozzi said. 'We just alibied him.'

'Then we've wasted your time here. I'm terribly sorry for that, but terribly grateful, too, for what you did tonight.'

Now that he was close to heading for home, Gino was feeling magnanimous. 'You did pretty damn good yourself,' he told her. 'Not bad for your first day, Iris Rikker.'

She flashed him a grim smile. 'Yesterday I would have

been hiding in a closet, speed-reading the manual, trying not to get sick. You'd be surprised what you can learn in a day, watching good officers do their job.'

It was a great thing to say, and Magozzi started really liking her for the first time.

'Listen, I won't keep you long, but I really need some advice, and I would very much appreciate your professional opinions.'

Aside from food and sex, not necessarily in that order, the best way to worm your way into Gino's heart – or any man's heart, come to think of it – was to compliment him professionally. Magozzi wondered if Iris's phrasing had been intentional or if it was just knee-jerk. Sometimes he thought all women were born with a special strand of DNA that made manipulating men effortless and instinctive.

Gino gave her a paternal smile. 'Anything we can do, Sheriff. Ask away.'

Iris took a deep breath. 'Well . . . how much stock would you put in some of the things Laura was saying?'

Magozzi and Gino looked at one another. 'There could be some truth to it.'

'Would you drag the lake, come spring?'

'That's totally your call, Sheriff.'

'Thank God,' Gino added tactlessly. 'I wouldn't want to touch that for a million bucks.'

Iris looked a little disappointed, but the wheels in her head were still turning. 'Under normal circumstances, I probably wouldn't give a second thought to what Laura had to say, given the clear evidence of her diminished capacity, but the bones really bother me.'

'What bones?' Magozzi asked.

Iris looked surprised. 'Sampson didn't tell you?'

'Haven't talked to him since he called me out of bed this morning, and all he said then was that you were tracking Weinbeck from your place to Bitterroot, and if we wanted in on it, to get up here. I got the feeling things were pretty tense on your end when he called.'

Iris nodded. 'We were moving pretty fast then. But it turns out Weinbeck wasn't the only thing in my barn. We found what was left of a body in a locked room under the barn floor – little more than a skeleton, really. Sampson thinks it was Emily's husband. He disappeared decades ago.'

Magozzi's brows shot up. 'Murdered?'

Iris shook her head a little and Magozzi smelled orange again. *Definitely shampoo.* 'We didn't have a spare second to look at the time. Weinbeck was running then. The BCA's coming out later this morning to take a look.'

Gino had a funny look on his face. 'A locked room, you say?'

'It was worse than that. More like an underground prison cell, no windows, a single trapdoor in the ceiling, no way to reach it.'

'Oh, man, I've got goose bumps. Jeez, that's creepy.'

Iris nodded. 'It's the connection that's giving me the willies. I'm living in a house where a woman very possibly imprisoned her husband, perhaps killed him, and it turns out she just happened to be the niece of another woman I just interviewed because she also killed a man tonight, and claims to have killed others, and I have to ask myself, what the hell are these women teaching their daughters?'

Magozzi turned completely around in his seat to look at her, and noticed for the first time. Gino was right. She was a looker. 'What are you thinking? Some kind of twisted family legacy?'

Iris rubbed at her face. It felt like years since she'd washed it. 'I don't know. I just know that it has me wondering about what really might be at the bottom of Lake Kittering.'

Magozzi and Gino were both silent for a moment, taking it all in, then Gino shrugged. 'So what's the down side of dragging?'

'It's a big lake, Gino,' Magozzi reminded him.

'An enormous lake,' Iris amended. 'It stretches from the county offices on one end, over to the back of Bitterroot property, all the way to the land behind mine. The cost would be astronomical. The worst part is that whether or not we found anything, the dragging operation itself would make people believe the worst, no matter what the results. If we found something, bad ending. And if we didn't, a lot of them would say we just hadn't looked in the right place. They'd never stop believing there were bodies in that lake, and politics still rule up here. I think they'd find a way to shut Bitterroot down.'

Gino blew out an exhale that almost moved his brush cut. 'Really tough call. What are you going to do?'

'I was hoping if I asked nicely, you'd tell me.'

Magozzi smiled a little, and then went serious. There were too damn many moral questions to this job. Most of the time you knew which side of the line you were supposed to walk, but sometimes, the road on one side of it looked just as crooked as the road on the other.

'Shit,' Gino grumbled when she left the car. Apparently she and Sampson were headed over to her place to wait for the BCA. 'I sure as hell hope nobody ever asks us for advice again.'

'Me too,' Magozzi said as he shifted into drive and heard the snow crunch under the tires.

He was really depressed now. Iris had half bent getting out of the car, and he'd gotten a good whiff of her hair. Fresh air, no orange; so it wasn't shampoo. Another unsolved.

30

Magozzi pulled out his cell and snapped open the cover. 'Magozzi.'

Gino raised his brows when Magozzi pulled over to the shoulder and flipped on the emergency lights. This was not a good idea, especially on this narrow country road with snowbanks towering on either side. Gino wasn't a hundred percent sure they were on the shoulder, or if the road even had one, and this was absolutely not like Magozzi.

'Okay, Grace. Shoot.'

Well, that explained it. Gino leaned back in the seat and tried to relax. First thing was, he didn't like to hear his partner say 'shoot' to a woman who carried all the time; second thing was his door was jammed up against one of the stupid snowbanks and he didn't have a chance in hell of getting out when the car was hit by some bohunk driving a snowplow or a tractor or whatever the hell was going to come first.

'Jeez, Leo, get someplace a little safer and call her back, would you?'

Magozzi was listening hard, and just raised his hand to shut him up.

Gino closed his eyes and waited to die. Christ. Sometimes men were so stupid he was sorry he was one. Magozzi would take a bullet for him any day of the week, but if Grace MacBride called, all bets were off. No sense.

'Just hold it a minute, Grace. I'm in the car with Gino. I'm going to put you on speaker . . . okay? Start over.'

As if Grace would ever stop if someone told her to, because she was in the middle of a sentence.

'. . . so this morning we finally managed to pull the whole chat thread I told you about that kept mentioning the Minneapolis snowmen. You need to see this. How close are you to Harley's?'

'That's the thing. About sixty miles away, up in Dundas County.'

Silence for a second, then, 'Dundas County? Where they found the other snowman?'

'Right. The guy responsible for that snowman was just greased by an old lady up here at Bitterroot. One of your clients, right, Grace?'

'That's right. We did some corporate security software for them last fall. How did you know?'

'We saw your logo on one of the programs. Did you know what that place was?'

'Some kind of mail-order business, why?'

'You didn't get the tour?'

'We were there to work, Magozzi, and only on weekends, when the place was closed. We saw a couple people and the inside of the computer room. That's it.'

'There's a whole town behind the corporate building, Grace, and what it is, is one giant safe house for abused women.'

'Oh, Lord.' Her voice was a mere whisper, and she covered the phone for a moment and said something, probably to the rest of the Monkeewrench crew. When she came back, her voice sounded tense. 'Magozzi. Bitterroot was the subject line on that chat thread. We didn't know what it meant at the time, but it's starting to make a sick kind of sense. I think they're killing abusers.'

Gino forgot about dying under the blade of a snowplow and leaned forward. '*Who's* killing abusers?' he demanded.

'We don't know that. Yet.'

Magozzi closed his eyes. 'Read us what you've got, Grace.'

She took a breath that sounded fractured. 'Okay. This came off a private chat room within a very private site we haven't cracked yet, but the conversation is what we wanted anyway. The thread goes back for months – these two people have been talking for a long time about the legal system not being able to protect their daughters from the men who were abusing them. Frustrated blather, mostly . . . no, not blather, really, because it's true and it's sad, but what you need to hear are some of the last entries. Like this . . . "Do it exactly the way I told you, then put the body in a snowman. We did it here, you can do it. They'll look for a serial."'

Gino and Magozzi looked at each other.

'Are you there, Magozzi? Did you get that?'

'We got it, I'm just not sure where it's going . . .'

Grace just blustered on. 'One of the correspondents is here, in Minneapolis, and the handle is just a bunch of numbers, but the one responding calls himself "Pittsburgh."'

'Oh, Jesus,' Gino murmured. 'The Pittsburgh snowman.'

'So we pulled up the Pittsburgh police reports . . .'

'You *pulled* them?'

Grace sighed, exasperated now. 'They're computerized, Magozzi, and they keep pretty current, which is a good thing. But someone out there was sure asleep at the switch, because they never ran the victim, or if they did, they left it out of their reports. The guy had a sheet, and every one of them was for domestic assault. He kept trying to kill his wife.'

'Anything else on that website you want to read to us?'

'There's only one more entry after the one I just read to you. All it says is: "We do what we have to do. We take care of our own."'

Magozzi and Gino exchanged a troubled look as they remembered Laura saying those exact words not an hour ago. It was starting to sound like a motto.

Magozzi closed his eyes and took a deep breath, almost afraid to keep prodding, although he didn't know why. Just a feeling. One of those bad feelings he hated. 'Keep trying to trace that thing, will you, Grace? We need a name, we need an address.'

'We're working on it. I'll call if we get something.'

'Call Iris Rikker,' he told Gino as he pulled the car off the shoulder and started moving again. 'Get directions to her place.'

'Whoa, buddy, hold on just a second. Think this through. Grace finds a few spooky connections and all of a sudden you decide what? That Bitterroot's an enclave of secret assassins that run around greasing abusers?'

'Goddamnit, Gino, don't make it sound stupid and simple. It isn't either of those things, but we've had nothing but big fingers wagging in our faces pointing up at Bitterroot all along, and we just keep trying to get out of here. This time we're staying until we get some real answers.'

Gino made a face. He didn't like the sound of that. I mean, shit, there wasn't even a decent motel up here.

He got out his cell as Magozzi braked hard, spun the wheel, and did a one-eighty right there in the middle of the road.

31

A long, long time ago, before there were bodies in snowmen and living rooms and maybe even in lakes, Iris had made chicken soup and tucked it in the freezer. She nuked it for five minutes while she was cutting fresh vegetables and getting out the noodles, then put it on the stove and let it rip.

She could hear Sampson's heavy tread as he paced around the downstairs like a man trying to walk off a problem. He'd volunteered to make all the calls they had to make, and that had suited Iris just fine. She was starving.

He came back into the kitchen carrying Puck, who seemed delighted with the situation.

'You like cats?'

'Not really.' Sampson slumped at the kitchen table and settled the purring mass of black fur in his lap. 'She kept winding between my legs every time I took a step, damn near put me on my ass a dozen times. Seemed safer to pick her up and haul her along.'

Iris smiled as she ladled out two bowls. 'We're having soup for breakfast.'

'Thanks. It smells great.' He spooned with one hand and stroked Puck with the other. 'The hospital agreed to put Weinbeck's remains in the cooler for the day. Neville posted a man there, so we're okay. BCA says they won't make it out here till noon, at the earliest. They'll process your barn first, then pick up Weinbeck on their way back into town.'

'What about the scene?'

'They're still collecting and printing. Neville's staying there until they're finished.'

'So we have time.'

'More than we've had in a while.'

They were both into their second bowl when Gino called Iris to ask for directions.

'They're coming back?' Sampson asked her.

'Apparently. He didn't say why, just that they'd be here in a few minutes, and could we wait for them.'

'Huh. Wonder what that's about.' He leaned back in his chair and looked down at the cat in his lap, wondering why it felt so good to pat the dumb old useless thing. He'd never liked cats; never liked chicken soup much, either, but for some reason one of them felt pretty damn good on the inside of his stomach right now, and the other one didn't feel all that bad curled up on the outside. It was the stuff going on inside his head that was eating at him. 'You should shit-can me, you know.'

'Excuse me?'

Sampson pressed his lips together and looked around the kitchen. 'I like this room.'

'Thank you. I do, too. Why should I "shit-can" you?'

'I bailed on you back there. Just took off, and left you to handle everything.'

Iris sighed and pushed her bowl away. 'You went to protect your sister, Sampson. I would have done exactly the same thing in your position.'

Sampson looked straight at her. 'Don't do that. Don't ever make excuses for a cop walking out on his partner. Ever. One of them does it, you fire their ass. That's your job, now.'

Iris put their empty bowls in the sink and leaned back

against the counter, arms folded across her chest. 'A lot of us were working alone out there. There was too much ground to cover in twos. Besides, Magozzi and Gino and about a hundred other officers were there. I was hardly alone.'

He just sat there looking at her, shaking his head.

'Babysitting me is not your job, Sampson.' For some reason that made him smile a little.

'Well, that's where you're wrong. It was exactly my job. I made a deal.'

'A deal with whom?'

'Bitterroot.'

She puzzled over that for a second, decided she wasn't getting anywhere, then sat down opposite him and waited until he met her eyes. 'What are you talking about?'

'Sheriff Bulardo was going to pull Bitterroot's gun permits.'

'Why on earth would he do that? You said yourself you never had a single trouble call out there.'

'He was pissed. His wife checked into Bitterroot last summer.'

Iris felt her eyes getting bigger. She couldn't seem to stop them. 'Oh, my.'

'Trouble is, no one would run against him. The guys in the department who might have knew damn well they'd lose their jobs afterward unless they beat him, and beating him was impossible. No way this county would elect a deputy over a sheriff when from the outside, the sheriff seemed to be doing an okay job. And then out of the blue, this brand-new deputy on dispatch that nobody knows puts her name on the ticket.' He grinned a little. 'That was a David and Goliath move if ever there was one. Why the hell did you do that, anyway? You had to know it was career suicide. Most of us figured you for some kind of hotshot crusader. The martyr type.'

Iris shook her head. 'It was nothing that noble. Bulardo caught me in a supply closet my second night on dispatch and made some pretty offensive advances. So I slapped him. Really slapped him. Now *that* was career suicide.'

'You slapped Sheriff Bulardo?' Sampson was trying not to laugh.

'I did. And that's when he promised that I would never, ever get off the dispatch desk as long as he was in office. See what I mean? No nobility at all. I didn't have a thing to lose by running for sheriff, and I did it for all the wrong reasons. I was just thumbing my nose at a man who'd hurt me, and no one was more surprised than I was when I got elected.'

Sampson was still smiling. 'We got lucky there. Most people stopped bothering to vote in the sheriff's race a long time ago. But this time Bitterroot voted in a block. Every single one of them made it to the polls that day, a lot of them leaving the complex for the first time since they arrived. It was a big deal. And it was just enough to turn the tide.'

Iris closed her eyes. 'Terrific. Bitterroot got me elected to save themselves, and now I'm the one who has to decide whether or not to start an investigation that could shut them down.'

'Yeah. I didn't see that coming, either.'

'What am I going to do, Sampson?'

He tipped his head and looked at her for a long time. 'The right thing.'

'I don't know what that is.'

'You will, when the time comes.'

*

Magozzi pulled to a stop in Iris's circular driveway halfway between a big, weathered barn and an old-fashioned, white-railing porch that looked like a great place to drink lemonade and pass the time on a steamy summer day, although that was a hard scene to imagine this morning.

He put the car in park, but didn't turn off the engine; he just sat there with his wrists draped over the steering wheel, squinting hard out the window, as he always did when he was really thinking something out. Blocks of color was the way he thought of it. The devil might be in the details, but unless you squinted every now and then, you'd miss the big picture. Which is exactly what had happened.

Magozzi's eyes and head shifted back into close focus and he tapped a finger on the windshield at the falling snow splatting on the glass. 'Snow blind,' he said to Gino. 'That's what we were.'

'What do you mean?'

'I mean we followed the Weinbeck connection because it was the easy trail. The path of least resistance . . .'

'Now, just wait a minute, Leo. We can't beat ourselves up for that. We had a third snowman, for Christ's sake. We had no choice but to look at Weinbeck, and for a while, he looked pretty damn good.'

'Yeah, but that's *all* we looked at. What we should have been paying attention to from the get-go were the victims and their families. That's the first place we always look, but this is the one time we didn't, because Weinbeck stormed onto the scene so fast. Pittsburgh made the same mistake, probably because they were figuring copycat.'

Gino was genuinely confounded. 'What the hell are you talking about?'

'I'm talking about your average homicide, and how you

usually don't have to look very far to find the murderer. You know how rare stranger killings are.'

'Sure, but Deaton and Myerson were not average homicides . . .'

'The way they died wasn't average, but the motive probably was. We weren't even in the forest, Gino. Not even close.' He looked over at his partner. 'Get on the horn to McLaren. Have him check 911 calls and ER records at local hospitals for Mary Deaton.'

Gino's expression cleared slowly as it dawned on him what it was Magozzi had been trying to say. 'Holy shit. Mary Deaton. The nose job.'

Magozzi nodded grimly. 'That maybe wasn't a nose job.'

Gino was shaking his head miserably. 'Goddamnit, Leo, Deaton was a cop.'

'It happens, Gino. A lot. You know it does.'

He thought for a moment. 'No way Mary Deaton had anything to do with this. She doesn't have the physique, for one thing, and she's got that abused-woman mentality going, or she would have put his ass in jail a long time ago.'

'I wasn't thinking of Mary Deaton.'

Gino looked at him for a second, then flipped open his phone and dialed the office.

They sat in absolute silence in Iris's driveway, waiting for McLaren to call back. It didn't take long. Gino listened for a few minutes, nodding occasionally, but not bothering to take notes. 'Thanks, Johnny,' he finally said. 'Follow it wherever it leads.'

He hung up and looked over at Magozzi. 'Mary Deaton went into Hennepin County ER for a broken nose two nights before her husband was killed. First time they'd ever seen her. No 911 history, either, so McLaren got a wild hair and started calling other ERs. She had a file in every one of them, one visit each. He got up to five and called us, but he's still checking. You know how many hospitals we've got in the Twin Cities area? And here's something interesting. Guess who took her in every time.'

'Her husband. Tommy Deaton.'

'No cigar. His partner, Toby Myerson. Son of a bitch. That bastard had to know what was happening.'

'He's not the only one.' Magozzi turned and looked at him head-on. 'What would you do if it was your kid, Gino? If it was Helen?'

Gino didn't answer him.

By the time Magozzi and Gino finally got out of the car and headed up to Iris's porch, a weak sunrise was trying to lighten the dingy, snow-speckled sky. Iris and Sampson were both peering out at them through the kitchen window, probably wondering what the hell they'd been doing in the car for so long.

As Iris opened the door to gesture them in, the smell of homemade soup nearly knocked them both down. Gino smiled a little sheepishly when his stomach roared loudly enough for everybody to hear. 'Sorry.'

'Sit down,' Iris grabbed two clean bowls from a cupboard above the stove.

Magozzi was suffering the ill effects of skipping breakfast, too, just not as audibly as Gino. 'We appreciate it, Sheriff, but we really don't have time.'

'Where are you going?'

'Bitterroot. Your jurisdiction, so we'd like you both to come along.'

'Fine.' She slapped spoons in their hands. 'Then spoon it

right out of the pot while we get our boots and coats on. You both look like you're ready to pass out.'

Gino's resolve weakened the minute the spoon hit his hand, and he was on his way to the stove when Magozzi's voice stopped him.

'Not even time for that. We've got to get back out there before Bill and Alice Warner leave.'

Iris's brow furrowed a little when Magozzi mentioned the names. 'The relatives who were on their way to Laura's?'

Sampson had his coat halfway up his arms, then let it drop to his chair. 'Relax. Our deputies just checked in from out there. The local doc ended up giving Laura a sedative when she got a little wild, and the Warners are babysitting until she comes around. You've got time for a bowl, and you'd be crazy to pass it up.'

Gino was a happy man, already at the stove, working the ladle.

Iris was standing by the door, one boot on, one in her hand.

'Their last name is Warner?'

'Right. Bill and Alice. They're the in-laws ... *were* the in-laws of one of the cops we pulled out of the Minneapolis snowmen. Tommy Deaton. We just found out he was abusing his wife big time.'

'Oh, man,' Sampson was shaking his head. 'This isn't good. It keeps coming back to Bitterroot.'

'Tell me about it. Every time we try to get away from this place we keep getting jerked back. I'm starting to feel like I've got a rubber band around my ankle and Dundas County is holding the other end.' Gino delivered a bowl of soup to Magozzi and started slurping his own. Sure, it looked like they had a little time, but Magozzi never took things like that for granted, and he'd be pulling him out the door in a second.

Iris was pulling her second boot on in slow motion, and Magozzi knew how that worked. Back in the days when he still thought jogging was sensible, he'd be humping it around one of the city lakes at a good clip, thinking about a case, and pretty soon he'd find himself moving like a snail. When the mind was really working, the body slowed.

'Alice Warner was the name on the deed to this house,' Iris said, straightening and looking at Magozzi. 'The daughter of Emily, who owned this house and probably killed her husband. And now you tell me she's the mother-in-law of a murdered abuser? Now I'm *really* wondering what these women are teaching their daughters.'

Sampson looked at Magozzi. 'You like the Warners for your two snowmen?'

'We're leaning that way.'

'How sure are you?'

'Not at all. That's what we're going to find out. We'll tell you the rest in the car.'

32

They didn't call ahead this time; just stopped at the big gates and waited for Liz, the guard they'd met yesterday, to check them in.

'We've got to get back to Laura's house, Liz,' Sampson told her when he rolled down the driver's window.

She looked tired today, frustrated. 'You and every other cop in the free world.' She bent to look in the SUV, nodded at Iris, then Gino and Magozzi in the back. 'Same crew as yesterday?'

'That's right. How many of our people are still out here?'

Liz actually scowled at him. 'We had to keep the gates open when you people first started moving in so fast. First time since the fence went up. I have no idea how many people came in, or how many went out. Every bit of security we had on the perimeter was gone in a heartbeat.'

'Sorry, Liz. We didn't have a choice.'

She found a little smile for him. 'Yeah, I know that. It's just a little weird, you know? All these strangers tromping around, and nobody knows who anybody is . . . We're not used to that.'

'We'll clear out as soon we can.'

They parked next to the few other squads left in the lot, then took the shortest route around the corporate building and followed the narrow road out to Laura's house.

It occurred to Magozzi that he'd never heard the old woman's last name. Not that it mattered much at this point, it just seemed a strange omission. You always asked for a full name and the correct spelling, whether you were interviewing a doer or a witness, because if you sent in a report without those details, they'd ship you back to night classes on investigation.

'Damn, I'm sick of this,' Gino complained as they slogged through the new snow that just kept piling up. 'These pants are so wet my legs are getting moldy, and it just keeps snowing.' He stomped his feet when they made it around the building and hit the little plowed road.

'How do want to handle this?' Iris asked as they made their way through the little patch of woods and out into the open. Laura's farmhouse was visible just ahead.

'Gino will lead on the interview,' Magozzi said. 'We're feeling our way here, and don't want to spook them with the recorder, so we'll need good notes from everybody. Words, yeah, but reactions are going to tell us a lot, too. Wait until Gino closes down his end if you think of something you want to ask.'

Bill Warner opened the front door. He looked exactly as he had that day at Mary Deaton's house. Neat gray brush cut, good physique, a cop's eyes in a tired face. He would have been told they'd been here before, of course, but he looked a little surprised to see them back.

Good, Magozzi thought. *Got him a little off balance, anyway.*

'Come in, come in,' he widened the door and gestured them inside. 'Not fit for man nor beast, and all that. Detectives Magozzi and Rolseth, right? You remember me?'

'Of course, Mr Warner.'

'The name is Bill, remember?'

'Thank you. This is Sheriff Rikker and Lieutenant Sampson, Dundas County. How's your daughter Mary doing?'

'As well as can be expected, under the circumstances. We've got Tommy's funeral to go yet, of course, and Toby's. What happened here tonight isn't going to make it any easier, especially if there's some backlash against Laura we have to deal with.'

Magozzi said, 'I don't see that happening. It's Dundas's call, of course, but we were all on scene and agree that it seems like a pretty straightforward case of self-defense.'

'A pretty impressive case of self-defense,' Gino added. 'She did some fast thinking on her feet for a lady that age.'

Bill nodded. 'Laura's a pistol; always has been . . .' He faltered then, apparently realizing how inappropriate his choice of words had been. 'Unfortunately, her mind's been slipping for years now, but she still has her moments. Can I take your coats?'

Magozzi shook his head. 'Thanks, no. I don't think we'll be long.'

'Well, come in at least, sit by the fire and warm up.'

Once they were settled, Magozzi looked around. The body was gone, of course, and Iris's men had collected the area rug. Otherwise the place looked relatively untouched. He saw a few traces of fingerprint powder on some surfaces, but they'd cleaned up pretty well.

Bill Warner followed his eyes. 'The crime-scene unit left about fifteen minutes ago.'

'Is Maggie Holland still here?' Maggozi asked.

'She left right after they did. Probably went home to pop a Valium or something. I know I would, if I'd had her night.'

Magozzi smiled. 'Did your wife come with you today?' he asked, as if he didn't know the answer.

'Yes, of course. Laura's her great-aunt – I'm guessing

Maggie told you that. Alice just went back to the bedroom to make sure she was still asleep.'

As if on cue, Alice Warner's footsteps sounded in the hall, and she stepped through into the living room. She did a little double take to find it filled with people who hadn't been there when she had left. 'Hello?'

Magozzi, Gino, and Sampson stood up when Bill introduced them. They hadn't gotten much of a look at her that first day at Mary Deaton's house, let alone met her – she'd been totally focused on comforting her daughter when Bill had stepped aside to talk to them. She was almost as tall as her husband, and something about her was very nearly elegant, very self-possessed. She had a strong handshake and a stronger gaze. 'Detectives. It's a pleasure to meet you at last. Did Bill thank you for being so kind to our daughter on that terrible day?'

'He most certainly did,' Gino stepped in with an attempt at suave and friendly. 'I know you must have had a trying morning, but do you have a moment to sit and chat with us?'

She gave Gino a gracious smile that made Magozzi think they were treading water here and maybe way over their heads.

When they were all seated, Bill and Alice Warner next to each other on the sofa, Bill looked at Magozzi and gave him a sad, friendly smile, and Magozzi realized he'd already pegged him as the one playing good cop. 'I was surprised to hear you two were so far off the beaten path up here.'

Magozzi smiled back, and felt false. He hated this. 'We followed the third snowman, the one Weinbeck built around the parole officer he'd killed. We thought at first it might be connected to your son-in-law and his partner.'

Bill made his eyebrows go up. 'And was it?'

'I'm afraid not.'

'Which is why we wanted to talk with you and your wife,' Gino interjected, and the atmosphere in the room changed abruptly. Iris Rikker and Lieutenant Sampson pulled out their notebooks, and the Warners noticed.

Gino continued. 'First, Bill, let me say this. I've got a daughter. Coming up on sixteen, this year. And I'd rip out the throat of anybody who hurt her.'

Bill and Alice Warner didn't even flinch.

'So I get that. I get it big time. Now my question to you is this: Did you know your daughter was being abused?'

It was a slow, disdainful blink. 'Of course I did, Detective. You think I'm stupid? Blind? What? Twenty-five years on the force. I've seen it a thousand times, just like you have. You think I'd miss that?'

Gino nodded. 'So I'm thinking, you and me, we're a lot alike. We've both got daughters, we're both cops, we know what's going on, I'm guessing you weren't going to just sit idle while Tommy beat up Mary whenever the spirit moved him, and the guy was escalating. The ER visits were clumping up. He was going off.'

Bill gave him a flat stare. 'You're going the wrong way, Detective. I know you have to look at it, but I spent a lot of years enforcing the law, not breaking it.'

Magozzi thought that was a pretty mild reaction from a man who just learned he was a possible suspect in a double homicide. Then again, a controlled response was the hallmark of any good cop, and Warner would be a cop until the day they put him in the ground.

'So when did you first learn what was going on, Bill?' Gino asked him.

'For sure? A few months ago. And once we knew, we did what we could. Tried to get Mary to leave Tommy, tried to get her to press charges, begged her to come up here to Bitterroot, and when she wouldn't do any of those things, we went all over the legal system, starting with some friends of mine who are still at the Second, but without Mary's testimony, everybody's hands were tied. After that, there was only one thing I could do.'

'And what was that?'

Bill Warner smiled a little. 'Exactly the same thing you'd do in that situation, Detective Rolseth. I went over there and beat the shit out of him. Told him if he ever hurt my daughter again I'd kill him.'

Gino was working hard to keep his expression neutral. Sure, he felt for the guy, he got it big time, but even when someone's hurting your kid, you can't just go out and plug him, right?

What would you do if it was your kid, Gino? If it was Helen?

He shook his head a little, dislodging that question, because the answer didn't matter. Couldn't matter when you were a cop trying to nail a killer.

'And you know what Mary did?' Bill was saying. 'She kicked us out of the house, told us she didn't want to see or talk to us again until we apologized to the son of a bitch, and she didn't. Not until the day Tommy died.' He sagged back on the sofa as if the telling had exhausted him. Alice Warner patted his hand, but her expression remained impassive.

Gino gave him a sympathetic look. 'I think it's pretty obvious you've both had a hell of a time, and we're damn sorry for that, but the thing is, we've still got an unsolved double, and like you said, Bill, we have to look at everything.'

'I know.'

'So. You were at the Second when the Snowman bust went down, right?'

That seemed to surprise him, but he recovered quickly. 'I was.'

'So you knew all about it.'

Magozzi was watching Bill Warner closely, and saw the skin tighten around his eyes.

'Along with about a million other people. It hit the papers, the TV news.'

'But you followed the case closer than most, I'll bet, because Tommy was a key witness.'

'I suppose.'

'Let me tell you how it went, Bill. After Tommy and Toby were killed, we got some information that maybe the Snowman was knocking off some witnesses before his trial next week, putting them in snowmen to scare off the other witnesses. But then we caught wind of a few things that started us thinking in other directions, and the Snowman stopped looking so good for it.' He paused to give that time to sink in. 'That's when we started toying with the idea that maybe there was somebody else out there who wanted Tommy and Toby dead for other reasons, and they used the Snowman as a blind. And, hell, framing a scumbag like the Snowman for murder – who cares? He's probably going to do life anyway. It was a pretty sweet setup, when you think about it.'

Bill Warner snorted. 'Pretty damn elaborate setup, especially for the kind of pinheads who usually go around killing people.'

Gino smiled. 'That's exactly what we thought. At first we thought the killings were pretty clean – not perfect, mind you – but almost' – he saw the Warners glance at each other, then quickly away – 'so you start thinking who knows enough to leave a clean crime scene?'

Bill shrugged. 'Anybody who reads or watches TV, for starters. *CSI* is killing us.'

'Tell me about it. But the field narrows a whole lot when you start asking who would want Tommy and Toby dead.'

Warner had had enough. He leaned over his thighs and drilled Gino with a glare. 'Stop treating me like some yahoo on the bad side of an interview desk, Detective. I've been on your end for too many years, so let's cut to the chase. Alice and I were home together Friday night. All night.'

Alice nodded, frighteningly calm.

'That's good to know, Bill. I'm writing that down. Because the thing is, we just might have whoever murdered Tommy and Toby for a similar murder in Pittsburgh.'

It took him a second too long to respond. 'Oh?'

'Yeah. Pulled some stuff off the Internet, you know, from one of those super-secret chat rooms no one else is supposed to be able to get into? Only it can be done, of course, you just have to have the right people working on it, and we've got some good ones. They're doing a trace on the sources now.'

Warner's eyes narrowed and his forehead wrinkled as he thought about that for a minute, then he leaned back in the sofa and almost smiled. 'That's interesting, Detective, but you know how it is. People say all sorts of things in those chat rooms for all kinds of reasons. Fat people claim to be thin, hustlers claim to be doctors . . . they lie like crazy, telling strangers they've actually done the things they only wish they could do.'

Gino held his eyes. 'Is that how it works?'

Warner nodded. 'That's how it works.'

Smart, Magozzi was thinking. *He just set up a reasonable explanation for what he said in the chat room, just in case they traced it back to him. Not that it mattered. Online conversations were clues, not proof, and he probably knew that, too.*

'Anything else, Detectives?'

Iris waited half a second for Gino to say something, then jumped right in with a timid little smile that Magozzi thought was absolutely disarming. 'I have one question for Mrs Warner, if you don't mind, ma'am. It's totally off the subject, more a matter of curiosity than anything else, just because I bought your mother's house. It's also very personal, so I completely understand if you'd rather not respond.'

Alice Warner actually smiled back at her, and the smile was genuine. 'What is it, Sheriff?'

'Well, I was wondering ... we were told that you were raised here at Bitterroot by your grandmother Ruth, and Laura. But your mother lived so close.'

It was the first time Magozzi had seen Alice Warner exhibit any emotion at all. It wasn't a bit hostile, but it wasn't pretty, either. She looked down at her lap to hide it, then took a deep breath and met Iris's eyes. 'I was sexually abused by my father. My mother sent me away. Here, where she knew I'd be safe.'

'I'm very sorry.'

'Thank you.'

'And I'm also very sorry to tell you that we found the remains of what may very well be your father in my barn this morning.'

Magozzi had never seen anyone's eyes glitter before. Oh, you read about it in books, and people used the expression all the time, but he'd never really seen it on another human face.

'Oh, my,' Alice Warner said. 'That's very disturbing.'

But she didn't look disturbed. Not at all.

33

They went through the village on their way back to the car. The snow was getting too deep to walk anywhere but on the little plowed road, and it was still coming down; big, fat flakes that belonged on a kid's tongue.

But today there were no kids, and the village was silent. Kurt Weinbeck had done that.

It was a sad thing, Magozzi thought, when you finally learned that the one place you always felt safest wasn't that safe after all. Any burglary victim had a taste of that when they came home to see their doors or windows shattered, their home trashed, their possessions missing. Here, Magozzi had to multiply that feeling by four hundred souls who'd lived a lot of their lives in fear, and thought they'd finally found sanctuary. He wondered how long they'd stay locked in their houses.

None of them spoke until they got back in the county car, and Sampson had started the heater. 'I have a problem with this one,' Gino said. 'Half of me wants to book those two and toss them in the can for life; the other half wants to turn my back and pretend I don't know what they did.'

'Half of you is going to get its wish,' Magozzi said.

'Yeah, but which half?'

'It doesn't matter. Half of you is still going to end up pissed.'

Iris turned around in the front passenger seat. 'I don't understand how you can be so certain they're guilty. They didn't actually say anything incriminating in the interview. Even admitting that he threatened his son-in-law doesn't seem to count for much. Any father would have done the same.'

'Or brother,' Sampson added from the driver's seat. 'I said it myself a few times. But it isn't what they said. It's the way they were.'

'What do you mean?'

'Faces,' Magozzi said. 'You do enough interviews over a long enough time, you learn to read the faces first, and listen to the words second.'

Iris turned back around in her seat and stared out the windshield. 'I'm not there yet.'

'Well, jeez, Iris Rikker, you've been on the job for almost two days already,' Gino said. 'How long is it going to take you to catch on?'

She smiled a little at that, but didn't let him see it. 'Do you have enough to get a search warrant for the Warners' home?'

'Maybe if we strong-arm a judge and do some fancy stepping with probable cause, but Bill Warner's a cop. No way he'd leave a crumb behind.'

'Which leaves us exactly nowhere,' Magozzi said. 'We have nothing on them. No forensics, no ballistics, no witnesses, and even if we trace that chat room right back to Bill's PC, it doesn't prove a thing. And those two sure as hell aren't going to give each other up on the alibi.'

Gino nodded. 'They're pretty much Teflon.'

'So where do you go from here?'

Magozzi shrugged. 'Where we always go. Back to the scene. Back to the beginning. We do it all over again.'

Iris cracked the back door. 'Sampson, would you mind

giving the Detectives a ride back to their car? I want to stay until the last of our people have cleared out. It's time to give these women back their town.'

'No problem. I'll be back in half an hour to pick you up.'

Two dozen deputies had stayed on at Bitterroot, going house-to-house for the second time, reassuring the frightened occupants that the intruder had been apprehended. Most of the women already knew that Kurt Weinbeck hadn't exactly been 'apprehended' – he'd been dropped in his tracks by a very old woman with a very big gun – news traveled as fast in this small town as any other – but still, the deputies had to go through the motions.

Each deputy took one side of a block, working opposite sides of the narrow, curving, snow-clogged street. Except for Kenny. He was working the town alone, after the other deputies had moved on.

He wore his hat-brim low against the falling snow, which hid most of his face, but he had the badge high on his department-issue parka so the women wouldn't be afraid to open their doors. Every single one of them thanked him politely and informed him that another deputy had already stopped to announce that the danger was over. Invariably, Kenny smiled, touched the brim of his hat and apologized for disturbing them twice.

He knew a little about the town layout, but never before had he seen the insides of the houses. Some of them were a little larger than others, probably for the women who had kids and needed extra bedrooms, but otherwise the interiors were almost identical. After peering over a dozen women's shoulders when they opened the door, Kenny had it down. Living room in front, kitchen in back, bedrooms on the left.

There had to be over 300 of them in the town, and by his fifteenth stop, he began to wonder if he'd have enough time to find her. He was moving a lot faster than the other deputies, but as soon as they finished and cleared out someone was bound to wonder why one man lagged behind, checking houses that had already been covered. He could probably bullshit his way out of that, but he didn't really want to get put in that position. He started to move a whole lot faster.

The twenty-sixth house didn't look a whole lot different than the first twenty-five, but the minute a woman opened the door it felt like home to Kenny. In one quick, powerful motion he shoved her aside and stepped into the house, closing the door behind him.

'Hello, Roberta.'

Some things never changed. She just stood there for a second, eyes cast down, every bit as still as the bronze statue of that pioneer woman in front of the library. That's what she'd always done whenever he'd come up on her suddenly, and he used to do that a lot, just to see her like this.

Christ, it was the middle of the night, almost sunrise, and she still looked good; the kind of woman who turned men's heads no matter how many years were on her. They hadn't just had a decent life together; they'd had a perfect one, until the night she'd left that shitty little note and . . .

'Goddamnit, Roberta!'

She was moving now, backing into the little divider that separated the foyer from the living room, and she wasn't allowed to do that. She had her eyes on him now, too, instead of looking down at the floor like she was supposed to, and he didn't like that one bit. 'Stop right there.' And she did, but she was still watching him. He decided to let that go, because this was sort of like training a not-too-bright hunting dog: you had to balance punishment and praise just so. 'That's good, Roberta. That's real good. Now put your coat and boots on and we'll get you home where you belong.'

She didn't move for a minute, then she shook her head, and damnit, she was still staring right at him.

'Do not do that Roberta. Do not make me repeat myself, Goddamnit.'

Roberta knew what was going to happen now. She'd been through it a hundred times before. Halfway through that hundred, the fear had stopped escalating to terror, and downshifted into a black hole of apathetic resignation. After that, whenever Kenny got that wild look that advertised her near and terrible future, all she hoped was that he'd hurry up, hit her and get it over with. The actual impact of fist or boot was almost better than the fearful agony you went through waiting for it.

There would be pain and blood and probably broken bones, then hours later, or sometimes days, the apologies, the loving words, the promises never to do it again, and of course, the question: *Why do you make me do that Roberta? Why do you make me hit you?*

The first thing they started to teach you when you came to Bitterroot was how to protect yourself, how to fight back, and Roberta had been a very good student. After three months she could overpower anyone in the defense classes, even though most of them were younger, and the sense of empowerment filled her with a great resolve. She would never back into a corner again. She would never drop to the floor and cover her head and curl into a fetal ball and wait for it to be over. Not ever again.

Until this moment she had actually believed that. It was only now, with Kenny this close, that she realized the truth. If a stranger ever attacked her, she wouldn't hesitate to slam her heel into his instep and break the bones in his foot, or jam her thumbs into his eyes to blind him – but to do these things to Kenny? It would be unthinkable. She didn't know why.

There was nothing left for her to do, except what she had always done. Find a corner, because where walls came together they offered a little protection from the roundhouse swings; then drop, curl, cover your head and pray. There was just such a corner in the living room. She'd kept it clear of furniture, as she had kept another corner clear in her old house, and whenever another Bitterroot woman visited her, she would find that corner with her eyes and look at Roberta as if they were sharing a sad secret. Almost every house in Bitterroot, the safest place in the world, had a corner just like hers – empty, waiting, just in case.

Kenny wasn't expecting it when she moved so suddenly. I mean, Christ, he hadn't even raised a hand to her, hadn't even *thought* of raising a hand to her, and she was running anyway, scooting into the living room really, really fast.

That was the thing about Roberta. Everybody always said she was built like a ballerina, but man, she scurried like a spastic rabbit when she got scared. Kenny had always thought that looked kind of funny. She was ten steps into the living room by the time he closed his hand around her forearm and jerked viciously.

Roberta didn't have enough breath to scream, so she actually heard the sharp cracking sound of her bone breaking within the sheath of her arm.

She didn't feel the puppet-like flopping of the part of her

arm that swung uselessly beneath the break, but Kenny did, and it grossed him out.

'Jesus Christ, Roberta, you stupid bitch, look what you did!'

She'd hurt herself again, and that always made Kenny angry. *Now it begins*, she thought, but then she saw the arc of his big, hard fist driving toward her head, and thought instead, *And maybe now it ends.*

34

As Iris made her way down one of the still, silent village roads, she started to feel very strange – her limbs were suddenly hollow and weak, her head was light, and sparkles danced in her peripheral vision. Even her skin felt all wrong, crawling with a hot, itchy tingle that made her think of centipedes. It was probably just plain exhaustion, topped off by one big, bad adrenaline hangover, and her body was telling her to slow down. And she would, just as soon as she finished her last round of Bitterroot.

She forced her shaky legs to plod along for another couple blocks, then paused to rest at a tiny cross-street, looking up and down in both directions at the rows of quiet little houses. Bitterroot had been turned upside down and inside out this morning, but bizarrely, the only evidence of all that had transpired here were messy trails of bootprints, and they were already filling in fast with snow, like wounds healing before her eyes. Their physical presence would be erased within an hour; but their psychological presence would probably linger for a long, long time.

He radio unit crackled, and she heard Deputy Neville's tinny voice talking through the plastic box on her shoulder. 'This is two-four-five. We just gave the all-clear to the last house. Heading out. Over.'

Iris punched her call button. 'This is Sheriff Rikker. Are you the last team in the town?'

'We're it, Sheriff,' Neville answered. 'Where are you?'

'On the northwest grid. I'll see you back at the office.'

As Iris walked back toward the parking lot to wait for Sampson, she noticed that lights blazed in every house she passed, but there was no sign of life in any of them. She suddenly felt very lonely in this silent, snow-shrouded village and found herself wishing desperately for a glimpse of just a single person, a dog in a yard – anything that would make this place seem a little more normal, as it had yesterday, before Kurt Weinbeck.

She never knew what made her single out that house in particular, but as she turned her gaze toward it, she caught a flash of movement inside, through the open louvers of a mini-blind. She paused and squinted through the snow, and saw two figures: a woman, and goddammit, was that a deputy? As she moved closer, she could make out the unmistakable shape of the county hat, and the badge glinting on the side of his parka. Maybe a straggler who hadn't heard the all-clear call?

Suddenly, she wasn't tired anymore, just furious. He had no business being inside that house, even if he had missed the all-clear – she'd given direct orders to all the deputies not to enter any domicile in Bitterroot under any circumstances, and yet here was one of her men, blatantly disregarding his superior officer, and she was going to have to march right up there, pound on the door, and knock her first head as Sheriff . . .

But as she stormed up the front walk, she saw something else, and that something else was a gun rising in the deputy's hand, then coming down hard.

Iris had no idea what made her grab the knob and throw open the door – certainly not a cop's experience, since she didn't have any; and certainly not courage, because she'd never had any of that, either. She wasn't even sure how her weapon had come to be in her hand, how her body had found the shooting stance without her mind's direction, or if that was really her voice – a little shaky, but roaring nonetheless, shouting at this huge man, 'DROP THE GUN! DROP IT!'

For a split second she had a glimmer of the feeling she imagined any cop would feel, what Sampson must have felt when he'd stormed into her kitchen when she'd been cowering, terrified, with her back against the wall and a butcher knife in her hand. She felt strong and just and full of purpose instead of flat-out scared to death, and that's when she made the mistake. She forgot the first lesson. *Worry about the perp first; the victim second, because you can't help the victim if you're dead.*

But Iris's eyes darted of their own accord to the woman held upright only by the choke-hold the man had around her neck. It was such a short glance, just a flicker, really, but it was long enough to see the blood streaming down her face, the floppy, broken arm, and the sad flash of relief in her eyes before they fell closed and the deputy tossed her aside.

Oh God. The deputy. He was a law officer, too, and he hadn't forgotten the first lesson, because now he was spinning toward her, leading with a handgun a lot bigger than hers, and fast, so fast, he had it pointed directly at Iris's chest and saw the red light in Sheriff Kenny Bulardo's eyes that Roberta had seen for most of her life.

Iris felt her finger close on the trigger, and heard the deafening blast of a bullet breaking the sound barrier.

He'd been smart. Nobody could say he hadn't been smart. Kept his hat and his department parka, filched an extra deputy badge from the stock in the basement, and bought a new, bigger weapon on his way home from turning in his department issue 9-mm. He'd been ready and waiting for the smallest of chances to take back his wife if not his county, and last night it had come in the form of a phone call from one of the men who was still loyal. For the fist time since the fence was built, the gates to Bitterroot were wide open, and no one was checking who drove in.

Ex-sheriff Kenny Bulardo stood over Iris Rikker, watched the blood seeping out of her body onto the tile floor, and felt the grin crawling across his face.

He hadn't really intended to kill anyone – certainly not a sitting sheriff, even if it was the bitchy little snip who'd stolen his badge. Hell, he hadn't known the person he was shooting at was Iris Rikker until the bullet had left the barrel. When you live most of your life as a cop you learn early that you don't hesitate when someone breaks in on you screaming, pointing a gun at your face. You turn and shoot first and ask questions later. That's what they'd taught him all those years ago, and no one would blame him for doing exactly what a trained cop is supposed to do to save his own life, not even at his trial, if it should come to that. Roberta had been out cold by the time he'd pulled the trigger, so it was his word against a dead woman, who God damn her anyway had actually taken a shot at him – they'd find the slug punched into a wall or the floor somewhere – and his word had been good in this county for a long time.

Of course she wasn't quite dead yet, but the way she was bleeding, it wouldn't be long, and all he had to do was stand here quietly and wait for it to happen.

Except it was taking too long and he was feeling a little wobbly in the knees. He should have expected that. He'd felt the same way when he'd shot Billy Hambrick just before the stupid, drugged-up kid had slipped a knife into the stomach of one of his deputies. You didn't want to shoot, but sometimes you had to, and it always left you weak and a little dizzy and not thinking right.

He closed his eyes, just for a second, and heard the steady drip-dripping of Iris Rikker's blood hitting the tile, but that wasn't right. She was lying down, and the blood hadn't been dripping, just sliding out of her without a sound. God, he hoped it wasn't Roberta, but that couldn't be. He'd only hit her a few times; just that once with the barrel of the .45, but goddammit he could still hear that drip, drip and it was driving him crazy.

He tried to open his eyes, managed a slit before too dizzy to stand up anymore, and had just a second to look down and see the puddle spreading around his boots before his knees gave way.

Even inside the closed house, the shots had been very loud in the quiet town. Deputy Neville was less than a mile away when the 9-1-1 'shots fired' call came over the radio, and for the rest of his life, he would never remember the miraculous 180 turn he made on that narrow, snowy road, or the wild ride back to the Bitterroot parking lot with his accelerator jammed to the floor.

He didn't even shut off the car; just jumped out and started running around the big building, knees pumping high through the snow, heart pounding, gun drawn. Someone was broadcasting a location through his shoulder unit and his spirit sank as he raced toward the street Sheriff Rikker had been walking when he'd talked to her last.

Two blocks away, then one, then he turned the final

corner and stopped dead. The narrow street was filling with people, a sad, rag-tag army of women with hair flying as they ran, some dressed for the weather, but most wearing a hastily donned jacket over pajamas and slippers. They were all converging on the fourth house down, gathering at the front door in absolute silence for the briefest of moments, and then, as he watched, they burst through the door and poured into the house where the gunshots had been fired such a short time ago. He didn't even have time to open his mouth and scream at them to wait for the officers, professionals, goddammit, didn't they know there was a shooter in there?

He put his head down and ran toward them, waiting for the gunfire to start.

Iris was flirting with consciousness, sometimes aware, sometimes not, as if life were a dance partner with an outstretched hand held just out of reach. Occasionally she saw a searing, painful light; more often, there was complete and utter darkness that pressed down on her, making it almost impossible to breathe. Scraps of frantic conversations drifted around her head like busy gnats.

Is she alive?

Just barely . . . too much blood . . . we need a line here fast, and more of those gauze pads . . . how's Bulardo?

Silence for a moment.

Dead. But Roberta's coming around, Doctor. She's going to make it. The ambulance is on its way, but the roads are bad . . .

We can't wait. Get the stretcher.

And then there was a more familiar voice, and something about it made Iris feel safe; safe enough to drift away into sleep.

I'll take her. Let me take her. Iris? Oh, God, Iris . . . DOCTOR?

Busy, chilly hands around her face, so much commotion, and then the unmistakable sense of rising up, up . . .

We're losing her! Out of the way, Sampson, please!

Deputy Neville took Sampson firmly by the shoulders and pulled him away from the stretcher. 'Sir? Let them take her up to the lot. We need to get up there and get the squad ready to take her to the hospital.'

Sampson felt his head move in a stiff nod, and let Neville lead him out the door.

Other officers had responded to the call, more were racing in, snow flying from their boots. They arrived in time to see a stretcher coming out the front door of the little house, held high by women, so many women. Those who weren't actually bearing the load still reached out with their hands to touch the cold, steel frame of the stretcher, as if touch itself would make a difference. There must have been over a hundred of them.

'That's the damndest thing I ever saw,' one of the officers murmured, and then for some reason, he took off his hat and held it over his chest.

35

Homicide was deserted by the time Gino and Magozzi got back, and that was all wrong for the middle of the day. They found everyone down the hall in the media room, huddled around one of the new oversized computer screens. McLaren was there, Tinker, and a few others – even Chief Malcherson, looking totally out of place next to all the forty-dollar sport coats in his blue pinstripe.

'You might want to take a look at this, Detectives,' he said when Gino and Magozzi came into the room.

'What is it?'

McLaren tapped the computer monitor and Tinker slapped his hand away. 'The home videos from Theodore Wirth Park keep coming in as people dig themselves out from the storm. This one's from the sledding hill the night our boys went down.'

'You can't see the location of either snowman from that sledding hill,' Gino said. The woods curl right around up at the top.'

McLaren nodded. 'Yeah, but in this one a couple of baby Spielbergs took their video cam on the sled with them, all the way to the bottom. They got a sweeping shot of Toby Myerson down there when the camera was bouncing around. It's a ways off and it's fuzzy, but we got a couple frames that aren't bad. God bless auto-focus. See?' He touched the monitor again, and Gino and Magozzi leaned forward, squinting at the screen.

Four people building a snowman – the kind of happy, idyllic scene that took place in Minnesota every day of every winter, except this time the people were packing snow around a dead man.

'Jesus,' Gino whispered.

'It wasn't this clear when we first looked at it,' McLaren went on, so we sent it over to the BCA lab for enhancement, got it back a few minutes ago. No chance in hell . . . sorry, Chief . . . no chance we can make any kind of an ID off this – they're dressed for the weather, ski masks and the whole bit – but BCA managed to calibrate the size of our four happy sculptors against the stats on Toby Myerson. All of them are five six or under. They're either kids, midgets, or women, every one of them, and from the rack on that one, I'm going with the women.'

Chief Malcherson looked at Magozzi and Gino. 'Detective McLaren said you had your eye on Bill Warner and his wife for this.'

Magozzi nodded. 'Right up until the minute we looked at that shot. Bill Warner goes nearly six feet, and his wife's almost as tall.'

Gino was staring at the monitor, at the four female silhouettes, his lips pressed into a nowhere line. 'Bitterroot, damnit. It's gotta be.'

They were all silent for a moment, then McLaren spoke. 'There's one more thing.' He used a pencil to point at the frozen photo. 'See that white smudge on one of the figures? BCA did some pixel work on a close-up.' He pushed a few keys and an insert frame popped up on the side of the screen. 'The white smudge turned out to be some kind of printing on a scarf. W-T-C, and this last one's a zero. There's more to it, but there was a shadow and BCA can't pull it. This is the best we're going to get. Mean anything?'

Gino was scowling. 'I'd say it's part of a plate number, but that's dumb. Who'd print their license-plate number on a scarf?'

McLaren nodded. 'Nobody. So we were thinking monogram. Somebody makes a scarf for somebody, puts on their initials and the date, and we can only see part of it.'

'Possible.'

'World Trade Center, oh-nine-eleven-oh-one,' Tinker said, his thoughts taking their usual path down the darkest lane. 'You see that a lot of places. Bumper stickers, T-shirts . . .'

'Which would make it generic and impossible to trace.' Magozzi looked at Gino. 'Let's run the initials through the Bitterroot roster, see what we get.'

'Couldn't hurt.'

Chief Malcherson turned his head, white hair shining like a beacon in the darkened room. 'The way I understand it, the Bitterroot roster is confidential information. You'll need a warrant to access that.'

'Maybe you could call one of your judge friends, pull a few strings.'

Malcherson sighed. 'We have one piece of solid evidence on this case, Detective. A rather blurred video image showing four unidentifiable figures, possibly women, at our crime scene. Over half the population of this country is female. I've read all your reports very carefully, Detective McLaren has kept me fully briefed on your investigation, and your speculations. What I have gleaned from that information is that only the demented ramblings of a diminished elderly woman make you seriously suspicious of those at Bitterroot.

I couldn't get a warrant on Hitler's bunker with that kind of conjecture.'

Gino rolled his head around and stared at the Chief. Man. It wasn't really a joke, but it was damn close.

'We're still going to look at it,' Magozzi said.

The Chief didn't even bother to ask how. He didn't want to know. 'Then I advise you to step very carefully on this one, Detective Magozzi.'

After the Chief left the room, Johnny McLaren looked up at Magozzi. 'The Monkeewrench people?'

'Burn me a copy of that disk, Johnny, will you?'

36

Snow was still coming down hard when Magozzi and Gino left City Hall with the disk and headed for Grace's. The program they needed was on her home computer, and she'd promised to meet them there.

'Man, I can't believe it's still snowing,' Gino said, tightening his seat belt as Magozzi fishtailed onto Washington Avenue. 'What do you figure we got so far?'

'Probably close to three feet since it started Friday.'

Gino pressed his face against the window and looked skyward. 'What if it never stops? What if this is global warming and we're entering a new ice age?'

'Maybe we should start looking at high-rises.'

Gino fiddled with the heater controls for a minute, then flopped back in his seat. 'You know, the Chief kinda pissed me off today with that little lecture about the whole search-warrant deal. I was just about ready to fly off the handle and say something stupid, but then he threw me with that crack about Hitler's bunker. Did you catch that? He actually sounded like a cop.'

'He is a cop.'

'You know what I mean. An actual human-type cop. Anyhow, I'm not so sure he's thinking this through. What we got is a hell of a lot more than an old lady going on about offing her husband – that and the bones at Rikker's make you think it could be a family thing, you know? All the women in one family popping off their men over the generations. It was the other thing that really creeped me out, because if there are bodies in that lake, Laura was talking about killing other people's husbands, and that ain't self-defense any way you look at it. Plus, if we tie that video to Bitterroot, you're not looking at one family anymore, you're looking at a whole damn town that might be justifying murder, and that scares the crap out of me. I don't want it to be an ex-cop with a clean service record; I don't want it to be a bunch of women who think they're saving their own lives, but, man, the stuff keeps piling up, just like this snow. It's cumulative, Leo, and that ought to be worth something.'

'The Chief can't support a warrant without cause.'

Gino grunted. 'Maybe not, but he could have supported our reasons for wanting one. It probably doesn't matter anyway. To tell you the truth, I don't hold out a lot of hope for the monogram thing.'

'I don't, either, but we'll have Grace pull the roster for us anyhow. What I really wanted was for her to play around with that disk. BCA might be a top lab, but I'll still put my money on Monkeewrench magic.'

They didn't hear Charlie's customary welcoming woof before Grace opened the door, and Gino's face showed his disappointment. 'Hey, Grace, long time no see. Where's my dog?'

'He's still at Harley's. I'm on my way back there as soon as we finish here. Hi, Magozzi.'

She was wearing her usual black T-shirt and jeans instead of plastic wrap, and she wasn't holding a martini. Magozzi smiled at her anyway. 'Thanks for doing this.'

'No problem. Come on in the kitchen and get a cup of coffee before we get started.'

Magozzi and Gino sat at the table while she stood at

the counter and filled three mugs. 'You said you needed a couple things. I've got the photo-enhancement program up and running. What else?'

Magozzi said, 'The roster from Bitterroot. The names of all the current residents.'

She turned around and looked at him. 'You think somebody who lives at Bitterroot killed your two cops in the park? Just because Bitterroot was the subject line on that chat thread?'

'There's a little more to it than that. Turns out one of the cops was abusing his wife, and it was getting worse. She has family at Bitterroot, hell, her great-grandmother and aunt founded the place, and this may not be the first time those people have killed to save a woman.'

Grace sat down between them and looked from one to the other. 'You said Bitterroot was basically one big safe house for abused women, right?'

'Right.'

'And all the women who live there are abuse victims.'

'Looks that way.'

'Then it's impossible. Both of you know the psychology of abuse victims. Those women don't fight back. They're incapable of it.'

'Almost all of them are,' Gino put in. 'But once in a blue moon it happens, especially when they're trying to protect someone else, like family, like Tommy Deaton's wife. She was one of their own, hell, her mother grew up there, and she wouldn't take their help. We think they might have taken the proactive route.'

Grace shook her head. 'That sounds like a really big leap to me, Gino.'

'There's a lot more backstory, Grace,' Magozzi said.

'Reasons to think maybe some of the women at Bitterroot have killed other men in the past to protect themselves. We're not sure about that, but it's possible. Right now we need to focus on the two murders we *know* happened, and for that, we need the roster.'

'I don't have one. I don't even know if such a thing exists.'

'Of course it exists, Grace. It's a corporation, and it has to keep corporate records. You've been in and out of their computer system installing your software, so you know how to get it.'

'You want me to break into a client's confidential records?'

'Yes.'

That surprised her. It wasn't the first time Magozzi had wanted information from some illegal site, but he never said it out loud. 'Why do you want it?'

'We're looking for murderers. They might be on that list. Is that reason enough?'

She didn't hesitate long before getting up from the table and leading the way back to her office, but Magozzi could tell that the hunt had changed for her, just as it had changed for all of them when they realized they weren't looking for a crazed psychopath; they were looking for desperate women trying to save their own lives and the lives of people they loved. You had to be careful not to think about that too much, not to let yourself slip into that gray area where sympathy could step all over the simple fact that in the end, murder was murder, no matter who did it or why.

It only took a few minutes for Grace to bring up the roster on the screen. She rolled her chair sideways to give them a clear view. 'There it is. What are you looking for?'

Magozzi handed her the disk. 'This is a home video from the park the night of the murder. There are a couple frames on here that show four women building a snowman around one of our dead cops at Theodore Wirth. BCA enhanced them enough to get some initials off what looks like a monogram, and we want to match them against the roster. In the meantime, we want you to try getting some more detail out of these shots that might help with a specific ID.'

Grace closed her eyes briefly. 'Four women?'

'That's right.'

She didn't say anything after that; just took the disk and slotted it into a drive and fiddled with the image that came up on an adjacent monitor until it was clear. 'That's about as good as it's going to get. I see W, T, C . . .' She stopped speaking.

'Yeah, yeah,' Gino said. 'And then a zero. We know that. We were thinking it might be a date, only they couldn't clarify the rest of it. So how do you make this thing page down?' He pointed at the monitor showing the roster.

Grace reached over mindlessly and pushed the scroll button. Gino and Magozzi hunkered close to the screen, watching the names go by until the list finally ended on somebody called Muriel Zacher.

'Nothing, damnit,' Gino muttered, straightening up and pressing his hands to the small of his back. 'Back to the drawing board.'

'It was a long shot,' Magozzi said. 'But we had to try. What do you think of the photos, Grace? Any chance you can show up the BCA on enhancements? Maybe get some bone structure from under those masks for your facial-recognition program?'

Grace nodded without taking her eyes off the video frame on the second monitor. 'I can try. Give me fifteen minutes alone with it.'

37

'Holy shit.' Gino was peering out Grace's living room window, looking up at the sky like Chicken Little. 'It's the end of the world. It stopped snowing. Has it been fifteen minutes yet?'

Magozzi was flopped on the couch, arm over his eyes to block the daylight. 'Jeez, Gino, relax, give her some time. That program is slow.'

'Relax, he says. Are you kidding me? This friggin' case is driving me insane. We've come at it in four ways and we're still empty-handed. We went through Weinbeck, the Snowman, the Warners, and Bitterroot, and we can't prove shit.'

'That about sums it up.'

'So where do we go from here?'

'I don't know.'

Back in her office down the hall, Grace was going through the motions with her own advanced photo-enhancement program. The computer assessed probabilities, adding pixels of color in the most likely configurations, but there was no hope of getting enough off the poor-quality shots to justify using the facial-recognition software. All it had been able to accomplish was clarifying the rest of the monogram on the close-up of the scarf, but that was all she needed. W-T-C-0-0-0.

Cops were so single-minded sometimes, she thought. They got the idea of numbers into their heads and couldn't let go. It never occurred to them that the zero wasn't really a zero; that maybe it was the letter *O*, imperfectly stitched by the shaky hands of a very old woman. She pushed her chair away from the counter and closed her eyes, remembering the last day she'd worked at the Bitterroot offices last fall.

It's lovely, Maggie. Thank you.

Just a little something to remember us by. I told Laura you admired mine on your first visit, and she insisted on making you one.

Laura?

Yes. She's one of the original founders of Bitterroot. She's very old now, and her needlepoint isn't what it used to be, but she's always so flattered when someone appreciates it.

What does this stand for?

It stands for what we stand for. Bitterroot, and all the places like it. W-T-C-O-O-O. We Take Care of Our Own. Laura makes them for all our girls.

At the time it had seemed like such a wonderfully human motto in a world where corporations were usually so impersonal, and it wasn't such an unusual phrase. People said it all the time about their families, their communities, their countries, so it hadn't rung any bells when she'd read it on that chat room thread. Now the motto on the scarf seemed a lot more sinister.

Magozzi and Gino went to join her when they heard Grace leave her little office and go into the kitchen.

'Did you get something?' Gino asked hopefully.

She turned to face them, and Magozzi thought her eyes were empty, as if she'd used up everything behind them. 'Do you have any idea of how many women have been murdered by their partners in this country since you walked through my front door?' she asked quietly.

Magozzi's eyes held hers. 'Tell me how many minutes it's been and I'll tell you how many women. We know the stats,

Grace. It's our job to know them. It's also our job to change them. Ours, and every other cop's. Nobody else's.'

Grace thought about that for a moment, then nodded. 'You said an old woman killed someone at Bitterroot this morning.'

Gino said, 'That's right, but it was self-defense, plain and simple. Well, not exactly self-defense. The guy had a gun on another woman.'

'And I can make sense of that,' Grace said. 'It's one thing to kill someone who breaks into your house with murder in mind, like the old woman did this morning. But seeking them out to kill them in advance, like Tommy Deaton? It's almost like . . .'

'Hunting,' Magozzi said, and he felt his heart speed up. She'd found something, something that connected the snowmen in the park to Bitterroot. 'But for what's it worth, if people from Bitterroot were involved, they probably thought it was the only thing they could do to save Mary Deaton's life. Even Gino and I were having problems with that one. Half of you knows it's murder, the other half gets it.'

'Exactly. But then you have to start multiplying.'

'What do you mean?'

'How many abused women are at Bitterroot?'

'Four hundred,' Gino remembered.

'Okay. And for every one of them there's probably a man out there who might kill them one day. If you start making excuses for Deaton's murder, you have to make the same excuses for three hundred ninety-nine others.'

Gino stared at her. He'd had his head wrapped so tight around what he would do in Bill Warner's place that he'd almost lost sight of the job itself, and why he did it.

Grace pushed herself away from the counter and went to a drawer, pulled out the soft, folded scarf and laid it on the table between them.

Gino pulled it closer, fingered the imperfect embroidery, then sucked in an audible breath.

Oddly, Grace almost smiled at him. 'It wasn't me in that video, Gino. It wasn't the same scarf. Just one like it.'

He exhaled slowly. 'I knew that,' he grumped. 'Jeez, Grace.'

'They gave it to me the last day I worked there. Apparently the old woman makes them for all the women out there, and those aren't zeroes, those are *O*s. The inscription stands for the Bitterroot motto. "We Take Care of Our Own." We found that phrase in the chat-room thread I read to you, remember? I just didn't make the connection.'

Magozzi and Gino just stood there for a minute, looking at each other. Normally the big break in a tough case was cause for jubilation. That didn't happen this time.

Gino shoved his hands in his pockets angrily. 'Goddamnit, Leo, I was half-afraid of this. I mean, a town without men creeped me out at first, but the thing is, that place worked, and you can't tell me all the women up there are in on this. So what you've got is a few bad apples ruining a really good thing for a bunch of scared women who have no other safe place to go. We're going to get a warrant on Bitterroot out of this, and then there's going to be an investigation, and the scandal will shut that place down forever, whether or not we find the evidence to nail the real killers.'

'I hate this,' Grace whispered, and Magozzi wondered if abuse was part of her past, which he still knew nothing about after a year of loving the woman. 'But one of those women passed out free murder advice in that chat room that led to the Pittsburgh killing.'

Magozzi shook his head. 'We think that was Bill Warner, Mary Deaton's father. He may not have been at the scene, but he sure as hell was in on the planning, and now he's spreading his know-how.'

'Yeah,' Gino said. 'Probably to some other poor schmuck of a father who lies awake at nights waiting for the call that his own daughter's dead . . . Christ, I don't know who to hate and who to feel sorry for. This case turns me in circles one more time, I'm going to look like a corkscrew. I'm going to go warm up the car.' He stomped down the hall, grabbed his coat, and slammed the door on his way out.

'Gino's having a really hard time with this one,' Grace said. She was looking down at the floor.

'So are you. We all are.'

She walked him to the door and watched him shrug into his coat. She looked as exhausted and troubled as he felt, and he knew that this was one of those times when Grace had to be alone. She didn't work her way through problems or sadness the way other people did, by talking about it. She just retreated someplace to which Magozzi had never been able to follow.

'You want to forget dinner tonight?' he asked her.

She opened the door for him. Her eyes looked faded in the bright light from the outside, and he couldn't read them. She reached up and touched his cheek, then kissed him on the mouth very briefly, a peck, really, like the kind a woman might give to her husband in the morning when he left for work.

'Bring your pj's,' she said.

38

By the next morning the close-up of the four women building a snowman around Tommy Deaton's body was the lead shot on every local television station newscast, and on the front page, above the fold, on every paper in the Midwest. The politicos behind the scene at MPD did what they could to trace the leak, hopefully back to the BCA and not to one of their own, but in a matter of hours the damage had been done. Bitterroot hit the national airwaves.

Magozzi and Gino ignored what they could, gritted their teeth at the rest, and did their job. Monkeewrench had finally traced the chat-room thread to its origin – the Minneapolis Public Library computers. Anyone could walk in off the street and use those computers, which left them nowhere as far as pinning accessory charges on Bill Warner.

For fifteen days, more than fifty officers from MPD, Dundas County, and the Department of National Resources searched every house, every building, every one of the thousand acres owned by Bitterroot. They found a lot of weapons, all of them registered, not one a ballistics match to the slugs the ME had pulled out of Officers Tommy Deaton and Toby Myerson. They also found hundreds of scarves like Grace's, like the one in the photo. The Minneapolis Crime Lab and the BCA each sorted through the scarves, comparing them to the freeze-frame Grace had enhanced – there were subtle differences in each scarf, created by the tremors in an old woman's hand – but they found no definitive points of comparison. Certainly there were a lot more out there somewhere – Laura said she'd been stitching them for years, ever since they'd founded the place – but the search for a match was fruitless.

Every day that the search went on, the press gathering outside the gates grew larger and more vocal, demanding entrance, demanding answers. The media wouldn't let the story go. When current news gave it a rest, the talk shows picked up the ball and ran with it. The idea of abused women turning killer was simply too salacious to leave alone. The Dundas County Council meetings were mobbed by residents and politicians alike, demanding what would certainly be the inevitable end to the story – the closure of Bitterroot.

Gino and Magozzi interviewed each and every current resident of the place, but they kept coming back to Maggie Holland. As longtime manager of the complex, it seemed reasonable to assume she had knowledge of everything that happened there, but after the first interview, their questioning became a simple exercise of going through the motions. She quickly became impatient with the process, but she submitted without complaint, kept her hostility under wraps, and kept what she knew, if anything, to herself. More than once, Magozzi caught himself almost admiring her courage and endurance. If she were truly a murderer, she wasn't the kind he and Gino were used to interrogating. There wasn't a doubt in his mind that if they ever latched on to the kind of solid evidence that would connect Bitterroot to the crimes, this woman would take the fall all by herself, whether she'd been involved or not, in the hope that it would help keep the place open.

It was their last day in Dundas County. The search teams

were packing up their gear and their dogs, getting ready to pull out, and Gino and Magozzi were sitting opposite Maggie Holland's desk for the last time.

She was standing at the window, looking out across the fields in the direction of the gated entrance. 'So you're leaving.'

'Yes, ma'am,' Magozzi said.

'And you found nothing.'

'Not yet. The case is open. It will stay open until it's solved. We still have two murdered police officers, one of whom, I'd like to remind you, was not abusing anybody.'

Her head moved in a nod, but she didn't turn around. 'But you accomplished one of your goals, didn't you? They're going to close us down.'

'Our only intention was to catch a killer.'

She turned at last, came back to her desk and slumped in her chair. For the first time she looked almost beaten. 'Have you considered, Detectives, that even if some of the women at this complex took it upon themselves to do what they felt they had to do to save a life, the others might be totally blameless? Totally unaware that such a thing had even occurred.'

Gino nodded. 'We've considered that a lot.'

'When those gates close for the last time, those particular women, those innocents, will have no safe place in this world. The journalists outside that gate will follow every one of them, convinced that each one is a cold-blooded killer.'

Gino leaned back in his chair and folded his hands across his belly. 'You know, I've been keeping a pretty close eye on the coverage of this thing – all the TV shots of the press hammering at the gates, locked out of the place that does God knows what inside – and I've been thinking that you're crafty in a lot of ways, Maggie Holland, but in other ways, you're just about as snow blind as we were during this whole damn case.'

Her gaze sharpened. 'Really.'

'Yeah, really. You know what I'd do if this was my place? I'd open the damn gates, let the press inside, let them see what you're really about. Show them the other side of the story. And show them your neck, Maggie. Show them the scars that built that fence.'

Maggie was silent for a long moment, and although her gaze remained hard, there was something new in her eyes – an almost imperceptible flicker of light, of hope, as she considered what Gino had said. 'Sheriff Rikker goes home today,' she finally said.

Magozzi smiled. 'We know.'

'Of course you know. The nurses tell me you've both been at the hospital every day.'

Gino shrugged and looked away. 'Yeah, well, we were up here anyway. It's a cop thing, you know?'

'It's a human thing, Detective.'

'Whatever.'

Back in the car, Magozzi turned to Gino. 'You're supposed to be a hard-ass. I can't believe you told Maggie Holland to court the press. Great idea, by the way.'

Gino shrugged. 'Yeah, I thought so. The way I was figuring it, we couldn't bag the Warners, we couldn't bag Maggie Holland or anyone at Bitterroot; that basically we couldn't do shit to close unsolveds on a couple of cops, and the one and only thing we managed to accomplish with this whole investigation was to close down a place that really did some good. Total loss, beginning to end, and it pissed me off. This was kind of a salvage operation.'

'Well, you sure opened a can of worms.'

'Good. Maybe people will look at it. And maybe some of those people will call the useless sacks of nuts in the legislature and get them to stop releasing the other useless sacks of nuts we've been trying to keep locked up since we first put on the blues.'

Magozzi faced front, smiled, and started the car. Gino always was a dreamer. 'I suppose that would be some kind of a happy ending.'

Gino snorted. 'Bottom line? We got people out there who got away with murder, Leo, and Pittsburgh's in the same boat we are. If it really was Bill Warner in that chat thread, he's a damn good tutor. There is no happy ending to this case. I told you that, right from the start.'

Magozzi pressed the accelerator and the squad crunched its way out of the lot. 'We do what we can, Gino. It may not turn out perfect, but sometimes, it's not half bad.'

39

Sheriff Iris Rikker was standing on the shore of Lake Kittering, watching the water lap at the brown sand beneath her boots. March had blown in on a stiff, warm wind, more lamb than lion, and the ice, along with the second lottery car, had disappeared into the spring-fed depths a few weeks later. An even, white chop ruffled the surface of the lake today, and Iris thought that it didn't look much different than it had back in January, when the waves had been suspended in ice.

She heard Sampson's heavy footfalls squishing on the soaked lawn behind her. 'It's a little early to go swimming, Sheriff,' he said as he came up beside her.

'Actually, I was thinking about going fishing.'

'Bass opener isn't for another month. Suckers and bullheads are about the only thing you can pull out of there now. Nobody eats them because they taste like mud, but they're good sport.' He stooped, picked up a piece of driftwood, and started poking at the sand. 'But I never really had you pegged as the sporting type, come to think of it.'

She sighed and fixed her gaze upon the distant shore; the shore closest to Bitterroot. 'I'm not.'

Sampson poked his finger into her arm like a little boy. He'd been doing that a lot lately. 'Do you want to show me your scars?'

Iris smiled, but she didn't look at him. 'Maybe some day.'

Sampson dug his foot around in the sand, making a big footprint. 'Do you think they're down there?'

'I don't know.'

'Do you regret it?'

'Not dragging the lake? No.'

Sampson stood up, pitched the driftwood into the water, and nodded. 'Probably just as well. We've had fifteen drownings in that lake over the past twenty years, and they never found one by dragging. Had to wait until they floated, and not all of them did. You're as likely to find Mike Jurasik's grandson as you are to find anybody else.'

'I got the lab results from the bones in my barn today, Sampson.'

'Oh yeah?'

'There's no way to identify them. Even DNA needs something for comparison, and there isn't a trace of Emily's husband left anywhere in the world.'

'It was Lars. Nobody else it could have been.'

Iris started moving her own boots in the sand, looking at the patterns she had made. What was it about the human animal that wanted so desperately to see their footprints in any medium that would duplicate them? 'He starved to death in that little cell, Sampson. That was the official cause of death.'

Sampson didn't say anything at first. He just folded his arms against his chest, trying to hold in the imagination that would show him what that kind of death would be like. 'You know what I think?' he said at last. 'I think Emily locked him down there to save herself, and maybe to save her daughter, too. It's kind of funny, when you ponder it. Emily was the only one in that family who couldn't kill to save herself, so she did the only thing she could. She locked him away where he couldn't hurt anybody, as if that kind of life was better than death, and then when the cancer got bad, she decided she had to kill him because there'd be nobody to take care of him after she was gone. In a way, it kind of makes you believe in a God that sees suffering and believes in payback, because he dropped her in the driveway with the gun in her hand, before she could put Lars out of his misery. And say what you like, the bastard probably got just what he deserved.'

Iris looked at Sampson, horrified by what he'd said, so certain that no one deserved that kind of life and death. It took her a full second to forgive him completely, because a man like Lars had done terrible things to Sampson's sister, and left a painful twist in Sampson's mind.

She looked back over the lake, thinking of all the horrible secrets she'd discovered in this one tiny little spot on the globe, wondering if every other spot held just as many.

read more

P. J. Tracy

WANT TO PLAY?

Monkeywrench – morden

Hide and Seek. And Kill.

Minneapolis, a brutally cold autumn. And a killer is at work. Two bodies are found, two slayings that the police treat as unrelated. But games-creator Grace MacBride knows different. The murders are exact copies of those in a game she is designing – one that already has hundreds of eager players. As the copycat killings mount up, Grace knows that she is both suspect and potential victim. And with the serial killers getting closer, she is drawn into a murderous game of cat and mouse …

Want to play?

'A thrilling page-turner with a nail-biting finish' *Sunday Telegraph*

'A fast-paced gripping read with thrills and devilish twists' *Guardian*

'A powerful thriller and an ingenious plot' *Observer Review*

read more

P. J. Tracy

LIVE BAIT

Do you know evil when you see it?

Springtime in Minneapolis and with the thaw comes murder: an elderly man executed with a gunshot to the head and another literally frightened to death. But when Detective Magozzi calls on the analytical skills of Grace MacBride, it appears not only that the killings might be connected but also that the victims might be something other than they first seemed. As more deaths follow, Magozzi and Grace must quickly discover what secrets these men shared – and with whom – if they are to bait their trap and catch their killer…

'Impressive … P. J. Tracy is about to become a household name' *Daily Mirror*

'A winner. Don't forget to take it on holiday' *Time Out*

'A tense edge-of-your-seat thriller' *OK!*

'Brilliant … *Live Bait* proves that the phenomenal *Want to Play?* was no fluke' *Amazon*

read more

P. J. TRACY

Dött lopp

DEAD RUN

If you go down to the woods today …

It should have been a simple journey – a drive from Minneapolis to Green Bay, Wisconsin. But a couple of unplanned detours lead Grace MacBride, Annie Belinsky and police deputy Sharon Mueller deep into the northern woods, far from civilization and a mobile phone signal. Then their car breaks down.

The nervous search for a landline and a mechanic leads the women to Four Corners, a sleepy crossroads town. And a place they soon wish they'd never stumbled upon.

Because something terrible happened in Four Corners.

Grace, her senses honed by a lifetime of paranoia, sees sinister stories in details that even Sharon misses. But it's Grace's instincts that might save the women's lives when they become witnesses to a chilling scene – and party to terrifying knowledge that they might never be allowed to leave with …

'A writer with all the credentials to sit firmly in the upper echelons of top crime novelists' *Amazon*